ESCAPADES OF
A Self-Styled Gandhian

VITHAL RAJAN

INDIA • SINGAPORE • MALAYSIA

Notion Press

Old No. 38, New No. 6
McNichols Road, Chetpet
Chennai - 600 031

First Published as 'Sharmaji Padmashree'
By
Writers Workshop, 2006;
Konark Books, 2013;
Re-published by Notion Press 2018
Copyright © Vithal Rajan 2018
All Rights Reserved.

ISBN 978-1-64429-551-9

This book has been published with all efforts taken to make the material error-free after the consent of the author. However, the author and the publisher do not assume and hereby disclaim any liability to any party for any loss, damage, or disruption caused by errors or omissions, whether such errors or omissions result from negligence, accident, or any other cause.

No part of this book may be used, reproduced in any manner whatsoever without written permission from the author, except in the case of brief quotations embodied in critical articles and reviews.

Disclaimer: Please note all illustrations in this book are artists creations and used for explanation only and not to the scale.

Other books by the author:

Holmes of the Raj

The Year of High Treason

The Legend of Ramulamma

Jungu, The Baiga Princess

Les Mangues de Tara [translated in French]

The Anarkali Diary [play]

Not So! Stories

Varadachary's Annotated Chess Masterpieces [plays]

Different Millennia: Three Plays

Dedicated to the memory of my dear father
Shri ***Srinivas Rajan****, I.C.S.*
A brilliant mathematician
with a great sense of humour

CONTENTS

1. The Happy Birthday 1
2. People vs. Pesticide 9
3. The Brother-in-Law 17
4. At the Barricades 25
5. Sharma*ji* and the Tiger 33
6. The Classes in Marxism 45
7. The Club 53
8. French Memories 59
9. The Peace Film 67
10. The Sabbatical 75
11. Wanted, a Brahmin Cook 83
12. Sharma*ji* Meets the Sisterhood 91
13. Human Materials Engineering 99
14. Sharma*ji* Gets Angry 107
15. The Storyteller 115
16. The Servant Girl 121
17. Sharma*ji* Stands Trial 127

Contents

18. A Day to Remember 139
19. Sharma*ji* Meets his Match 145
20. Sharma*ji* Meets the Learned 153
21. The Great Canadian Curd Churn 161
22. The NGO Living Book 167
23. Sharma*ji* of the SAS 173
24. Death and the Maiden 183
25. Sharma*ji* Battles Dark Powers in the Air 187
26. An International Wedding 193
27. The White She-Buffalo 201
28. Shanta Threatens Divorce 209
29. The Heart Attack 217
30. Desert Flower 225
31. Sharma*ji*, Padmashree 235

About the Author 243

1. The Happy Birthday

'**Happy birthday, Sharma*ji*, happy** birthday!' A chorus of good wishes voiced in varying tones and accents showered in. His staff burst into the sanctum sanctorum, unannounced for the first time in the history of the Society for Educational Resources Vitalizing Indian Community Entrepreneurs [SERVICE]. Shri Vedavyas Sharma, M.A. [London], sat in his customary cane easy chair, behind the long teak table piled with important-looking files. He received the congratulations and adulation of his staff with the modesty he always displayed, and never failed to mention, on such occasions. This was only his fifty-third birthday, though often before he had openly talked of his extreme old age. This was to make sure he got the respect he deserved and to allay any comment on the fatherly interest he took in his female staff. Rukmini, separated from her husband soon after marriage, had found herself without money, security, or shelter and had come to the village SERVICE centre, looking for any kind of work. He had taken pity on this young unskilled girl, trained her personally, and made her coordinator of SERVICE Women in Development [WIDS]. Now she came forward sinuously, under the arms of her male colleagues garlanding Sharma*ji*, touched his feet, drawing long finger marks with scented sandalwood paste, and then stretched forward gently to place a jasmine garland round his neck. He had to lean forward a little, and could smell a fresh perfume on her breasts, inches from his face.

After what seemed a long time, they all drew back respectfully, and Sharma*ji* looked at them, his handiwork so to speak, with satisfaction. They were his life, and he told them so. Gupta, his clever accountant who for some reason had failed to find work with the government or corporates, came dragging his polio-stricken left foot and carrying a plate of Bengali sweets he had especially ordered from home for the day. They all had one each, chattering that this was a family celebration, when they felt close to their leader, their guru, their father.

'Thank you, thank you, thank you,' said Sharma*ji*. 'My love and my blessings are always with you. But you must understand, I am nobody. Gandhiji—' and he paused as he always did when he took this name, 'Gandhiji wanted us to fight the Self, if we are to serve Society. I am an old man, and of course I love you as my children, but my thoughts should now be about God. What is it we have done here?'

At such moments there would be silence, and his staff would look at one another like children in a classroom. This day was no different. Venkat, tall and darkly handsome, who took more interest in Rukmini than Sharma*ji* liked, ventured a hesitant answer.

'We, we serve Society,' said his coordinator for SERVICE Thrift Entrepreneurship and Savings [TEAS], glancing at his colleagues for reassurance.

'No!' said Sharma*ji* with much satisfaction. 'We serve God, for in people we see God. All this we see around us, people striving, people fighting, people agreeing, pain and pleasure, all, as Adi Shankara has taught us, is *maya*, illusion. If it is all *maya* why should we do anything to help people?' He hurried on, knowing that they needed his message. 'We serve Society, because through this we serve God. This is how we come to know God.'

They looked stunned at this revelation.

'It is our very, very good luck,' said Seshadri, his Admin Manager, 'that we work under you, that God sent us to you.'

Here was another opportunity for Sharma*ji* to teach his staff something.

'You serve with me, with me, never under. I am the least of your colleagues.' With this he signalled that they should leave so that he could return to weighty matters of serving the people, and Mother India. Alone, he heaved a happy sigh. He knew they would celebrate his birthday, although he had given them no inkling that he expected anything. He was a humble servant, the man who washes the courtyard of the temple so that others may pray. And he had moulded them into a good working unit. There were some problems of course, as in any human organization. This Venkat, he was too self-willed, and unable to appreciate that in his own best interests he should listen attentively to his master.

And then, Rukmini, what was to become of her? She was fresh as a flower; the image of a ripe fruit came to his mind, but he discarded it as too worldly a symbol. He was no traditionalist; he would have liked her to re-marry. If only she had been fair, he might have found a suitable boy, but she was dark, in fact black with even black lips, enclosing a melon mouth that never failed to startle him when she sang a SERVICE song. He would call her over this evening and speak about her prospects. Perhaps, through Christians Everywhere, he could send her on a training programme to America for a month—no, that was too long, say, two weeks, for how could WIDS get along without her for a whole month?

When at the village SERVICE centre office, he always wore a spotless white *kurtha* and *dhoti*, a hallmark of service coming down from the days of Gandhiji. When he retired to 'his unit,' actually a nice little cottage with a drawing room, a bedroom, a bathroom and a kitchen attached, he liked to lounge in a full-sleeved shirt over a pyjama. He would sit in an armchair in the deep veranda at the front of 'his unit,' an occasional table with a telephone and pad by his side, and would summon Rukmini. He took a fatherly pleasure in seeing her tall, trim form walk across the SERVICE campus, and then, only because it gave her pleasure, he would ask her to make him a cup of tea and *pakodas*.

Sometimes, if it was later in the evening, she would come of her own accord with a basket of flowers. She would sit on the steps of the veranda, at his feet, and thread the jasmine into flower-strings for all the SERVICE women to wear. She would tell him all the local gossip, the diamond in her right nostril twinkling as she talked. Then she would raise the jasmine to tuck it into her hair with her breasts rising under her sari. Somehow, one day, he must tell her not to wear such low-cut blouses, for you could almost see everything. But these were ladies' matters, and he was too shy.

'Hello, Sharma*ji*, the years come around, eh?' cut across his reverie, and he saw Robert's long, thin face poking round the mesh door. 'I've brought something very special for you.' Robert, dressed as usual in a careless loose shirt with the sleeves rolled up, over khaki shorts and sandals, thrust his thin British body unceremoniously into the office, and flung himself into a chair, putting a long jute bag on the table.

'My motorbike failed somewhere near Shadnagar, and it took me a couple of hours to find a mechanic who had even heard of a Harley-Davidson. So, I left it in his tender care and took a bus, Sharma*ji*, to bring you this.'

He pulled out a full bottle of Teacher's Scotch. Sharma*ji*, gripping his hand in gratitude, quickly slipped the bottle into a special lower compartment in his desk. Robert had been forever in India, first as something low down in the British Council establishment, then for several years in an ashram in Rishikesh. Then, he and the development agencies mutually discovered each other. He was an instant hit with village people, simple, charming, painfully helpful, and surprisingly efficient. He had recently taken over as Regional Director for Christians Everywhere. But he was also totally mad.

'Robert, thank you, I can't say how much,' said Sharma*ji* sincerely. 'You know, it is years since I have had a glass of genuine Scotch. Indian whisky is good, I won't say anything against it, but Scotch is Scotch. You will stay for dinner and a drink this evening?' Robert expressed his inability to stay for more than half an hour. He had to catch the next bus to Thummalakunta, for all the drinking water wells there were dry, and he must fix the pumps. 'Robert, you know, it was Professor Headley,' said Sharma*ji*, his tone reminiscent, 'who first taught me to sip Scotch gently. Those days, London was beautiful. We Indian students were much liked. I remember Lord Cornwallis—a descendent of one of our Governor-Generals—invited all the Indian students over for tea. He questioned me very closely about living conditions in India. I remember...'

Robert had come round the table, his lanky blond moustache falling like a curtain over his laughing mouth. 'Another day, Sharma*ji*, for these stories of ye olde England. I must get on with these pumps. I am sure you will find someone far better than an

Englishman to split the bottle with.' And with a vulgar wink and a slap on the back, Robert swung out of the room.

Robert was undoubtedly mad, why else would he be in this godforsaken hole? He could have lived in England. Sharma*ji* still treasured every memory of those never-to-be-forgotten nine months he had spent in London; those parks, that sharp chill in the morning air, the politeness and discipline of English people, his own appearance: fully dressed in jacket, tie, overcoat, hat, and carrying an umbrella. His uncle had sold nine acres of his father's lands to enable him to get a foreign degree in London, and those acres had given him more than an education. They had set him apart as 'foreign returned,' as a man, who, though all the world was open to him, returned to serve his country. This point he never failed to drive home, to his staff, his family, his donors, and to supercilious government servants, some of whom even dared to make fun of his M.A. [London]. Of course, every evening had not been spent at tea with Lord Cornwallis. He had saved money by eating *dosas* at the India Club, at the edge of Waterloo Bridge. And there was also the secret, confused memory of the ample bosom and energetic embraces of the Austrian cook who made the *dosas*. How did his wife know? She always threw out these dark references, whenever he spoke of London and his studies there.

Mallanna, his attender, as a peon was politely called these days, stood before him. 'I am going to the village to post letters. Can I get you anything, Sir?' he asked.

Sharma*ji* placed a podgy hand on his stomach and groaned slightly. 'Bring two bottles of soda round to my unit,' he said in a feeble voice. 'I have some pain, and soda will help, I think.'

Mallanna gave him a knowing look unnecessarily, and left. He was a smart young dalit, whom Sharma*ji* liked to showcase when visitors came to the Village SERVICE centre. 'He is like my son,' he would say. 'We eat from the same plate.' This was very far from the truth, Sharma*ji* only allowing him to wash the utensils after he had finished dinner. But the key point was that the thought was there. All in all, it was a very Happy Birthday, with a bottle of Teacher's arriving just at the right moment.

2. People vs. Pesticide

Rukmini and Venkat sat on the stone platform built around the base of the large *peepal* tree in the heart of the SERVICE campus. Dapple morning sunlight fell on them through the dancing leaves as they sipped their morning cups of tea and shared a plate of hot *pakodas*. Rukmini was still in her blue housedress, while Venkat was already quite ready for work, bathed, shaved, and dressed in jeans.

'The old goat wants to impress the foreigners with that silly play he has written,' said Rukmini. 'It is so silly. I am afraid everyone will laugh and we will look ridiculous.'

Venkat was giving her a strange look, a half-smile on his face. 'Oh, I thought you were his pet lamb,' he said. 'Have you fallen out with him or something?'

'What do you mean?' she asked, arching her eyebrow. 'I have never fallen into him. This is a very good job, Venkat, or even you wouldn't be here for half a second. If I can get a permanent job in a good company, I would be off.'

'Don't put me off,' said Venkat, still smiling. 'Has he made it with you? Come now, you can tell me the truth. We all know what's going on.'

'Nothing is going on,' she said shortly. 'I won't sit here and have you insult me.'

'I don't want to insult you ever, Ruku,' said Venkat softly. 'Just wanted to know if he has had the courage to make a pass at you. Is he any good?'

Rukmini drained her cup, got up, and flicked a long finger against his cheek. 'No one is as good as you,' she said, walking back to her room.

The campus was beginning to fill up with gaily decorated bullock carts, and choruses of traditional songs could be heard from groups of women, who were sitting down in circles to light a fire and make their breakfast. Sharma*ji* had declared a *mela*, and all the poor women and their children were invited from all the neighbouring villages, which he dominated. Of course, many of the men were also there, driving the carts, putting up *shamianas*, supervising the work.

Nagaraju came striding across from between the groups of squatting women. He was tall and handsome, with a full, black moustache, oiled and curved. Even his village-made *chappals* looked masculine, the way he stood with his left foot thrust out. 'Rukmini amma! I am looking for you all over,' he said, smiling into her face as she came out of her room, freshly dressed in a printed nylon sari. 'Nothing will be done right, unless you come and stand there. They have not even started to cook the big meal, and the stage is falling to pieces!'

Three of the London Directors of Christians Everywhere were to arrive any minute at the village campus of SERVICE. It was rumoured that Lady Scilly, Chief Patroness, herself might come, and bring along some European donor friends as well, to witness the empowerment of poor rural women. Everyone had worked for weeks, preparing a spectacular *tamasha* for the occasion. Venkat was printing out the latest micro-credit figures in the low *godown* converted into the SERVICE TEAS office. He saw Rukmini hurry away to the cookhouse, almost rubbing shoulders with Nagaraju.

That man needed to be taught that he was only a villager, and that too a Dalit villager, promised Venkat to himself.

Finally, Lady Scilly's cavalcade was announced with a blare by turbaned trumpeters, arranged in a glittering line on a nearby hilltop. When she drew up in a cloud of dust, tutored village women surrounded the vehicles, garlanding the guests, daubing large dots of *kumkum* on their foreheads, sprinkling them with *attar*, and slapping sandalwood paste on their arms. Lady Scilly, an old NGO hand dressed in a beige *salwar-kameez*, got out of the car with folded hands, smiling and saying 'Namaskaram! Namaskaram!' to everyone, but Jeneke van Boren shrank away a little from such easy familiarity. She was new to such greetings, and concerned that the colours would ruin her clothes, and remained unconvinced by the reassurances whispered by Lady Scilly. Gert Wolfowitz, a tall, well-built, bespectacled German in a blue safari suit and with an abstract air, seemed neither happy nor embarrassed at the reception. In fact, he seemed far away in thought.

The village women then formed a cordon round the guests, singing and clapping their hands, and led them with din and confusion through the sights of the SERVICE campus, past the windmill which remained obstinately still without moving an inch, past the solar panels and the biogas plant, through the medicinal herbarium, and the dryland micro-watershed demonstration, to the biodiversity fields. The procession stopped at a little forest of messy plants to discover Sharma*ji*, totally oblivious of the noise, on his knees in the mud, patting a seedling into place, with three women whom he seemed to be instructing.

'Welcome! To SERVICE village, Sally,' he said familiarly to Lady Scilly, getting up with some reluctance from the wet earth, his *dhoti* muddied up to the knees. 'I would have come to welcome you at the gate, but this planting must be done at this hour, according to local tradition.' He held up folded hands when introduced to Jeneke and Gert. 'Please forgive me for not shaking hands, but this is Indian village. We touch mud all the time as it is the skin of our mother, Mother Earth.' Jeneke was smiling at everything now, resigned to paint, and mud, and noise, and pollen. Gert said nothing at all, but just nodded, mostly to himself.

Sharma*ji* then escorted them all the way back to the low buildings which formed the office. He loudly declaimed over the general hubbub how multinationals had stolen the indigenous knowledge of peasant women, and the scientific work of several hundred generations of women farmers. Lady Scilly was seen nodding in gracious acknowledgment, while Jeneke seemed wildly enthusiastic at every expected revelation of multinational deceit and heroic grassroots resistance. Gert kept talking in German into his cellphone.

Sharma*ji* stopped at a low door with a brass-plate that read 'Ramulamma, President.' He knocked timidly, and then, as if hearing permission to enter, led them into a small carpeted room. A middle-aged dalit woman sat perched on a metal chair behind a large desk, which had an in-tray with a few papers in it and two telephones, one painted red. A large photograph of Lady Scilly, wearing a garland of marigolds, hung behind Ramulamma. There were only three chairs in the room, so the guests sat on them.

Sharma*ji* stood humbly by the desk of his President and translated Ramulamma's short answers at great length. Thanks to the Internet, and Sharma*ji*'s highlighting and translating, the women knew everything—all the ploys of multinationals, to patent people's knowledge under the new WTO regime; to thrust their rotten GM technology onto India's sacred land by bribing corrupt politicians; and to poison people with their pesticides. Jeneke's eyes showered on Sharma*ji* the devotion owed to a *guru*, while Gert continued his inaudible German conversations over his cellphone. When a particularly important call drove Gert out of the small office, Sharma*ji* thankfully took the vacant seat. Lady Scilly sat serenely facing her photograph, in fact, dominating the proceedings though saying not a word. At a break in Sharma*ji*'s efforts, she turned to Jeneke and said for all to hear that SERVICE's biodiversity programme had to be supported. She, that is Christians Everywhere, would support fifty-five percent of the total cost, and would Jeneke pick up twenty-five percent? Jeneke was too overwhelmed at this gracious offer of participation in a planet-saving exercise to say anything but beam with watery eyes. Gert ducked in, made inaudible German calculations between marks, pounds and rupees, and said yes, he could manage the remaining twenty percent, and went outside to continue his calls.

The business of the day accomplished, Sharma*ji* led the foreign delegation to the feast that had been laid out under flapping *shamianas*, while Ramulamma locked the deserted President's Office and went to help in the kitchen. Changed into clean white clothes for lunch, Sharma*ji* stood in the centre of the tent, holding a plate in one hand while he stuffed his face with the other, explaining to his guests the nutritional value of every dish, the origin of the recipes, the obscure names of the local landraces of grains from which the culinary creations had emerged, and the battles he had fought to retain these grains in village storehouses, under constant threat from secret agents that worked for those multinationals. His loud voice competed with the women's singing, leaving Jeneke straining to catch his words. Gert, with one small, untouched helping of a single dish, stood scribbling in his notebook while he spoke on his cellphone. Lady Scilly seated herself in a comfortable cane chair, surrounded by the village women, who sat in a circle on the ground around her chair, and ate a hearty lunch, nodding and smiling as though she understood what the women said.

It was then time for the play, which had been a spontaneous creation of all the women, said Sharma*ji*. The covered stage was set like a court of law, with the village women arranged on the wings like a great body of jury. In the centre was a gold-painted chair, to which some women led Lady Scilly with great ceremony. She was clearly to be the judge, and everyone laughed when a big black shawl was draped round her shoulders. Lady Scilly seemed to be enjoying herself immensely. In the dock stood three boys dressed in suits too big for them and wearing black cardboard top hats with the American flag painted on them. To make sure everyone understood, the boys had placards slung round their necks, reading 'MNC.' The prosecution witnesses were all girls, each symbolically carrying the stalks of a plant.

The star seemed to be a short girl with two long sheaves of rice tucked behind her ears. She rolled on the stage, weeping loudly how she had been ravaged by the bad MNCs in the dock, torn out of her soil, and thrown away as if dead. Jeneke was much affected and said it was very good that the women had thought of the gender question as well, for gender and biodiversity were inseparable. Sharma*ji* beamed his agreement. 'Cotton' was a tall girl, who lunged to tear out the eyes of the MNCs, and had to be dragged away, screaming her hatred. 'Sunflower' had huge flowers in front of her face, and went silently bowing from jury member to jury member while depositing drops of oil onto their palms. A row of finger millets dramatically collapsed on the stage, and were literally swept away, dry and dead, with brooms. Every act of accusation was greeted with loud applause, till finally the jury was ready for the verdict. A black cap was put on Lady Scilly's head, and everyone laughed as the boy MNCs ran away in great terror.

Sharma*ji* gave a short speech in English as the shadows of trees lengthened across the grounds in front of the stage. He reminded the villagers that their foreign friends had come from across the globe to show solidarity in their just fight. The people would win for *dharma* was on their side. Gandhiji had always been sure of that and he, as a humble follower, had no doubts. He was especially grateful to Lady 'Iskilly'—he could not bring himself to pronounce her name any other way—for she was the *Devi Mata* of SERVICE. Everyone clapped.

Gert needed to take the plane that very evening to Delhi and Frankfurt, so after cups of tea, which Lady Scilly slurped happily in village India fashion, the cavalcade set off with all the women standing on either side, clapping their hands and waving. One girl came up to the window and said in English: 'Come again, please quickly, Lady Amma!' Then they were really off in a cloud of dust, leaving the tired women to clean up, while a few fights broke out about accounts and stolen food.

Some of the women had eased themselves behind the office building, and everyone was very angry, but what could they do, pointed out Rukmini, someone had left the toilets securely locked up. The *bhangi* women members had to clean up the mess, and everyone could hear them grumbling, and later shouting at the other women. Sharma*ji* had been successful in his mission of landing the money; he was exhausted, and went to his 'unit' to relax. He also had made sacrifices that day, not getting one minute to listen to the Test Match commentary.

3. The Brother-in-Law

The Brother-in-Law is a traditional figure of fun in South Indian folk literature and popular films. There was nothing funny at all about Sharma*ji*'s brother-in-law. He always brought problems that led to other problems. He would drop in at around seven-thirty in the evening, right when Sharma*ji* was about to settle down in front of the TV to watch his favourite serial. He would begin to talk endlessly about his office, the hostility he faced, the strange thing that had happened in the street that morning, and so many other annoying things, before he broached the problem. Then he would wait, drinking the third cup of coffee that Mrs Sharma served up, in full expectation that Sharma*ji* would solve it, and indeed that he would be happy to do so. Sharma*ji*'s evening would be ruined. The TV serial would remain unwatched while Sharma*ji* would have anxious moments that night wondering whether the heroine had been able to escape the clutches of the villain, or shed the calumny cast on her by her sister-in-law. Whether she had succeeded in teaching her competitive female friend a thing or two about matchmaking, or whatever.

This evening was no exception. His brother-in-law sat lightly poised on a straight-backed chair, balancing a cup of coffee in one hand and a lurid journal in the other, brought as a peace offering. It was midweek, and Sharma*ji* was back in the bosom of his family, in his large, untidy, third-floor city flat, and he was already feeling hot and sticky. His village SERVICE centre was so orderly, totally under his command, where he was treated with great respect almost verging on fear, though he was the most democratic and fatherly of leaders. But here in his own flat, he was just an ageing husband, father, or brother-in-law, suspected of eking out a livelihood by means that could almost be termed shady. None in his family cared to understand that he, with vision, daring, and sacrifice, had built an NGO, considered a jewel in the comity of world civil society organizations.

'I understand your need, Prasad,' he said, wiping his bald head with a handkerchief that was already greying in the city dust, 'and believe me, your daughter, dear Meena, is like a daughter to me. But how can I raise thirty thousand rupees by Monday to pay for her admission to this IT College? Can you not raise money through a chit fund or the bank? I believe banks are giving educational loans liberally.'

'*Bavagaru*, I have tried everything. The banks want collateral like gold, or my house, which is already mortgaged to pay for the housing loans. If I don't find the money by Monday, the college will offer the seat to someone else. The Principal, who is the cousin-brother of my friend, is actually doing us a favour,' said Prasad, making it sound like Sharma*ji*'s own problem.

'But what can I do?' went on Sharma*ji* gamely. 'My small salary just about pays for our frugal monthly needs. Many others in important positions like mine take huge salaries, but I said no! I am a servant of the people, and must live like them. I have no cash. I cannot raise money on this flat, for I am still paying off a loan incurred for sending my son Ashok to study abroad. I am helpless!' He pumped his arms, and spread out his hands in a gesture of anguish.

Prasad said something about whether there might be a possibility with SERVICE, but Sharma*ji* cut him short. 'Consider my position, it is a position of trust. I am in charge of a respected institution following in Gandhiji's footsteps.' He paused impressively on mentioning the sacred name.

Mrs Sharma came out of the kitchen. She was a large woman, a few inches taller than her husband, and not in the mood to mince words. 'You took money very easily from your Society when you got your sister's daughter married. Not a few thousand rupees, but two lakhs, I remember very well. Take from the Society now also. Everyone is doing it.'

Sharma*ji* was embarrassed at his wife for bringing up that matter. She had never let him rest after that, always suggesting he could draw money at will from SERVICE for all sorts of frivolous reasons, like buying her a new set of gold bangles. She had never understood that on that occasion, he had behaved with most scrupulous propriety. By an act of intellectual daring, equaling the perspicacity of Lord Maynard Keynes himself, he had found the money for his sister's daughter's wedding, as was his duty. For the dowry and the wedding feast and function, his sister had needed two more lakhs. She had come to him. What was he to do? If the money had not been produced, the wedding might have been called off, and that too to a Silicon Valley software engineer.

SERVICE had just then received fifty lakhs into its bank account from the Dutch Catholic Water for the World Mission, to undertake training of fifty communities in rain-shadow areas. By sheer chance, his cousin, the Secretary of an IT major, had dropped in from Bombay, and over the simple lunch that Sharma*ji* could afford had told him of the IPO about to be launched by his company. Everyone knew those days that the price of IT shares would take a quantum jump once they came on the market. He put his bold idea before his cousin as they were sitting fanning themselves after lunch, not failing to remind him that Sharma*ji*'s sister was like a sister to him also. Surprisingly, his cousin did not raise any difficulties. He had not applied to the full limit of his quota, for frankly he didn't have that much money. He would take five lakhs from Sharma*ji* and invest it in his own name. Having set out on this path, there was nothing for it but to carry it off with aplomb. Next day in the office, Sharma*ji* surprised his accountsofficer, Gupta, by demanding five lakhs as imprest cash, which he would personally distribute to all the grassroots NGOs involved.

'This is a very important project,' he had announced loftily. 'I want to make sure personally that every project head understands what he needs must do. It is the duty of the state to provide safe drinking water to all the people, but have they done so? No! It is now our responsibility. Gandhiji,' he paused as usual out of respect, 'would have wanted me to shoulder the task. It does not matter that it is hot. I shall go to every town, by bus or bullock cart, if necessary.'

With the money in hand, he raced to the airport to give the cash in person to his cousin. There should be no bank transactions, he had been warned. The next two weeks he took to his bed with a sudden attack of influenza. He was too weak to shave, or bathe, and could drink only *rasam*, every now and then. His staff came to visit him in his darkened bedroom, and he assured them that even death could not stand between him and his duty, but his wasted body kept him tied to his bed.

The very first day the shares came on the market, his five lakhs had been turned into eight lakhs. Fear and anxiety choked him, whether Murthy, his cousin, would keep all the money to himself and deny ever having received any cash from him. What a fool he had been not to see through Murthy's transparent ploy— he should have insisted on sending the money through the bank. Then, at least, Murthy would have been shamed in front of the family for sending Sharma*ji* to jail for doing his sacred duty by his sister. His bowels gave way and he had to run to the toilet three times that day. As if on purpose, the Municipality released no water that day, and he felt like an Englishman, having wiped himself with torn pieces of newspaper. He smelt in his bed, the sheets of which he had not been permitted to change for two weeks, in any case. But Murthy, good fellow, an ornament to the family, was as solid as his word. Seven lakhs were sent to him in a sealed package by courier—what a risk, in case the plane had crashed, there were so many rich people flying around whose *karma* deserved death. Sharma*ji* was out of bed in a jiffy, and cured of his debilitating flu at long last. However, he was in no state to travel to villages, everyone agreed, and he asked Gupta to go in his place and disburse the five lakhs. Well, God's blessings, and his own cleverness, had helped him to get his niece married off without a hitch to a Silicon Valley software engineer. Murthy had made a lakh out of the transaction thought up by Sharma*ji*.

Murthy had only played the role of a postman, so to speak and he could at least have shared that extra lakh fifty-fifty. But what do you expect with business types, what do they understand of service to society?

His wife had whisked herself back to the kitchen, though he knew that her ears were tuned to every word that was said in the living room. There was no point in explaining to her or Prasad, that the chance that enabled him get his niece married does not come round every day. He must think of some other way out, for his wife was an irresistible force when it came to her family and their needs. God had to show the way. Thinking of God gave him an idea.

'How many days of leave can you take?' he asked.

'I have ten days of casual leave,' said Prasad promptly.

'There is a project, a very important project,' Sharma*ji* started weightily. 'Christians Everywhere has asked us to undertake a study on slum living conditions, collect and tabulate data, and draw inferences for a typical slum. You are a Commerce graduate, but you took Sociology as a subject, and I can pay you post-grad going rates, say, three thousand rupees a day, rather high, but we want quality work very quickly, so that would be justified.'

Prasad looked totally dismayed. '*Bavagaru*,' he remonstrated, 'whatever I studied long ago, I have forgotten. I could never do statistics. And one would need assistants to interview these people, who are drunk most of the time. There are also *goondas* who could beat you up. *Bavagaru*, the people living in slums these days are terrible people, and their drains overflowing with shit, I tell you, it is hell in there!'

Sharma*ji* frowned thoughtfully. 'I started serving people twenty years ago under that good man, Dr Barclay, of Goodnews Friends. You know, I took a great risk, I left my permanent Government post to do it,' he said fiercely, his Section Officer's job in the Land Records Office being given by time the aura of an IAS Secretary's post. 'We never worried about dust or pain or inconvenience, or even grave risk to our lives. But what can I expect? Everyone is not made like me. Anyway, under Dr Barclay's personal direction, Goodnews Friends had completed a comprehensive study of the Keechudgally slum. A copy of that study I should still have among those files in the top shelf over the dining table. Let us use it; how do facts change in twenty years?'

'I am going to serve dinner any minute now, so don't throw dust all over my table,' shouted Mrs Sharma from the kitchen. 'Who serves all these people doing service all over the world? Me, I have to clean up, as if I was a *harijan*.'

Prasad intervened to pacify his sister. He tied one of Sharma*ji*'s *dhotis* to two chair-ends, as a screen protecting the dining area, climbed up onto a stool, and after some coughing and mutterings about useless paper, brought down a large yellowing file.

'This is the study,' said Sharma*ji* triumphantly. 'Photocopy it neatly, maybe make a few corrections to bring it up to date. Oh, and bring along your biodata, we would need that for our files.'

Next morning, as Sharma*ji* sat frowning over a fresh photocopy of the study in his office, Gupta hobbled in, dragging his game leg behind him. 'Gupta, you know that slum study required by Christians Everywhere?' he said. 'Well, I know one Mr S.V. Prasad, a Sociologist, who has intimate knowledge of the Keechudgally slum, really the archetypical slum in our city. I said, "Do the study, but I will not pay you!" He looked up at Gupta for effect, and noted that his assistant was suitably impressed. "If your study is of quality, I will consider suitable payment." This is the study. I am satisfied, though mind you, if I had undertaken it myself, it might have been better, much better. But with all this work, where do I have the time? What are the going rates, say, for ten days' work, though Prasad said he spent almost a month on it?'

Gupta suggested two thousand rupees a day. 'No, no, not for a study of this standard. We must be fair. Let us make out a check for thirty thousand rupees.' Then, something caught his eye. 'But I must make my observations also. Bring me a whiteout.' Prasad, the lazy oaf, had not even obliterated the date or the Goodnews Friends logo from the pages. Grumbling that all the hard work still had to be done by him alone as Sharma*ji* carefully corrected each page.

4. At the Barricades

Unlike all the others enjoying the bright summer morning in their casual clothes, Sharma*ji* was carefully wrapped up in his woollens with a long scarf wound round his bald head like a turban, for he feared the tricky European weather. They were a group of global protestors, expertly brought from around the world to form a picket line outside the Swiss chateau where the World Bank was holding a meeting to discuss food security in impoverished countries. The provocation for the protest was a leaked paper that a former president of Harvard University, and present advisor to the Bank, had written on the vital role of modern pesticides to increase food crops. Christians Everywhere had swiftly organized a civil response to this blatant corporate attack on the Planet itself, and Sharma*ji*, as was to be expected, was representing South Asia.

The Swiss Police in their neat grey uniforms had formed a cordon, leaving twenty yards clear of the wrought-iron gates. The protestors had been very politely informed that they could stand behind the police line, raise slogans if they wished, wave placards. But on no account should they surge forward or throw anything at the delegates, however harmless, on pain of instant eviction from Switzerland. Could they throw flowers, a girl from Mexico had asked, and the police had replied without a smile that they could not. A thin jeer, which almost sounded like a cheer, rose from the group as a cavalcade of black Mercedes cars swept through the gates towards the rather plain chateau deep within its grounds. Tall green trees shimmered in the sunlight, and beyond, to the left, were open fields with hardly a soul working in them. Just then a team of TV vans drew up and parked close to them. Cameramen with CNN, BBC, CBS and CBC logos emerged, led by a few brisk, important-looking women interviewers.

Sharma*ji* was enjoying being in Europe once again. His fears of violence, which had kept him anxiously awake during the long flight from India, were dissipated by the calm and authoritative assurance of the Swiss police. He had also worried about lodgings, but Christians Everywhere had thoughtfully provided him with a single room with an attached bath, TV, a coffee-maker and a welcoming bottle of red wine. Before dropping off to well-needed sleep, he had seen, to his delight, that even the normal pay channels that show a 'certain type' of movies, as he put it, were showing them without charge late at night. His hosts were not unaware that Sharma*ji*, for all his earnestness, found child-like enjoyment in the comforts and freedoms of European life. SERVICE was a valuable partner, and the work of which had netted one million pounds in personal donations in just one week before Christmas. What had done the trick was a single poster with Sharma*ji*'s squat figure in the foreground and what looked like a sea of poor sari-clad Indian women linking hands before a field of maize, carrying the slogan 'Will You Help Him Protect Their Fields?' And now, here he was giving a firm, non-violent Gandhian message in the very heart of opulent Europe. Who better than he?

Suddenly, Arturo Pereira from Brazil was standing in front. 'Sharma, Mr Sharma, they want someone from Asia, who knows—how we say—problems, problems about agriculture, to tell them why we are here—pesticides, dangers to health, land, crops. Here they are,' as a media lady bustled up. Sharma*ji* beamed, he was in his element. What could all these young people, laughing and jostling one another all round him, tell the world about issues? They needed a man of experience, of commitment, like himself, to lead them. Take this Pereira, for instance, just a young man out to have fun, nothing more. Last night, Sharma*ji* had excused himself early after dinner, he was tired, and in any case he did not need the 'orientation,' which was planned, about the dangers of pesticide use. Leaving the dining hall, he had gone up a flight of steps, and round the corner found this Pereira holding that Finnish woman, Helga, in a crushing embrace. Both had smiled and waved to him, and carried on. Such behaviour would never be tolerated in India, certainly never in his SERVICE centres. But you needed tradition to know how to behave, and where did they have tradition?

Cameras and mikes were being thrust at him. 'We are the people of the world, the simple people of the world,' said Sharma*ji* slowly, with a special accent he used when interviewed in Europe. 'What do we want? We are not like these rich people, who need so much money for everything. Last night's dinner, I could not believe what we paid! With this money, my people can eat for four months!' The interviewing lady nodded delightedly. 'And why do we need pesticides? To make Rich Feed, to feed your European pigs? No, the answer is always—No! Our land is for feeding our own people, with our traditional, simple food!'

'You have come here, Mr Sharma, from India, to protest the World Bank's policy of helping your country's farmers modernize their agricultural practices,' said the media woman. 'You are head of a civil society collective of poor women called SERVICE. Don't you think they would want to make more money by following modern agricultural practices?'

'Absolutely Not! They have an ancient, and spiritual relationship to their land,' he said firmly, and noted from her expression that he had scored another hit. He was now in full swing. 'Their land is their Mother. No one in our country poisons their Mother for money! I am determined for the sake of the people I lead to end my life here on Swiss soil, rather than permit pesticides on our fields! And my good friends here, who have come from all over the world, we all have the same focus. We have but one focus!'

'We have only one focus!' echoed the jubilant group, led by Pereira, who was looking fixedly at Helga's bosom. She gave him a dazzling smile from across the gathering.

After the TV people had packed up and left, the police informed them that they all had to leave then, for some reason that was not clear, but they could assemble again next morning. Sharma*ji* was relieved. There was no place even to sit outside the chateau gates, and what was the purpose of loitering anyway? He had saved some project money by very clever management of funds. The extra bank interest earned was due solely to his hard work, and really belonged to no one. He had drawn a larger travel advance with that money and now hoped he could buy an Omega watch with it. Saying something vague, that he had to report to the Indian embassy, he detached himself from the group and wandered around the clean streets of Geneva. That fountain of water foaming over the lake was a marvel. He sat and watched it for sometime. In Geneva he had no fear that he would be approached by some tout or other, or attacked, so he could let down his guard and just enjoy himself. He wandered past all the famous shops, gazing through the windows, wondering how much money one needed to be really at home in Geneva. A World Bank person would not be just looking at all that glitter; he would go in and purchase what he wanted. He entered a few watch shops, asked for Omega watches, held them in his hand, looked at the prices, and then went away. They were expensive, but he should have one, he had always wanted one. He would think about them, conjure up images of how they looked, go over the specifications in the brochures he had stuffed in his pocket, and then take a decision. He was cool-headed as always.

That evening they were all invited to dinner in a café by the lake. There was some music, and a few of the group danced. Pereira was dancing, but with a dark-haired Italian woman. What loose behaviour! As the waitresses in their red uniforms and white aprons came round to take orders, an officious Englishwoman stretched out a protecting hand and said, 'Remember, only vegetarian food for Mr Sharma. What do you have that is vegetarian?'

Sharma*ji* would not permit their hosts to be embarrassed. 'Please, no trouble, I can eat anything you serve me, and with gratitude,' he said in his saintliest manner. 'It is true I am a vegetarian at home, a strict vegetarian. But the Gandhian approach' – pause – 'the Buddhist approach, is to treat all food as sacred. Nothing should be rejected. We should not kill, but we should eat with gratitude—and pleasure—what is put in front of us.'

There was an appreciative silence. Some old Swiss ladies turned, looked at Sharma*ji*, nodded, and smiled. They even came round later, took his address, and promised to visit his ashram when they came to India. 'What shall I bring for you?' asked the smiling Swiss waitress. 'Filet de perche with tartare sauce and French fries,' said Sharma*ji*, in a soft, rapid whisper.

The next morning's protest was petering out very much like the previous day's when a middle-aged Swiss functionaire, in blue blazer and grey trousers, approached the group, and fell into conversation with Pereira and a few others. It transpired that the World Bank wanted to meet a few of the protestors, their delegation, if you like, to discuss whether differing opinions could be bridged, whether there could be rapprochement. The leaders naturally gravitated towards Sharma*ji* and the TV cameras swung round.

'Where is the question of compromise?' asked Sharma*ji* loudly. 'We are talking of values, and where values are concerned, there can be no compromise! We are not academics that discuss ideas! We here are the world's people, who wish to be heard!' He had raised his voice dramatically, and the group shouted 'Hear us! Hear us!' into the cameras. 'No! There is nothing to discuss but— as people—we are always ready for dialogue,' he said, even as the Swiss bureaucrat was turning away.

The question was who should represent the group, the people of the world, at the dialogue. They went to a nearby café to discuss and settle the issue. Sharma*ji* formed the centre of the decision-making circle; some others, the young European crowd, melted away, uninterested in serious dialogues. It was decided that Sharma*ji* would be the de facto leader of the dialogue group, which would have Arturo Pereira representing Latin America, and Lungi N'kolo representing Africa.

At the Barricades 29 'I will come along, if all of you want me to,' said Lungi, a rather straightforward woman in her early thirties. 'When I was at university in London, I thought talking to these people helped, but it does not. They know what they want, and they only want to hear their opinions from our mouths. But, OK, we have decided we will meet them in dialogue, so I shall come, but Sharma here must do the talking.' She gave a gurgling laugh. 'He is so good at it, I am not!' Sharma*ji* took this as a compliment—in fact weeks later back in India, he would recount how the Africans and the Latin Americans had no plan till he led them to put forward their ideas clearly and forcefully. The three were escorted to the chateau, where they were in time to join the international delegates to the food security conference at a lavish lunch.

Assembled round the conference table, Sharma*ji* and his two colleagues were placed importantly at the head of the table. 'We are now to hear from the people,' said the World Bank Director who was leading the conference. 'Ms N'Kolo, Mr Sharma, Mr Pereira, you will have our full and respectful attention over the next half-hour. All of us here believe in dialogue, and in helping each other to help others. Together we must help solve the food crises. We are not committed to any one particular food producing methodology over others. We are here with an open mind.'

It was Sharma*ji*'s show. He, in turn, welcomed such an open attitude to the most important issue facing humanity. All the delegates applauded at this point. He was willing to work with the World Bank—he paused at this point and looked at his two colleagues as if he had just pulled a rabbit out of a hat—but only, and only, he emphasized, if the World Bank was wholeheartedly willing to work only for the people. Again there was applause all round, a few Americans at the end of the table making quick notes on their pads. He would go wherever they wanted him to meet them, his age and health were no concern, but within the next few years, through rigorous discussions, they must jointly arrive at a solution to the problem of food security. The World Bank officials and others round the table were of the same mind. Lungi, to whom they paid extravagant respect, said the real matter was that poor people could not afford pesticides, they got into debt. Their lands were too poor to use all these chemicals, and pesticides affected children and killed birds. Ah! The birds! Madame was right, charmingly so! She had reminded these hardheaded businessmen that there was a world outside their office rooms. A toxicology expert from Pesticlor said that as a boy he had always woken up to the music of birdcalls. And now, most of time he was on the fifty-fifth floor of a glass and steel skyscraper in the middle of Manhattan. They crowded round Madame and extended invitations to several other conferences, but Lungi said no, she had to be with her children, and the other children of the women she worked with. Pereira spent most of the tea-break looking down the deep cleavage of a Venezuelan chief executive, who said a smiling goodbye, giving him two of her visiting cards.

When Sharma*ji* flew out of Geneva, he stretched out his left arm against the cold armrest of his seat so that he could see the glint of his Omega watch every now and then. In his pocket were the addresses, telephone numbers and email addresses of the World Bank Director, who had invited him to three international conferences later that year, at one of which he would be the keynote speaker.

5. Sharma*ji* and the Tiger

'**Society for Educational Resources** Vitalising Indian Community Entrepreneurs,' was read out slowly, with a pause at every word, by S.R. Rajagopalan, IAS, Principal Secretary, Forests. 'I don't see any mention of tigers here,' he said politely but dismissively, raising his head from the file he had been studying in total silence for all of fifty seconds.

Sharma*ji* was sitting bolt upright in the chair, directly facing the official across a wide table piled high with files and four differently coloured telephones. 'Sir, SERVICE is a training organization, with over twenty years' experience facilitating development work…'

'Excuse me,' said Rajagopalan, politely as ever, and picked up a telephone. 'Yes, connect me to the Home Secretary...hmm... what? He is away in Delhi attending a conference? Well, then connect me to the Joint Secretary Home. And yes, ask the Deputy Chief Wildlife Warden to come.' He turned back to Sharma*ji* expressionless, but apparently awaiting explanation.

Sharma*ji* gamely started once again. 'As I was saying, Sir, we are an old organization dedicated to rural and tribal training, and funds have been allocated to us from Friends of Tigers Everywhere to protect our tiger resources...'

'The Foreign organization cannot allot funds directly to a Non-Governmental Agency,' cut in Rajagopalan, still politely but with an acid edge to his voice. 'Without prior approval of the State Government and Ministry of Finance, Government of India will not sanction release of funds. It is for us to take a view on how best the money under Project Tiger may be utilized. I have gone through your application carefully and I do not see any relevance between your experience and tiger conservation. Excuse me.' The telephone had given a sharp tinkle. 'Hello, Balaji! Long time, *yaar*, since we met. You never seem to come to the Club, what's the matter? Purushottam keeps you hard at work? I see. Well, just check this out, will you? I have an application here from one Mr Sharma, yes, Mr Vedavyas Sharma of SERVICE, yes, the usual acronym fund-catcher...has Home given them permission to work in sensitive areas in the State? Do they have clearance under Foreign Contributions Regulations Act? Please send me a file on their record, will you? Thanks. And what else? How are the children doing? What? *Arre bhai*, put her in another school. What about Flower Garden School? I know they are expensive, but I know Mrs Singh, and I'll ask her to give you the special fee rate. I will speak to her.'

The Secretary looked up, vaguely surprised to see Sharma*ji* still sitting in front. The door opened behind Sharma*ji*, in his imagination almost a hundred yards away, and an ageing man in khaki with wispy hair shuffled into the room. He hung about uncertain whether to take a chair or not. The Secretary beckoned him round the table and gave him the file. 'I want a full report by tomorrow how this NGO, SERVICE, has been included in our Tiger Project proposal to Government of India. Hmm? OK, thanks,' dismissing the older man.

The Secretary looked directly at Sharma*ji*. 'Mr Sharma, I have asked for an immediate report from the Deputy Chief Wildlife Warden. We will look into this matter, and take a view on it. We will let you know our decision.' With that he rang the bell for the attender to show his visitor out. And that was that. Of course, no letter was ever received from the Secretary, nor could one be expected.

Sharma*ji* had felt somewhat aggrieved. He had spent a lot of his time, and SERVICE money, going up and down to Delhi, discussing the project at the Indian head office of Christians Everywhere, where, of course, he had been very cordially received as their key Indian partner. He had put it into their heads to recommend him as a partner to Friends of Tigers Everywhere, and that had not been easy. They had been worried about loss of focus. He had had to be subtle.

'Development and Conservation are like two eyes to a poor Indian,' he had pontificated. 'If we look at Gandhiji's work'—pause—'we find an astonishingly modern perspective. And why is this so? Because, environment—the land—is our Mother to Indians. And animals, even fierce tigers, are our brothers— our siblings,' he had rephrased himself swiftly, so as not to have the discussion divert into gender-related questions. Christians Everywhere considered him an Original, a personification of the artless Indians of the Raj Legend. Almost all of whom had disappeared in the hustle and bustle of growing Capitalism, but they had once abundantly populated the Jewel in the Crown. When Sharma*ji* had brought in the spiritual dimension linking tigers to Hinduism, they had decided he would be the best partner in the Tiger Project. He had been silently jubilant for a fat project with ample funds had been secured, but the administrative guardian at the gate had undone all his work within five minutes. But, he had reflected, this was all part of the game of doing development work. You win some, you lose some, and with that, Sharma*ji* had put away all the files connected with the project into the bottommost shelf of his cupboard.

Hence, he was taken aback to receive, several months later, an invitation from the Principal Chief Conservator of Forests to sit in on the special advisory committee of the State's Tiger Project. Soon he found out that this did not betoken a change of heart in the Secretary. The Principal Chief Conservator, whose office was half-a-city's width from the power centres of the Secretariat, had received instructions that one member of civil society had to be inducted into the new advisory committee, as per World Bank norms. Sharma*ji*'s name was the only one his harassed staff could discover quickly. The committee had to be constituted in haste before the visit of the American Director of World Wildlife, who was coming to inspect the newly set up Bhramananda Reddy Tiger Reserve, which had already consumed ten million dollars worth of foreign grants.

Sharma*ji* was very proud of the fact that on the day of the first committee meeting, a white Ambassador staff car with the national flag neatly rolled into its plastic cover, but erect as a penile symbol at the tip of the car's hood, had carried him to the Forest Department. He was then seated in the middle of the long conference table that was crowded with several high-ranking conservators. Two chairs had been left vacant at the head of the table for the Minister and the Principal Chief Conservator, who awaited the Minister's coming in his own chamber, in the meantime discussing with several relatives, over long-distance telephone calls, the impending wedding of his daughter. But the Minister did not come; the calls got extended, and the gathered conservators disposed of several rounds of tea and *samosas*. Sharma*ji* was in his element. Since none in the gathering knew what the status of this lone civilian was, or the political power he might wield, everyone was extremely polite and attentive, and Sharma*ji* enthralled everyone with his jokes and his anecdotes.

Finally, the rapid entry of several liveried attenders, flinging open the door, indicated the arrival of the Minister, who came in first, followed by the Principal Chief Conservator. Everyone stood to attention. Sharma*ji* pondered whether he, a representative of the people of India, should also stand up. As a concession, he lifted his ample bottom a few inches from the chair. The Minister was a tall, huge man whose starched *khadi kurta* stood out like a tent around him, tight under his fat breasts, and jerking as his belly moved with every step or word he uttered. His lower lip hung over a square chin, a picture of ruthless power. The thin, wizened Principal Chief Conservator, half his size, was almost lost to view.

The Minister was deeply unhappy. His voice slowly rose to a crescendo as he began the meeting. 'I am deeply disturbed. I am holding Independent Charge of a number of important portfolios. I am handling the Prime Minister's Tsunami Fund, the Jawaharlal Nehru Housing Scheme for Widows, the Indira Gandhi Adopt a Village Plan for Corporates, the Rajiv Gandhi Drinking Water Programme for Tribals, and also the Project Tiger. When I ask to see Tsunami victims, I am submerged in a sea of them. When I look around for villages to be given in adoption, there are half a million; there is no shortage of widows or tribals either. But when I ask you high-paid forest conservators to show me one tiger—just one tiger—you turn up here with excuses! What do you mean there are no tigers in the Bhramananda Reddy Tiger Reserve! We have just spent ten million dollars on it! And the Director of World Wildlife is to visit it next week accompanied by the President himself!' He gathered himself, visibly struggling to regain his composure. 'This looks to me like a political move to discredit me—whoever is doing this—and I can easily get to the bottom of this bad political game—he will suffer, I can promise. And you do this to me! I am the Minister who has created more jobs for conservators than anyone else. I said in the Cabinet, "I don't care if there are more conservators than tigers—I want two trailing every tiger, everywhere!" And now you do this to me—the keynote speaker of The Global Jungle 2012 Conference in Washington!' He was shouting by the time he finished.

There was hushed silence round the room, middle-aged men shuffling their feet and looking at their toes, like schoolboys.

An old conservator stood up at long last. 'Sir, we all know the urgency, the importance of the occasion. We have made all arrangements in the Bhramananda Reddy Tiger Reserve. The best cooks have been flown in from Delhi. There will be dances by tribal girls from Assam. They dance in all-important state events, and have received training in tribal dancing in Paris. The guesthouse is beautifully decorated. But tigers, we could not see. I am an old man, with diabetes and blood pressure. Sir, I walked over every inch of the area in the boiling heat. See, Sir, the blisters on my feet...' With that he moved out of his chair, removing his shoes and socks, to hold up lacerated feet for all of them to see.

The Minister was impatient. '*Arre, bhai,* I don't doubt your sincerity. But tigers are not to be seen by slow old men. They don't sit on the roadside for photo-ops. They hide. Someone has to pull them out by the tail when the American comes, or, I will close down the department. I will outsource the whole job to West India Hotels! If they were in charge, they would have brought tigers from Africa if I had asked them.'

The old conservator was not to be put off. 'Sir, the poachers, Sir, have played havoc,' he said bravely, in the pin-drop silence of the room. 'If you had not permitted that paper company to build those forest roads, Sir, I warned…'

The Minister quickly cut into this kind of thinking. 'Nonsense! I tell you, nonsense!' he yelled. 'Nation-building cannot stop just because of some animals, or careless departmental work. Now, what about that child that was attacked and killed in that village, what was it called, near the Reserve? TV stations made so much fuss. Anyway, that shows there was a tiger!'

No one spoke up but the persistent old conservator. 'Sir, it was a pig that bit the child. Sepsis set in, and since there was no doctor…' The Minister's belly almost jumped out of his *kurta*. 'A pig! I can't show a pig to the American!'

A young conservator, who had been wrestling with himself for some time to say something important, burst in brightly. 'Sir, I saw a leopard, only two weeks ago, leaping across a glade. It was gone in a flash.'

The Minister relaxed dramatically. He smiled, and leaned forward cordially towards the young man. 'There! I knew there will be tigers. Enthusiastic young men work! You will go far. Now, tell me, how do you know it was not a tiger? It was gone in a flash. Most probably it was a tiger you saw in the bad light. In a tiger forest there are tigers, not leopards.'

The young conservator, his courage evaporating, was unable to sustain a direct dialogue with the Minister. 'Sir, it was mid-day, Sir. It had spots, Sir, it…' he said confusedly.

The Minister would have none of this cautious prevarication. 'Spots, warts, how do we know? When a tiger leaps, stripes look like spots. Find this tiger; our American guest must see it next week. This must be done, whatever else you people do.'

Everyone turned towards the Principal Chief Conservator, who, after all, was their leader. He was a quiet thoughtful man with a faraway look. He began softly. 'When Lord Willingdon was Viceroy, he used to go on hunting parties, I believe…'

If there was a tiger anywhere in the vicinity, it was the Minister. He turned with a growl on the poor man. 'You are a conservator,

Sir, remember! Not the manager of a hunting party! My God, I am surrounded by incompetents. You will lose your job, and get the Prime Minister to dismiss me as well. Hunting is banned; you can't kill a rabbit without getting jailed!' Then, he spoke slowly in frozen anger. 'We-must-show-a-tiger-to-this-American, do you understand? Not kill one for sport!'

The Principal Chief Conservator, for all his small size and soft voice, had survived many vicissitudes in long, not undistinguished, years of service. 'My submission is that there is a solution, if Honourable Minister permits?' he said quietly, looking full into the furious face glowering over him.

By now the Minister was like a tiring baited bull. 'Of course, I permit. I know the solution. What is the solution?'

'A tiger used to be taken in a special compartment of the Viceroy's train so that it could be shot at the appropriate spot. In this case, since there is some urgency, and Her Excellency the President is also coming, I submit, if Honourable Minister permits, we procure a good tiger from a zoo.' The words of the Principal Chief Conservator fell into the pregnant silence like a bomb. Many around the table had started to think the same thought, but speaking it out loud and clear was another matter. That was why that little man was chief.

All could see the light slowly dawn in the Minister's eyes. 'Yes, yes, I leave details to you,' he said, with shy haste, like a man caught with his fly open. 'I know nothing of all this. But, remember, you can't show a tiger on a chain. It must somehow be free, in the jungle.' Here was a chance for the young conservator to show off his brilliant foresight. 'Sir, we will release it at some distance, and then with some noise chase it towards the road where you and the foreign delegation will be passing!'

The Minister turned back with a snarl. 'No! No! You will get us killed. Or my armed Black Cat guards will kill it in front of the BBC and CNN cameras. You will finish all of us. How many days of service have you left, before retirement?'

The chief intervened quietly. 'We will dope the animal, Sir, and lay it under a tree by the roadside. You will all see it!' He opened out his arms dramatically. 'You will be silent so as not to wake the tiger. He will be lightly doped, so you will see the tail twitching. My staff and I will duck into covered pits when we hear the cars approach. After Honourable Minister and the foreign delegation leave, we will come out, tie up the animal, and take him back to the zoo.'

The Minister was happy at long last. 'Excellent idea, Conservator Sahib! Old is gold as always. Young people go to cinemas, do nothing, get lazy. All forest officers must learn from you. Make sure it is a good-looking animal. And, mind, no accidents!' The Principal Chief Conservator assured him there would be none. He turned professionally to his staff.

'We must plan this meticulously. I want back-ups, at least two more young tigers kept in reserve. Tap all zoos. You all know what to do.'

The Minister made ready to leave. 'I knew it was all nonsense about there being no tigers. I will issue a press statement to the contrary. Pug marks have been seen all over the place, tiger shit, that sort of thing. Please make all arrangements. I must leave now. I have to address the Freedom from AIDS Society, and congratulate the Dutch delegation for helping us make this city the first AIDS-free city in India. I hope officials have more sense than last time, and don't bring these fellows onto the stage and make us all shake hands with them. Idiots!'

As they all stood up, his eyes sweeping the room caught Sharma*ji*'s. For all his bulk, he moved forward swiftly, and grabbing Sharma*ji*'s arm, requested him to accompany him in his own car. Everyone stood back respectfully, casting many admiring glances at the pair. A flurry of attenders, armed guards, and drivers opened the car door for Sharma*ji*, who found himself squashed beside the ample form of the Minister and whisked away through the city at high speed, sirens blaring.

The Minister leaned towards Sharma*ji*, almost squeezing the breath out of him. 'Sharma*ji*, we must maintain a diplomatic silence about our strategy,' confided the Minister. 'There are so many miscreants in the Press, who are happiest when defaming their own country.'

Sharma*ji* understood him instantly and completely. 'Minister*ji*, I am a patriot. In my own humble way, I am also a servant of the public, like yourself. We all know there are abundant tigers everywhere. But the skill to locate them, the indigenous knowledge, which our forefathers had, where is it now? Destroyed by globalization. We cannot let India down in front of foreigners.'

The Minister was very pleased with the response, though he was on his cellphone most of the time Sharma*ji* was displaying his patriotism. The Minister assured Sharma*ji* with a squeeze of the arm that they were like brothers. When the cavalcade drew up at their destination, where a large crowd awaited the Minister with garlands, the Minister first instructed the driver to take Sharma*ji* wherever he wanted to go. Then turning to Sharma*ji*, and looking him full in the eyes, he asked simply: 'Is there anything I can do?'

Sharma*ji* started to protest that meeting a great man like him was itself sufficient, when he remembered, and mentioned the incident with Mr Rajagopalan, Principal Secretary for Forests. 'I should like to serve the people, Sir, in the cause of tiger conservation also, and foreign funds are readily available, but some bureaucratic hurdles…'

The Minister had opened the door and was halfway out of the car. 'He will be transferred. Come and see me day after tomorrow.' Sharma*ji* was a happy man as he rode back in the Minister's car to his flat.

6. The Classes in Marxism

'**What was the purpose** in starting the Marxist classes, Mr Sharma?' asked Harbajan Singh, the Deputy Inspector General of Police, Special Branch, with extreme politeness. Sharma*ji* looked round the old office room in the police headquarters, with the noisy desert cooler in the window spitting droplets of water over him. With all his reservations, he was grateful it was a cool room, for a hot summer raged outside.

'As you know, a special focus of the work of our charitable organisation is education,' he started in measured tones. 'Raising people's awareness, their rights and responsibilities, to help in the democratic functioning of our state.' He had been summoned by the police for an urgent meeting with the DIG in charge of intelligence, and he had come prepared.

The police officer looked at him with a friendly smile. 'And you believe that the interests of the state are furthered by ordinary people learning about Marxism,' he said, more as a flat statement than as a question.

'Well, our constitution defines us as a socialist society,' said Sharma*ji* defensively. Mr Harbajan Singh looked up at his ceiling and smiled. He could be quite handsome for a Sikh, thought Sharma*ji*, if he would only shave a little.

'So in your definition, a socialist state requires people to study Marxism?' asked his interrogator, even more pleasantly.

Sharma*ji* instinctively sensed he was being led into dangerous waters. This smiling policeman was far deeper than most of his ilk—he had a plan, he wanted to trap Sharma*ji* into making some admission, but why? There must be a report against him, or SERVICE, or one of his stupid colleagues. He had had to engage university lecturers to teach the classes; he had been forced to select those who could make things a little interesting. God knows Marx was very boring, but he just couldn't come straight out and tell this smiling Sikh that 'Leonard the Leninist' had been harping on starting the classes. At last Sharma*ji* had given in with a semblance of enthusiasm, saying something vague about the eleventh thesis on Feuerbach, for he needed 'Leonard the Leninist' to approve his budget for Christians Everywhere. He had shrugged his shoulders metaphorically at the oddity of Christian development organisations being more revolutionary than the Indian communist parties. But now he needed to answer this policeman, somehow satisfactorily.

'We understand the compulsions of funding very well,' said the Sikh answering for him. 'Who better than the police, who always have to look for more funds to help us contain growing civil unrest?'

So the fellow knew, then why was he harassing him? Sharma*ji* wanted to see behind that smiling mask of a face doubly hidden by that zareba of black hair and khaki turban. He had to pick his words. It would be dangerous to be condescending, but to appear as frightened as he really was would be equally self-defeating.

'My record of public service speaks for itself,' said Sharma*ji* at long last. 'I have never had any intention whatsoever of fomenting disturbances through an educational media.'

The police officer looked at his desk with a serious frown. 'We should not talk about personal records, Mr Sharma, at this stage, that is better left unsaid, for after all it's our duty to know everything about people under surveillance, know everything.' The man was quite unsmiling, and Sharma*ji*'s stomach gave a queer lurch.

Suddenly the DIG of Police, Special Branch, leaned back and laughed happily, while ringing his bell for the police orderly. 'What can I offer you, Mr Sharma? Tea or coffee? I wouldn't recommend coffee, it's full of chicory, and I am sure you as a South Indian Brahmin would drink only pure coffee, and that too made with peaberry beans, right? And you buy coffee beans from Krishna Stores every second week, am I right? I know how particular you are. Good, let's have tea, they make it sugary sweet, but we Punjabis like only sweet things!'

After the differential orderly had deposited the tea and left, Mr Harbajan Singh looked at Sharma*ji* with a fond smile as he sipped his tea noisily through his moustache. 'We are not worried about common human failings, money, women, we all have them, makes us men, right? But National Security is another matter altogether, I am sure you agree?'

Sharma*ji*'s disjointed explanations were listened to between noisy sips of tea. Suddenly, the police officer broke into his rambling defence. 'Why don't you treat us as friends, Mr Sharma?

Why couldn't you come straight to us and say, look, Leonard the Leninist wants Marxist classes—you wonder how I know— my dear fellow, knowing is our trade. We are in daily touch with Scotland Yard, doesn't look like it, right, seeing these shabby walls? But we are. You could have come to us as an honest law-abiding citizen and we would have solved all your problems by giving you our Marxist lecturers. The disgruntled fellows you have got know little about Marxism, they know enough only to rouse the disgruntled. You mentioned the eleventh thesis on Feuerbach— well, Mr Sharma what are the other ten? You want to know? Here, read the book,' and he drew a Marxist text from his desk drawer and threw it on the table. 'Please wait, I shall be back in a minute.'

The Sikh police officer was not back for a full forty-five minutes, letting Sharma*ji* stew in his doubts and fears. When he came back, he was accompanied by his stenographer, to whom he dictated routine letters for the next half an hour. After his assistant had left, Mr Harbhajan Singh was immersed in some files for another ten to fifteen minutes. Then he lifted his head and seemed to discover Sharma*ji* for the first time.

'Well, Mr Sharma, are you willing to cooperate? You need to be absolutely frank with me. You are free to go your own way of course at any minute. We are a modern security force working for the people of the world's largest democracy, so everything is above-board. But in your interests, I must inform you that Delhi has asked us to take a view on whether your registration under the Foreign Contributions Registration Act should be renewed. We can only express an honest opinion, we can do no more, they take all the decisions in Delhi. They will decide whether you are to continue receiving foreign donations, or not. Well? What is it to be?' And he rang the bell for the orderly and instructed him to put all the files in the car to take home. Clearly, he was impatient to be gone. Sharma*ji* was totally confused and looked in bewilderment. The police officer looked at him quizzically over large folded hands, his elbows thrust aggressively in front on the table.

'Sharma, you have passed the test. If you had taken my meaning straightaway, I would have immediately suspected you of playing a deep game, but now I know you just want your money and your livelihood. What's wrong with that? I want a livelihood! I will spell out what I mean. For the next term, send all your lecturers back to their colleges where they can do minimal damage. They poison the children's minds, but when the kids leave college, they learn they have got to work to live, and soon forget all that nonsense. But these public classes are quite another thing, labour union leaders attend them, a few Muslims are starting to come— we are happy for them to be in their masjids— and then all these women. My God, they can set fire to the country in no time! And what do you think we can do? Some of them are wives of senior officers! No, Sharma, get rid of the lot, and we will help you recruit a new set of Marxist lecturers we have trained. They know more, they can quote chapter and verse, and send disgruntled people back home knowing that revolution is not child's play. One needs to study all of Marx, preferably in the original German, and also know in what philosophical context he wrote, that of Hegel, Plato, the Jesuit philosophers and the Taoists they studied, and all the rest of them. Revolution takes a lifetime, while setting a match to a house or starting a fight on Fridays, it's the work of a moment.' He snapped his fingers in front of Sharma*ji*'s face.

Sharma*ji* was caught in a cleft stick. This man was very, very dangerous. Sharma*ji* could smell the danger. The DIG would think nothing of shooting him out of hand right in that office, and have his decomposed body discovered in the Musi riverbed two weeks later. Most probably he had done that sort of thing before. And yet, his gorge rose at succumbing tamely to blatant threat.

'Well, if the people you recommend have qualifications, better qualifications, we, I, can consider…' he temporized.

'Of course they have better qualifications,' thundered Mr Harbhajan Singh jovially. 'You will be surprised when you meet them. One even has a PhD from the London School of Economics, eh, that means something to you, right? And we even have respected card-holding members of the communist party. Gilt-edged credentials to teach Marxism. Leonard the Leninist will double your budget. Come to think of it, I will fashion a special course on Lenin and the October Revolution—most of your teachers don't even know it occurred in November, poor sods!'

The DIG of Police, Special Branch, led Sharma*ji* out of the room into the open, with his arms round his shoulders for all the hangers-on to see. He stopped as if posing for a photograph.

'My dear Sharma, this has been a very good meeting. I am glad you will cooperate with us in the interests of national security. We both want the same thing, peace and progress, right? Good! And we will come to know who the potential troublemakers are in that course, and deal with them. Don't worry, old fellow, it's just the official lingo I use that gets in the way. No, no, no! We will give them remedial education, teach the fellows and some of the damned women, that there is a great deal of difference between social revolution—which is the stated objective of the State—and creating disturbances. Some of them are slow to learn, but they all learn ultimately, and go home, or wherever, quite happily, I assure you. Better this way.'

Declining the offer of a police car to take him home, Sharma*ji* thoughtfully made his way back. He consoled himself with the fact that the DIG Special Branch had left him no option whatsoever, and in any case, it had never been his intention to start a revolution, as that damned policeman said, that was a life-long business, better left to Leninists than be interfered with, and if these new teachers were qualified, what objection could there be? After all, the goal of the course was the understanding of Marxism, and who better than trained Marxists from the Party, from the LSE?

7. The Club

The exclusive Trivedi Club was located on the spacious premises of US Strips & Mines, which the company had bought many years ago for the use of its own officers. But with a quick change of mind for which they were famous, the Americans had given it on nominal rent to the elite official members of the club, named after the first chief secretary who had struck such a shrewd deal for the benefit of succeeding generations of IAS officers. Non-officials, that is the rest of humanity, never saw anything more of the Club than its high and closed wrought-iron gates. Members of the humbler services entered the premises only for five minutes at a time, to procure the signatures of their chiefs on urgent documents.

Hence, Sharma*ji* was extremely gratified to receive a personal invitation from the departing Chief Secretary, Mr Thummaiah, to attend a party he was giving at the Club to celebrate the birth of his first grandson. The CS, whose father had been a Dalit bonded labourer, had risen through sheer merit, forced open several educational gates normally closed to students who are not educated from their infancy in the English language, gained entry into the elite 'heaven-born service,' and then quietly made his way up. Despite disparaging comments made by his superiors for 'acting without abundant caution' when securing the interests of the poor and needy. He had taken a liking for Sharma*ji* for so eloquently voicing the plight the poor found themselves in, had helped him build his NGO in the early days with grants for which it was entitled, and introduced him to foreign delegations that visited his department. At the end of his official career, Mr Thummaiah felt it would only be right that Sharma*ji*, who had worked with him on several development projects over the years, should be at his last party in the Club.

The officiating member-secretary of the Club covered his surprise at Sharma*ji*'s inclusion in the guest list with practised ease. 'Uncle Tom is bringing one of his spooks to the party!' he announced with a laugh at the bar, and the other young bloods having a drink there chipped in with their own pet stories of 'Uncle Tom,' the affectionate and only slightly derisive sobriquet they had given their reserved and well-liked superior.

On the night of the party, Sharma*ji*, dressed in dark closed coat and trousers, and wearing shiny black shoes half a size too tight for him, sat in a dark corner on the lawns. Some of the high officials had perfunctorily shaken his hand, others had airily waved across the table to him, and many had just ignored him. He did not mind. He was all too aware of the unique honour done to him; he would embroider and recount the happenings of the night at several other dinners to come, and drop names at key meetings. For now, he just sat quietly, savouring his drink and the august atmosphere.

Mr Raghuram, the Principal Secretary, Finance, otherwise known as 'The Rajguru,' was a very small man, with an egg-like bald head, but his eyes and permanently distended nostrils exuded self-conscious power. Younger acolytes were gathered round him in an admiring circle, listening to one of his great exploits. 'Bearer!

Bring me another double scotch and soda,' he said, snapping his fingers over his head. 'Glenfiddich. Right. The bugger comes up to me with the greatest look of innocence, and a plan that would have netted him millions. I saw through his game straightaway. The Minister of course wanted the industry because it would bring thousands of jobs to his own constituency, and tried to force my hand, but I put a stop to it. That factory will not be opened in ten years, I give you my word! What happens after I retire, God only knows!'

'These business *wallahs* are always corrupt,' said Mr Sarangapani, Deputy Secretary, Industries. 'Well, not corruption in this case,' corrected The Rajguru, 'but think of his cheek. Trying to go behind my back to the Minister.' They all nodded agreement that the unpardonable had been done.

'How is your son doing in America, Sir?' enquired a junior officer trying to ingratiate himself with the Great One. Others leaned forward obsequiously.

The Rajguru lit a cheroot, leaned back and blew a ring into the dark sky. 'He is very clever—ahead of his examiners here—they never understood him, and I had given up hope that he would ever become a doctor; and as you know with my salary I can't afford to send him to a private medical college. When the fellow—all by himself, quietly—found out that Texas Oil, to whom we have given the off-shore concession, had set up this new scholarship for third world students. He went for the interview without telling me—imagine! Without telling me! Got selected, and comes home, saying, "Papa, I am off to the United States!" I was flabbergasted, I tell you.'

Everyone broke into appreciative murmurs, and 'a chip of the old block' was heard said distinctly. The Rajguru continued gleefully: 'It's a whopping big scholarship—the fellow is earning more than me already, has bought a car, and fancies himself as a host, throwing parties for his professors!' The conversation turned to how brilliantly everyone's children were performing. Someone mentioned the name of the late Mr Trivedi's grandson.

'Oh, he is the spitting image of the old man,' said Mr Banerjee, Special Advisor, Tourism Development. 'When he walked into my room, I was taken aback—he had that same confident gait. Mr Trivedi was my Collector, you see, when I was under training. He taught me how to exert power, and how to make deals. He had the vision to buy up these hills when they were just jungle. The old man made millions I tell you, and this boy will turn it into billions!'

'Did he get the contract to plan out foreshore tourism development?' asked The Rajguru.

'How could I refuse him?' asked Mr Banerjee in comic tones. 'It was like watching the old man standing in front of me. It was all I could do not to jump up.' Everyone laughed in shared amusement, and Sharma*ji* thought it was the right moment to slip out from his chair and collect some food from the buffet.

'Ah! Sharma! Our Man from Civil Society!' said Mr Govind Nair gaily, helping himself to *mutton biryani*. 'We hear so many stories about the on goings among NGOs that I don't know what to believe. Is it true that Father Ambrose was caught in a sex ring and had to give away one of his NGOs as part of the dowry of Mukund's daughter?'

Sharma*ji* eyed the secretary for food relief with caution, for he would continue to be indebted to him. 'I know nothing about it.

Sir, one hears so many untrustworthy rumours,' he started slowly, 'and the IG, Anti-Corruption naturally is not liked, so when he celebrated his daughter's wedding so lavishly, people talked…'

'My dear Sharma, none of us were born yesterday,' said Mr Govind Nair, leaning confidentially on his shoulder, 'we all know where the money came from for that wedding…*arre yaar*, Gopal! A word with you! I hear you are taking a trade delegation to China! Why don't you buy the tickets through my wife? She's just set up a travel agency, and will give you a big reduction. She tells me she can give you two nights in Bangkok—five-star hotel, trips up the river, evening entertainment, all free!'

The two officers started discussing the details, and Sharma*ji* exited to his chair in the dark corner. The big group had moved off to collect their dinner and a few others had deposited themselves in the vacated chairs, their plates piled high with food.

Mr Ram Narain, Principal Secretary, Rural Development, was seated next to Mr Chaturvedi, IG, Special Operations, the only one in uniform in the crowd. 'Tell me, *yaar*, I believe your boys just decimated three groups in two days—how was it done?'

The police officer silently ate a *kebab*. 'Nothing to tell, really. My men were on normal patrol duty, when they were fired upon. They shot back in self-defence. The bodies will be returned to their families after post-mortem.'

Mr Ram Narian was in a reminiscent mood. 'I remember Gowramma, beautiful, well-built girl, though dark like a Negro. She was only sixteen then, but she spoke up bravely, saying there was no food to eat in those villages. Remember that terrible drought? She wanted me—she was telling me—to open a food-for-work programme, but I had no allocation. And all those other women?'

'They were all well-trained armed terrorists,' said the inspector general flatly. 'You know I am in an impossible situation?' Mr Thummaiah came up to see if Sharma*ji* was getting on all right, and the group stood up to give him their best wishes. Sharma*ji* hurried off to collect his dessert. He was debating whether he should add a scoop of chocolate mousse or chocolate gateau to the *gulab jamun* he had already collected, when he was hailed respectfully by Mr Krishna Prasad, Director of the human resources training institute.

'Hello, sir! I am so glad to see a leading person like you in this Club,' said Mr Krishna Prasad, leading him to two chairs near jasmine bushes. 'We are too insular here, just meeting each other. We need people like you to tell us what is really happening at the grassroots. I want you to give a series of lectures at our next executive training programme.'

Sharma*ji* was suitably flattered. He suggested some titles for the lectures, but Mr Krishna Prasad paid scant attention, saying all such details could be left to the deputy secretary in charge. He reiterated that he now had sanction to pay the best national rates for each lecture, but he was even willing to consider international rates, seeing that Sharma*ji* was really an expert known throughout the world. As he rose to take his leave, Mr Krishna Prasad detained him with a hand on his arm.

'Sharma*ji*, my nephew is looking for a job. He is a bright fellow, you will see for yourself, but he cannot pass examinations. And you know how stupid the educational system is. Can he work with you? Keep him busy, you don't need to pay him, even. Just let him work and learn.' Sharma*ji* assured him gravely that it was against his Gandhian principles to extract work without payment—a workman was worthy of his hire—and that the nephew should come round to see him next morning.

He slipped out into the night, dismissed his driver, and walked home with his feet on air despite his pinching shoes. For a few hours he had been in the company of the rulers of an obedient billion people, and he wanted to savour the memory in the quiet of the dark night.

8. French Memories

Ramanujan Varadachary, the reclusive, spiritual-revolutionary centenarian, was all that Sharma*ji* imagined he would be—spare and fit, bright-eyed and clear-headed, dressed in a simple white cotton *dhoti* with a blue border and a cotton singlet, and living in a small ill-lit lower middle-class house, tucked away behind a *neem* tree and on the edge of a school building. What was unusual was the lively sparkle in his host's eyes as he carefully read the label of the bottle of red wine that he had been instructed to present as a gift before the interview.

'Made in India from French grapes grown in a vineyard near Bangalore, very good,' commented his ancient host. 'We will let it breathe for a while, and then taste it. We'll see what wine we can make—it's a lost Indian tradition, destroyed by the uncultured British, and now restored to us by the French! Wonderful! Let me get two wine glasses, which I have not used for the last thirty-two years.' With that, the old man scuttled off inside, to emerge polishing carefully two wine glasses, and clutching Sharma*ji*'s letter.

'Yes, certainly I can tell you a great deal about Sri Aurobindo and his ashram, and even more about his younger revolutionary days. He took over where Vivekananda left off; he fired the patriotic zeal of all young men of this country. I left the Presidency College, Madras after listening to his speech, and followed him to Pondicherry—the French gave us all shelter, from where we could attack the might of the British Empire!'

Varadachary carefully uncorking the bottle with a venerable corkscrew, poured out the wine, swished it around, sharply breathed in the bouquet, swivelled around a small mouthful between his perfect teeth, and gulped it down. 'Not bad at all. It will do, it will serve. Yes! A very good beginning! It is totally against our ancient culture to deny a place for wine on our tables. What do you think *soma* was? Not some kind of medicine as these theologians make out, but wine, sir, wine, from the southern slopes of the Hindu Kush mountains, grown and drunk by our great Vedic forebears! It was the source of their good health, and if I have lived to be a hundred, it's because of the French wine we drank in Pondicherry!'

'We are bringing out a collection of essays dedicated to harmony among all religions,' broke in Sharma*ji* mildly. 'We, in civil society, want to be proactive in this climate of communal violence. Several great people are sending us messages for inclusion, but our publication will not be complete without a short message from you, Sir. You are the last of our great freedom fighters, and more— Sri Aurobindo called you a Spiritual Soldier of India, and my request is...'

Varadachary waved him into silence. 'Of course, I shall write out a message, today, right now, as we drink this bottle of wine which you very thoughtfully brought along. The import of all real wine was stopped a long time ago and I didn't even know we had started to make our own. I must tell my grandson to send me another bottle along with his money order. Don't drink it like whisky—savour the bouquet, roll it round your tongue!'

Sharma*ji* dutifully tried to comply with these instructions, while Varadachary took up an old ruled notebook and blunt pencil and started to write. He put both down after writing a couple of sentences, and started to speak dreamily, pausing to sip his wine between sentences.

'This is the first Sunday of February, do you know where I was exactly eighty-seven years ago to this day? In Paris! Sunday, the first of February, 1925! It was my first winter there and it was dreadfully cold. I was not yet a French citizen then and the British were asking for my extradition to stand trial for sedition, so the Prefect of Police in Pondicherry told me to leave quietly for France. It was on this day, eighty-seven years ago, that I met the greatest chess player of all time—and saw him lose! Are you interested in this story; do you play chess?'

'I was a chess champion in my school days,' said Sharma*ji* insincerely, trying to ingratiate himself with his host.

'Then I shall tell you the full story,' said Varadachary, pouring himself another glass. 'Now that Vishy Anand is well known there is some interest in chess, but for decades no one in India cared for this king of games, invented by us, of course. This is good wine, and you deserve to hear this good story. Alexander

Alexandrovich Alekhine, the great Russian, was in Paris, and he declared that he would break the world record for blindfold chess by playing against twenty-eight players, twenty-eight groups of players, if you please!

'How did I meet him, you ask? Émigrés tend to gather together—to explore, to help each other. I was from India, the home of chess, from a very well-known family, and so was he, the son of a Marshall and a member of the Duma. His people had been wealthy, but in Paris we both had to make do somehow. We were young, and what exploits we had in that queen of cities!'

Minutes passed as Varadachary was lost in earlier more gallant times.

'But to return. He already had a reputation as a ladies' man—but only for older, wealthier women. He had already divorced two such women, and he would divorce two more rich older women, so people gossiped that he was after their money. But, no! Alekhine was a great romantic at heart, otherwise he could never have been the champion he was—he was drawn to women of experience, of mystery, as they were to his matinee idol looks and his piercing gaze. You do not believe? Behold! I will tell you of a little affair, conducted blindfolded, in front of all, with one who was very young and most beautiful!

'On that record-breaking day, I was his second, to take charge of his Turkish cigarettes and see that he had a constant supply of hot black coffee. The day was cold; we made a dramatic entry into the great hall of the Petit Parisien in our black cloaks, our large felt hats pulled down, and everyone applauded. The newspapers! The cameramen! M'sieu Fernand Gavarry, the President of the Federation Internationale des Échecs, were all there to greet us. Laying aside our gloves, hats and cloaks on the side-table, Alekhine went from table to table shaking hands punctiliously with all the contenders. He would linger at Table Eleven, the young people from the École Polytechnique, Paris. Among the shy students stood this girl, with clear green eyes and a rosebud mouth, her close black knitted cap pulled over her pale blonde curls, a tight dark pink pullover pushing up her highlighting perfect breasts, her soft white hands like lily stems, with long elegant, aristocratic fingers. I could tell that my friend, Alexander Alexandrovich, was powerfully affected. He was breathing with passion even as I blindfolded him.

'As he went mechanically from table to table, outwitting almost absentmindedly the rest of his opponents, his mind, his heart, was always at Table Eleven, with this beautiful girl, whom he could see perfectly in his mind's eye. "She is an unfortunate émigré like me, Rum," he would whisper when we paused for a cigarette or some coffee—he would eat no food during a contest, and he called me Rum, y'know, for Ramanujan, "she is a Russian princess, I am absolutely sure, and I have to be silent for hours, blindfolded, when I should be gathering her in my arms, consoling her!"

'Or, he would say, "I bent over the board just now, and I could smell her breath—it's of the cherry blossoms over the Neva, that much of the real Russia she has brought with her!" Between rounds, I had to whisper to him how she was looking, whether I thought she had sensed his great passion for her, and of course I had to say truthfully that not only she but others nearby also sensed his desire, for he trembled whenever he was near her. I consoled him by saying that she blushed whenever he drew near.

"Rum, I am going to marry her the moment this game is over," he said mid-way through the games. "But how can I go empty-handed to her, to ask for her? I have to give her something, something great, that history will record as a mark of my great love!" Remark! He was in love, deeply, like only a Russian can be, in a moment, as happens in Paris, even in February. This is very good wine, and you are a very good fellow.'

Varadachary had finished over half the bottle, and he filled another glass, not seeming to mind that Sharma*ji* was still sipping his first glass. 'Where was I? Yes, he was playing Queen's Pawn Opening against her team. Conventional moves on both sides, nothing more. She was the lead player of Table Eleven, of the École Polytechnique. She, quite rightly, playing against a great master, had castled defensively on the sixth move. He, in a frenzy, did the same on the eleventh, to hint how he felt, bottled up away from her! The eager lover he was, he sent out his cavaliers on the queen's side; and she, she had opened up her file on the bishop's column. On the twenty-first move, his heart lay open to her Queen. He sacrificed his knight to her bishop. But this he would have done even for a tavern girl. A supreme sacrifice was needed. The great Alekhine must surrender all, show he was vulnerable to her, only to her!

'As we neared to make our twenty-third move, I knew, instinctively, that Alekhine would stake all, even his reputation, for his love, which was maddening him! He sacrificed his Queen! He was bent low over the board, his fingers lingered, brushed against hers and even as she removed his piece, he murmured: "Ah, Mam'zelle! You have won my Queen, and you have conquered me! Only a Russian princess was destined to do so! And here I am your slave!" Who could resist? I was moved. Even M'sieu Gavarry, the President of the Federation Internationale des Échecs, wiped away an emotional tear!'

'The lady was totally overcome. She blushed brighter than the pullover she wore. She let Alexander Alexandrovich take possession of her hand. "Hi! I am Cathy Ferrel, from Iowa," she said brightly, looking up into his blinded face. "And my husband Jim is over at the next table. We are here in Paris for six weeks for French immersion." Alekhine brushed her hand with his lips, "Enchanted, Madame, enjoy your stay, and command me while you are in Paris," was all he could manage to say, as we moved on.

'The rest of those tedious hours were passed in silence. Believe me, it took me days to cajole Alekhine back to good humour. "Iowa! Iowa?" he would say. "Incredible! How can there be such a place?" Varadachary drained the last of the wine. 'This is the truth how the great Alekhine lost a match in 1925 to rank amateurs. It also proves that had the right girl come along, someone not in blessed Iowa, Alekhine might, just might, have married someone young and beautiful, and been happy forever.'

The old raconteur leaned back in his cane chair, his eyes closed and his mind far away. After a few minutes, Sharma*ji* reminded him of the still unwritten message.

'You want harmony between all peoples, and that is a very good thing,' said Varadachary kindly. 'But how do we harmonize with people with closed up souls, who are afraid to drink wine? This is just not possible. They must first learn to open up, to others, to Nature, to le bon Dieu, who has made us all. I will tell you what I will do, without being false to myself. I will think about something appropriate, and send it to you. I want to rest now.'

So Sharma*ji* reluctantly took leave of him, and published the collection of messages for communal harmony without a contribution from the only living spiritual-revolutionary centenarian of our times.

9. The Peace Film

The girl was tall, and pretty in a media sort of way, with short black hair curved in wings over her ears, from which dangled long, thin silver creations. She was dressed in a tailored black suit, with the flaring white collar of her silk shirt tucked out over the lapels of her jacket. She had flung herself into a large cane chair and was tapping the parquet wooden flooring of her studio with a pointy black shoe.

'Really, Mr Sharma, this is an opportunity of a lifetime,' she assured him with a bright smile, arching herself in a winning manner. 'You will introduce the film; before the start of every sequence, the camera will focus on you at different locations in your villages, doing whatever you do. You will tell the audience what they are going to see next, why it is important, to them, to you, and to the people of this country. In a real way, the film is about you, your values, and how a man like you speaks for all of India. So you see, the theme of the documentary, well, it is a documentary feature, actually—well, the theme is that the people of India and Pakistan should work together for peace and prosperity—*this* will be brought out as the theme of your own life, what you stand for, what you work towards. Really, I would go for it, if I were you.'

To say that Sharma*ji* was dazzled would be an understatement. He had received a conference call linking up Indian financiers in America, movie-makers in Bombay, and two politicians in Delhi, one in power and the other in opposition, and himself, of course. Very large sums were talked about with ease in several accents. A documentary that people couldn't fail to see was what everyone seemed to want, a documentary which would push the peace process forward. An emotional documentary, which would go straight to the hearts of the people of both countries. But an impersonal documentary was dullsville, said the film magnate, it should be about a real person's life and views, a special person who sacrifices every day for the people. There was no way Sharma*ji* could say, 'No,' after all that; a business class air ticket to Bombay was delivered the next day, and there he was in Bollywood, already being treated like a star!

The girl had switched on the LCD projector, and he saw a short video clip, with pictures of Gandhi and Jinnah, and then heard a searing tear, and there were two torn still photographs of the leaders against a black screen. 'It's of course about today, but also about how the two nations were formed,' the girl said. 'We will go back and forth in time. The film follows you as you grow up, how your own ideas develop, how your values mature, how you give everything up to serve people, and yet all the time, you want that torn photo to be miraculously rejoined!'

She then brought out an impressive cardboard file with the working script and they sat together for some time as she sketched out the flow of the film. Sharma*ji* was as much overwhelmed by the honour done to him as by her perfume. When he closed his eyes on the flight back, he could still see her bright fair face, her perfect teeth and soft red lips. The next seven weeks were given over wholly to filming on location. The several re-takes at every location had him tired and limp by the evening, and he would not have been able to work the next day had it not been for Rukmini's massaging his trembling frame. However much he rehearsed his lines, somehow the words just evaporated out of his head when the cameras rolled, and he would stutter, say the wrong thing, or just look awkward or stiff. The chief cinematographer, Pervez, was an old hand, and regaled everybody but Sharma*ji* with stories about stars and their stupidities. '*Arre bhai*! Don't worry, you should have seen some of those asses in the Bombay Talkies days! Thank your stars we don't have to deal with a female prima donna! They are the worst, especially if a producer is keeping them. I tell you! But you are not half as bad. What can we do, God made you like this, that's all!' Sharma*ji* hated Pervez's frankness, and forgot his rancour only after their third or fourth double whisky, later in the evening.

Finally, Pervez said he had taken enough shots of cows and cowdung to last him a lifetime, that Sharma*ji* was heroic to live among all that rural idiocy, and that he himself would be happy only when the plane touched down in Bombay. Later, Sharma*ji* had to rush to Bombay for re-takes in the studio for close-ups of his face, or for re-dubbing his own voice wherever he had muffed it. He had never realized filmmaking was such an ordeal, stripping a person of all dignity, all self-confidence. But at the end of each wretched attempt, the pretty girl would steadfastly make much of him, order real Scotch, or when they had packed up, take him to some sets to see stars in action. He was genuinely humbled to see their poise and self-confidence, the easy way in which they joked with everyone on the sets just before action. He himself had lain sweating in bed hours before he was called, desperately trying to remember his lines, how he should say them, and how he should look. At long last, when he thought the nightmare would never end, he was released from his ordeal and went back thinking he had earned every rupee of his handsome fee.

The commercial promotion of the film was handled in a very professional manner, with a series of sneak previews, teasers, interviews, and other journalistic puffs in newspapers and talk shows. The docu-feature film, as it was called, was premiered to a distinguished audience of high officials, business magnates, professors, and the social elite, on Gandhi Jayanti Day in the special studio theatre of the Department of Communications and Broadcasting. Titled 'Sharma*ji*'s Dream,' it wove a web of fantasy between historical episodes and Sharma*ji*'s life, using historic documentary footage and shots of everyday life in the present with artful camera angles showing Sharma*ji* dreaming, working, singing, protesting, and dreaming again in a fictionalized story of his life. Somewhere within his dream of yesteryear was a song and dance routine, with a starlet acting as his wife-to-be. He was lost admiring himself on screen; he had never realized how good he looked, and how eloquently he spoke. The film dripped with sentiments of peace and brotherhood, and Sharma*ji* got a standing ovation when the lights came on.

Mrs Viccaji of the Ladies Club was ready with a large rose garland. 'Dear, dear Mr Sharma, almost every sequence brought tears to my eyes. You see, I am old enough to remember the good old days; they were in reality good old days, you know, when all of us lived as a tight-knit community,' she said. 'I am going to kiss you in front of all these people for making such a beautiful, sensitive film. Walliullah Khan used to be our neighbour before

Partition, he married Gokul Chand's daughter, and the reception was held in my garden. I baked the wedding cake myself, and what a problem I had finding proper icing sugar! He went to Karachi, you know, after Partition; their marriage broke apart, and that poor girl was left with two children the government wouldn't admit back to our country, just think of it! It was settled only when I spoke to Nehru himself! None of us wanted any of this misery! Maybe your film will help bring back the old days. I hope so, dear Mr Sharma.'

The Chief Secretary, the Minister for Rural Development, Chandramohan Reddy of United Cement, all shook Sharma*ji*'s hand in turn, and people clapped again as he left, bemused, on a cloud. The film then opened in several select cinema houses across the country, and plaudits written by highly placed people kept pouring in. Sharma*ji* even began to think of pursuing a career in Bollywood, and started asking his wife every evening when he returned if anyone had called from Bombay.

The first sour note was struck when the secretary of the local Gandhi Bhavan wrote a letter in *The Hindu* lamenting the anti-national spirit of the film, which placed Mahatma Gandhi, the Father of the Nation, and Mr Jinnah, who was responsible for Partition, on the same footing. The tearing apart of the photos of both, right at the very start, made no distinction between right and wrong. More angry letters followed. A member of the Shiv Sena complained that the documentary's scenes of violence were so mischievously jumbled together that it made the Hindus look like culprits instead of victims of a historic wrong. Certain cinemas in Bombay showing the film were pelted with stones, forcing them to close down.

Maulana Wahid went on the air to say that what pained him the most was the singing of *Vande Mataram* by some Bengali nationalists—to which, of course, he could have no objection—

but this scene was followed by one of Muslims reading *namaz*. An unfortunate conclusion could be mischievously engineered that Muslims were now being forced to bow down during the song, which the community had steadfastly resisted for a hundred years. A *hartal* followed angry mobs closing down theatres in Gulbarga. Violence flared sporadically between people of 'two communities' in various towns across the country. An inconclusive televised debate on whether 'Sharma*ji*'s Dream' was anti-national had the opposition walking out during question hour in parliament after protesting that the film was a clandestine attempt of a tottering government to buy peace with militant Pakistan by denigrating the role of true Hindu nationalism in the Freedom Struggle.

During a meeting of the two Foreign Secretaries at Islamabad, the Pakistani counterpart requested that India should ban the provocative film since in a very unsubtle way it showed Pakistanis as churlish, while portraying Indians as magnanimous, which, as everyone knew, was contrary to all known facts. The talks were broken off when the Indian expressed his inability to enforce censorship in an open society. Bishop Neelaiah noted during a South Indian Christian Conference that dissolving the figure of Gandhiji onto the image of Christ on the cross hurt the religious sentiments of his flock, and requested nuns to form a silent peaceful human picket line in front of cinemas showing the film. Dalit leaders angrily noted that the hero of the film was one Sharma, a Brahmin, and linking him with Gandhi, a Bania, the film ignored the role of all other castes, and reaffirmed caste oppression as the ruling ideology. Sikhs in Amritsar held a rally against the film for showing only the massacre of Jallianwala Bagh and the killing of Sikhs running helter-skelter, thus deliberately glossing over the martial valour of their people.

One day Sharma*ji* was informed by the Director General of Police that an armed guard had been provided for his protection, and that he should not go anywhere without his gunmen. A starred question in parliament asked the Home Minister whether he had investigated the financial sources behind the film, and whether it was true that the underworld mafia had deliberately made the film to 'vitiate the atmosphere.' Finally, the Censor Board retracted its certificate from the film and the agitations died down bit by bit, but it was another four months before police protection would be withdrawn from Sharma*ji*'s residence.

10. The Sabbatical

Hilda had taken a sabbatical—well, actually a long break for six to eight weeks—for reflection, spiritual renewal and community service. So naturally she chose to come to Sharma*ji*'s SERVICE Rural Centre, since he was, perhaps, her best project. She was received with all ceremony and outward shows of ecstasy at the airport, with rural women forming a loving circle around her and putting flowers in her hair as they sang a traditional welcome, while Sharma*ji* himself placed a large garland of marigolds around her neck and tried to hand her luggage over to Abraham, but she would have none of it.

'Sharma*ji*! Thank you, thank you, thank you all,' beamed Hilda. 'I will carry my own stuff. Look at me, I have come equipped to serve!' She pirouetted round between the tightly packed taxi cabs, and indeed she was quite a sight. A large horn-rimmed glasses separating her dyed auburn hair from her freckled nose, large white and yellow teeth grinned between the wrinkles that creased her cheeks. A dark green seaman's rucksack was strapped to her back, a laptop case was clutched in her hand, and a large floral shirt ballooned over floppy breasts and straggling over khaki shorts, out of which protruded two very long, very white thin legs, ending in ill-fitting sandals. She put down her laptop and exuberantly kissed Sharma*ji* on both cheeks, while his staff grinned round him. He hustled her into the Project SUV (which most of the time did shopping duty for his wife), with an eager declamation that they had a lot to discuss, and he was looking for her help at a crucial theoretical juncture in the affairs of the nation.

The long, dusty ride slowly brought them both to silence, gratefully acknowledged by Abraham and Rangulamma, riding at the back, who nodded off to sleep. That evening over dinner Sharma*ji* went over the recent history of his Society, with which in any case Hilda was well acquainted, and they parted early, since she had had a long intercontinental flight, and he could escape to his 'unit' to watch his favourite TV serial. When all was said and done, thought Sharma*ji* that night as he fell asleep, it was a stroke of luck that such a powerful lady had chosen to spend her 'sabbatical' working on his project; the word would spread, he would see to that, and donor money could easily cascade, so he would gallantly put up with her rather irritating chatter.

Early next morning, when the sun had still not risen, and the first birds were beginning to call, Sharma*ji* was almost jolted out of his bed by loud thumping on his door.

'Sharma*ji*! I'm ready,' called out Hilda, and he saw peeping out of the window that she had changed her shirt for a bush jacket, and her feet were encased in white trainers, and that she was ready, but for what?

'I wanted to be up before you,' she said happily. 'I know you leave early every morning to work in the bio-diversity fields, and you can teach me everything about your system. I am going to Africa in October, and I want to tell them about you.'

He, now, remembered regaling her and several others over dinner in London with details about his daily work routine, but it was no use regretting it now; he had to get ready fast, though he had not had his morning cups of coffee, or read a newspaper, or even moved his bowels. She didn't seem to notice his bleary eyes or puffed face as he staggered along beside her. The women in the fields looked up in surprise at both of them, but with tact continued to work as if it was a daily occurrence. Hilda got down on her knees straightaway, laughing with the women and being shown what to do, while Sharma*ji* after a few vague attempts pretended to inspect the health of the plants further off. Dasgupta came to his rescue with papers in a file, and after feigning displeasure at being called away, Sharma*ji* left the fields to retreat for a cup of coffee and a lazy wash. Hilda was still very happy and energetic when he came back a couple of hours later, and she told him that she had learnt a lot from the women, though she knew not a word of Telugu. He guided her round the fields, and it was a totally successful morning except when he wrongly identified a castor patch as potatoes, but then, as he said quickly, his eyes were failing him now, the result of long periods of study.

The next few days, the same regrettable routine was followed, but he was braced for it, nobly feeling that any sacrifice for the people and the nation was worth it. But he did see to it that Dasgupta interrupted him every day, to his obvious annoyance, after he had spent a few minutes in the fields.

However, he was quite unprepared for the next thunderbolt Hilda was to deliver. Lunch the third morning was quite tasteless, and his face clouded in a thunder of rebuke for the kitchen staff when Hilda, sitting at his left, broke in, chuckling: 'You don't know what struggles I have had in the kitchen. Finally, I had to put my foot down and physically take charge of all those chillies, and salt and sugar, and measure out tiny, tiny quantities. It is still not as *sattvic* as it should be, but I will personally supervise the cooking till we get real macrobiotic *sattvic* dishes.' She beamed at Sharma*ji*, who mumbled his appreciation, and ignoring the inedible food, satisfied himself by launching into a glowing lecture about the wisdom hidden in traditional Indian recipes. Later that afternoon, when Hilda was taking a siesta, which he had insisted upon, wisely telling her that she needed to be careful in the tropics and it was his duty to watch over her health. His driver cycled in from the nearby village with a flask of hot well-sugared tea and a plate of deep-fried chilli *bajjis*.

As the weeks wore on, Sharma*ji* congratulated himself that he had managed to negotiate his way round the impracticalities imposed by Hilda, while his staff understood that it was important to humour this important lady, and that after all she would have to return home some day, and they could all look forward to that. But imagine his shocked surprise one afternoon, and how much more shocked Dasgupta was, when Hilda proudly marched into their low-roofed office building with thirty of the women, saying they had come to inspect the accounts.

Hilda announced that she, with Rangulamma's help, had been training the women selflessly to understand accounts, and their joint responsibility to exercise the right of inspection. She was happy that the first bunch was now ready to help Sharma*ji* and his staff with the onerous duty of keeping accounts. Sharma*ji* looked sharply at Rangulamma, whose young, guileless face looked up at him artlessly, and he dismissed the thought that she had played politics. Rather, the blame was his that he had not detailed a mature person like Rukmini to chaperone Hilda. There was nothing for it but to go through the accounts, and Hilda whooped with pleasure when the women discovered a discrepancy: last week's savings collected from them had not yet been entered in the books. In fact, this was a time-honoured practice, the money being held in 'a suspense account' to meet unforeseen contingencies, which in fact regularly occurred as there were dinners to be given to Sharma*ji*'s guests, journeys to be undertaken by him, or things to be purchased for his house, as urgently demanded by his wife. Once he had even put the money on a sure tip he had received from a punter, who knew all the jockeys and had always been known to win, though not on that unfortunate occasion. It would be foolish to withdraw savings from his bank account, such as it was, and in any case Dasgupta was highly skilled in moving money around; otherwise he would not have tolerated the insolent fellow for so long.

Sharma*ji* gravely reprimanded Dasgupta, who said that for the first time in thirty years of service he had temporarily used the funds to buy seeds for the bio-diversity fields so that they would not miss the planting season. Sharma*ji* nodded when Dasgupta added he could not allow the women's fields to fall into the hands of money-lenders; again gravely thanked the women, and, brushing aside all remonstrance, insisted on issuing a check from his own account to make good the shortfall. Dasgupta was much moved, and dragging himself to the window, shook out his handkerchief and wiped his eyes.

The next evening a council of state was held in Sharma*ji*'s 'unit,' with Dasgupta and Abraham sitting in chairs round a small cane table, while Rukmini as usual sat at his feet, her deep, dark cleavage highlighted by the tight white blouse she wore, distracting him at that serious moment.

'She is training the women to vote representatives to the Executive Council,' said Abraham gloomily.

'Women cannot be handled in Western fashion like this, Sir,' chipped in Dasgupta slowly. 'It is against culture, and stress is being created.'

'I disagree. Hilda is doing very important work, work which we should have undertaken over the last several months,' said Sharma*ji* in slow seriousness. 'But what to do, so many new crises keep interrupting us in our work of empowerment...so how do we get benefit for the women from Hilda's noble efforts?'

'The women are very unhappy, Sir,' said Rukmini, twisting round, her black silky skin rippling over her long bare middle.

'They respect the older women you have nominated for the Council. Illiterate or not, they are respected and they think voting will destroy their unity.'

Tearing his eyes away, Sharma*ji* caught on to the last word. 'Yes, unity is important, all-important. This cannot be sacrificed. Hilda's motives are very good, but after all she is a stranger to our culture. We must hasten wisely, yes. Now, how to convince her that her methods are not appropriate?'

No one seemed to have any idea. The discussion dragged itself out to no conclusion, with Dasgupta retreating into speculative silence. Sharma*ji* had a troubled night.

The morning after next, when Hilda went out briskly towards the fields, she was surprised to see Sharma*ji* and Dasgupta already up, and talking in low voices with three young men. When the huddle parted, she saw with some alarm that the young men, boys really, were carrying what looked like automatic weapons. Sharma*ji* rapidly interposed his small rotund body between her and them, said something to them rapidly in pleading tones, seeming to make a promise, and led her away.

They didn't go to the fields that morning but sat on the veranda of his unit, sipping coffee and eating hot *idlies*. Sharma*ji* was unusually bitter, while Dasgupta stared stolidly at the floor.

'See how I waste my life, my efforts! This is what has happened to me over the last thirty years' said Sharma*ji* savagely. 'When I am on the brink of success, not even that, just reaching some satisfaction over a job well done, everything has to stop because of someone else – someone who doesn't understand, who has no clue! These boys, what do they know about national priorities? Or about our history? They don't want—they don't want—white people in the village—that is racism! And like this they think they will bring about revolution!'

Hilda put a restraining hand on his arm. 'You are a wonderful man, Sharma*ji*,' she said earnestly. 'And your staff are wonderful. I know you are frustrated. I would have liked to stay, I was getting along so well with the women, but the Western world has a lot to answer for. Some of us who are white know that, and we are trying to change things in the West, so that at least we don't feel inferior when we meet people like you.'

Sharma*ji* was moved to tears, which he made no attempt to hide, as the SUV rolled away in the morning light, carrying their honoured guest. He was genuinely sad at her departure, but then he cheered up—spices and chillies would return to his meals and he could start to taste them again.

11. Wanted, a Brahmin Cook

The phone call came early in the morning, before Sharma*ji* had finished his first cup of coffee. Vijay Kumar was at the other end. 'Hi! How are ya? I hope I didn't wake you up or anything, but we figured you would be drinking morning coffee, right? Dad! You were right, he is drinking coffee, would you believe that? We are sitting down to dinner. Sharma*ji*! The good news is that Dad and Mom will be coming over for a month's holiday, now that it is cool enough over there, and go visit friends, places. Sharma*ji*, could you fix them up with a convenient self-managed apartment suite sort of thing? ...you can? Wonderful! That's what I have been saying, things are levelling up so *faast*, there would be no difference between there and here pretty soon. But there is a problem... listen, listen, Mom wants a Brahmin cook for the month they are there, could you fix that? ...no problem? Great talking to you, and listen, while money is a problem everywhere now that the boom is over, I guess I can afford anything they may ask over there. So long! Will be writing a detailed email to ya! Bye!'

Sharma*ji* had been shouting his answers over the phone, in the belief that a long-distance call, particularly from as far away as California, required extra lung power, and also to convey his eager compliance to Vijay. His wife came out of the kitchen with a frown.

'What do you mean by telling them it is easy to arrange a Brahmin cook?' she asked indignantly. 'There is no Brahmin cook available anywhere in town. And why do they want a Brahmin all of a sudden, after eating cows and pigs and God knows what else in America? Hypocrites! A *harijan* cook will do for them. These NRIs are worse than *harijans*. I warn you, you will not find a Brahmin cook, and don't you send my sister chasing out for one; she has enough troubles of her own!'

Sharma*ji* rarely took his wife seriously, and he ignored her this time as well. It was important to make Vijay Kumar's parents happy and comfortable, for the Silicon Valley prodigy had exerted himself in forming a Friends of SERVICE Club, who sent over an annual Divali donation to the Society, which, while not much, could be freely used by Sharma*ji* to meet his many incidental expenses. Further, Vijay Kumar had also paid his way over a couple of times to talk to the group about development, enabling Sharma*ji* to visit Hollywood and Disneyland.

In short order, Sharma*ji* had booked a suite in an apartment hotel with a nice view of the city, and also engaged a taxi and driver for the month, and paid an advance. He asked a few friends, and they promised to line up Brahmin cooks for him to interview. But days passed, and no one turned up for the job. He rang Vasanti, who ran a training institute for destitute girls.

'Sharma*ji*! Your requirement has been at the top of my mind for the last three weeks,' squealed Vasanti in her usual excited manner. 'First I wanted only middle-aged men or women, you know, respectable types for your foreign guests, but they are all engaged. You see, the problem is that everyone these days wants a permanent job; no one is available just for a month. And as you know, young girls will not do, you know what I mean? They are mad about going to America! God knows what wiles they may use with a susceptible older man, and having been in America, with its constant high-pitched focus on sex, most probably he may also want a fling? No, no, I know they are not like that, but neither you nor I want to be caught up in any nasty business, paternity suits, cases of sexual harassment or worse, you know what I mean? I know a lot of very respectable poor Brahmin families in the districts, and I have asked my contacts to select a very dependable type, famous in cooking, and send him over for a month. All right? Don't worry, everything will be all right.'

Sharma*ji*'s sense of confidence drained completely on the Monday before the weekend of the couple's arrival back in India. He tried Vasanti once more, but her assistant after some hesitation told him 'madam was not available.' He tried all his friends in turn, and he got several and varied reasons why Brahmin cooks were just not available. The season was wrong, said one, and everyone was busily engaged, taking large orders for sweets. A widow was available but she flatly refused to stay for a month in a faraway apartment with people she did not know. Yes, it was true that Sharma*ji* had been most generous in saying Americans would pay whatever was demanded, but money was not so much an issue as jobs; now if he could have promised a job in America for a university-educated son, a Brahmin cook could have been arranged within an hour. In fact, there would have been a mob outside his house. Good cooks were always available, but Brahmin cooks on the loose were a scarcity. They were going into so many other professions, now if the younger fellow from Silicon Valley was coming, a Brahmin sex worker woman, of any proportions, could easily have been arranged.

Sharma*ji* rang off. All this was not helping. He thought for a bit. He dared not ask his wife—that channel of information was out. But why should he only ask other fellows like himself? Why should he not consult a cook to find another cook of his choice? This struck him as a very good idea, and he walked out of his apartment with resolution.

But the problem was that he did not know any cooks, and he would once again have to consult all his friends over the phone. None seemed to know any cook on a first-name basis, except an old classmate of his at college—Wajid, who was most reassuring. 'You want a Brahmin cook, you will get a Brahmin cook before the day is out. During the days of the Nizam, there used to be a whole retinue of Brahmin cooks to make local delicacies. Someone in their families must still be cooking. Come around at four, and I shall take you to the spot.'

As evening was falling fast, Wajid drove Sharma*ji* round to see Iqbal, whom Wajid said he always consulted on any matter of importance concerning food. A pleasant half-hour was spent in Iqbal's establishment, tasting various dishes even as they were being prepared for some party Iqbal was catering for that night.

'Sahibs, the person you want is Pandit Ram Charan's eldest son, Ravi, who failed all his exams, but remains a cook, a truly gifted cook. The poor fellow is out of work, for he has the habit of taking a little bhang after work…who can blame him? But people don't understand, they say he misbehaves, and won't believe that he is very dutiful and respectful of elders; only under bhang, he may joke a little; they should take it easy…' Sharma*ji* quickly intervened to say that while he himself saw no harm in a little bhang, these people were from America, had forgotten all about India, and he wanted to be one hundred percent confident about anyone he put in that apartment for a whole month.

Iqbal sighed, and said he didn't know how he was to help old Pandit Ram Charan's son, Ravi, if even old Hyderabadis saw anything amiss in some casual taking of bhang after work, for relaxation. Could Sharma*ji* fix him up with a job in his Society, or recommend Ravi for some government post? Sharma*ji* abjectly promised to help old Pandit Ram Charan's son Ravi in any way he could, but could Iqbal think of anyone else?

'Why not? *Arre*, it is not as if we have driven out all pandits!' said Iqbal indignantly. 'Every *mohalla* in the olden days had a *bahman-ki-galli*—they were very particular; no sweeper could enter from the front. Their womenfolk would wash the street themselves. But we Muslims were always treated as brothers. But now, all those old streets and customs have been broken up, families have moved away, the thinking of young people has changed!'

Wajid and Iqbal lamented the failings of the younger generation for a while, with Sharma*ji* joining in, in a desultory manner. He veered the conversation round to his urgent need of a Brahmin cook. 'You just don't want any Brahmin cook, you want a superior Brahmin cook,' said Iqbal with conviction. 'These are special friends from America. They are returning after God knows how many years, after eating only hamburgers and chips. They are looking forward already to tasting the dishes they relished in childhood! Where are they from? What is their native place? You don't know, Sahib? Arre, that is the first thing we should know, otherwise how can we find a suitable cook? Go home, call your friends, find out these particulars, and we will surprise them with an excellent cook who will make the dishes their grandmother used to make!'

Thus reassured, Sharma*ji* returned home in better spirits than when he had left it. He tried to call Iqbal several times during the week, but the master chef was not to be found. When he heard from Vijay Kumar that the old couple had taken off from San Francisco airport, he had himself driven straight to Iqbal's place, without even waiting to consult Wajid. Iqbal refused to hear a word till he had refreshed himself with a cup of tea, some *samosas* and *kachoris*, and a dish of *phirni*.

'Your guests are coming day after tomorrow, no problem,' said Iqbal with a big smile. We will give them such a cook, they will remember even after death, for a few lifetimes. Call Rashid! Rashid is like my own son, I have personally taught him everything I know. I will do this big thing for you, the close friend of Wajid *mian*. I will give them Rashid for a whole month, never mind my problems!'

Sharma*ji* felt he was in a nightmare. Controlling his temper, he said what he wanted was a *Brahmin cook*, they wanted a *Brahmin cook*, no one other than a *Brahmin cook* would do.

'You mean, your guests want a Brahmin, a person of *Brahmin caste*, not someone who can do Brahmin cooking?' asked Iqbal with scientific precision. 'This puts a very different problem before us. Why did you not say so in the first place?'

Again, with great difficulty, Sharma*ji* said evenly that such was the case, and he was looking to Iqbal to help him out, and that too urgently, since the couple was already aboard their plane headed east.

'You should have made things clear a long time ago,' said Iqbal slowly. 'But even if you had, no one could have helped. There are no Brahmin cooks available. Times have changed. Did I ever tell you that in the days of the Nizams we had so many Brahmin cooks...I did tell you? Well then, you see how times have changed for the worse.'

They sat in silence, Iqbal lost in deep thought, Sharma*ji* in the hope that even now at the last minute Iqbal might find a solution.

'I know what we will do, there will be no problem,' said Iqbal beaming at Sharma*ji*. 'I will still send Rashid to them, no, listen, but we will call him Ravi, son of Pandit Ram Charan. Who is to know? And in fact, Rashid was as much a son to Panditji as to me. He will be dressed like a Brahmin, he will wear the sacred thread, he knows the rituals, he saw Panditji perform them in his kitchen so many times. Don't worry, we Hyderabadis never let one another down. Everything will be all right!'

But Rashid refused to accept the masquerade at first. 'What do you mean it is against religion!' thundered Iqbal. '*Arre!* Idiot! This is acting! It is like the *natak* you did at school—you once acted as a girl, then, did you lose your balls? It is not against religion. You are pleasing some old people, you will give them food. You will do good, and Allah will be pleased. What do you know? I know, I am a five-times *namazi*, not like you youngsters, drinking, seeing cinema, immoral films, when you should be reading the *Koran Sharief*. I take full responsibility! You are my son, and you will do as I say!' There seemed to be nothing further for anyone to say.

When finally Vijay Kumar's parents left for America, his mother was profuse in her thanks. 'Sharma*ji*, I will tell Vijay how you looked after us both, like a dear brother. A blood brother could not have done more. It brought back so many happy memories of the old days. Best of all was the young Brahmin boy you found for us. He cooked all our traditional dishes to perfection. And so religious, it brought back our faith in the motherland! Every morning he, in his wet *dhoti*, would clean the *puja* room, light the lamps, apply *kumkum* to the Gods, and take *arthi* without being told. A very good religious boy. My husband offered to bring him to America to help our local *pujari*, but the boy's old mother is dependent on him, so we gave him five thousand rupees as a gift, and advised him to learn Sanskrit. I think they are calling our flight. Thank you very much once again. Bye! Bye!'

12. Sharma*ji* Meets the Sisterhood

He sat, the lone man, on the other side of a long curved desk at the Global Sisterhood Centre. It was housed in an old bungalow with peeling whitewashed walls and old-fashioned flagstone flooring, and was shaded by large sprawling trees, which were home to a cacophony of quarrelling bird colonies. Five of the most powerful women in the country sat facing Sharma*ji*. While they had all been frigidly polite, none smiled at one of his inane remarks, but acknowledged his apparent discomfort with a quick compression of lips and neutral looks.

'Mr Sharma, it is good of you to come at such short notice. All of us wanted to meet you, and help, if at all possible,' said Professor Radhika, the current chair of the centre, but he was left in no doubt that there was not much likelihood of help from any quarter to a fellow like him. She was a large, powerfully built, dressed conspicuously and plainly in a simple cotton sari, and who gloried in her thick shock of short greying hair, styled in a carefully casual manner. She shook her head absently, letting thick gold earrings glitter among the grey curls. 'We have been asked by the Ford Foundation to help them assess your work and the work of your Society, to progress your application for corpus funds. We are being very frank about this, Mr Sharma, because as you may know the Sisterhood Centre works in a transparent manner. The traditional male approach has been to play power politics; we oppose such attitudes in politics, in the workplace, in the home, and in the working of civil society organizations. Women—please don't think I am making an essentialist statement—suffering through socially experienced oppression have learnt to be transparent, to be inclusive, to be supportive. That is why we requested you to meet with us, so that jointly we may come to an understanding.'

Sharma*ji*, with several years of experience in dealing with soft-spoken high government officials, had no doubt in his mind that he was in the dock as an accused, not just in an ordinary trial but in an inquisition, in which the least slip on his part could lead to a disastrous fate. Even if the large funds he had been angling for over the last few years could be forfeited, a damning reflection on his work, casually passed on over a cup of tea in any corridor of power by any of the women who sat opposite him, would ruin his name for good.

'Professor Radhika, it is my good fortune that you are all taking a real interest in my humble work,' said Sharma*ji* unctuously. 'I am very glad that thanks to Ford I shall receive the benefit of your advice. I wouldn't have had the courage to disturb you by myself.' He laughed deprecatingly, and saw that he had won no support from any of them.

'Frankly, Mr Sharma, we have no interest in the working of an NGO,' cut in Dr Krishnakumari, who would be shortly retiring as Director of the National Education Foundation of India. 'In my opinion, my personal opinion, no civil society organization should be permitted to receive foreign funds, creating a backdoor entry for imperial interests and destabilizing our democracy, because, frankly, none of you are accountable to the people, are you?' She had been a card-holding member of the Communist Party of India for over three decades, and had risen to her high position partly through her family connections and partly because her male superiors dreaded a whiplash retort from her tongue. She was tall and thin, wore thick glasses, and was defiantly dressed in a rich brocaded silk sari, for, as she reminded everyone, she would support Indian weavers, and she celebrated Indian traditional crafts. 'Though I personally have no expectations of public benefit from the work of NGOs. I do insist that certain minimum standards be followed.'

Sharma*ji* was now sure that they were all in the know about some damning incident, some allegation, or some malign rumour, but he was unsure which one. He started to sweat that he may be unable to think of a glib riposte. 'Mr Sharma, your style of functioning is unacceptable to us, as a group of concerned women,' said Mrs Janaki Prasad Rao, a beautifully preserved woman who gloried in her marriage, her husband's fame as a Supreme Court advocate who took up pro bono cases in the public's interest, her wonderful son's wonderful ad agency, and the intelligence of her peerless dog. 'Women cannot be denied their rights, their right to equality, their right to sit at table.' She wiped away a tremulous tear. 'You totally control your organization. You do not share power with women. You must learn to do this, dear Mr Sharma, it will do you good, you will find women so supportive.'

Sharma*ji* heaved a non-transparent sigh of relief. So that was it. He was enough of a politician to know that an approach had been made. 'Madam, I couldn't agree with you more! SERVICE would have reached the skies under women's leadership! But the work is tedious and humble, and I have failed in my attempts so far to secure even the passing interest of any lady whose guidance we have sought. Now that you are taking an interest, my burden is lifted. Thank you! Any of you are welcome to join the Board, or all of you, why not! I will step back and be happy to be of any service, at your command.'

'We are all very busy people, and we do not have the time to work with any NGO,' said Jyotilakshmi Devi, former Minister for

Women's Welfare and currently a Member of Parliament waiting for a berth. By her irritation she showed plainly she understood Sharma*ji*'s game-plan. She had been whispering into her cellphone till that moment, and clearly was unhappy with both conversations. She spoke rapidly, in tones she used to harangue junior bureaucrats: 'It is for you to find suitable women members for your Board and not have us solve your problems. Why have you not done that, so far? All right, whatever the reasons, how are you going to improve matters in the near future? We have to say something to Ford—I would like to say something positive, for after all it is investment in our state—but my hands are tied when you are not gender-sensitive at all! How can you ignore the gender question? Do you know how many dowry deaths occur every year because men, even top officials, are insensitive to the gender issue?'

Sharma*ji*'s stuttered explanation that all his decisions were taken only after detailed consultations with village women was brushed aside as of no consequence. The fifth woman at the table was a young person, a Dr Sujatha, an anthropologist from Stanford, who had moved back to India with her American husband, the regional head of Times Warner News. She broke in rather mutinously: 'It is not a question of explanations about past issues,

Mr Sharma,' she said in Americanese, 'it's more a matter of taking farsighted action to prevent violence against women. And when I say violence I mean violence. When women are not in power, or even consulted, violence inevitably happens against women. Even this Centre has lost a member to domestic violence, despite all the support it offers, right, Radhika?' She reached over and touched the older woman's hand compassionately.

'Nothing could be done to help Mythili,' said Professor Radhika with another impatient shake of her head, which shot light off the gold earrings. 'She was obsessed with her man! I warned her how it would be. I told her to leave him immediately, and we would form a support group to fight the divorce, custody of the child, money for maintenance, everything. But no! She wanted to give him another chance, a third chance. Some women just crave to be objects! Nothing can be done for them, we just have to move on.'

Dr Sujatha would not let go. 'Well, I don't know. Women also have a right to love, and some men are weak, they need support too. Maybe if some of us had stayed with them while they were going through their crisis...'

Dr Krishnakumari burst in with an incredulous look. 'Who has the time, my dear? We all have our own hassles in our own homes, we just sweep it under the carpet and carry on. There are the larger public issues to contest, like enveloping globalization. My God, it is wrecking the country. Everyone is all that much poorer than ever before, and in the middle of all this, we cannot be perennially babysitting a stupid—I am sorry, but I must say it—a stupid woman!'

'Though none of us can sit in on your Board, Mr Sharma, perhaps, we can recommend one of our subordinates,' said Jyotilakshmi Devi with decision, switching off her cell-phone. 'I think Vijaya could monitor gender concerns in your organization. Call Vijaya!' An attender women hanging about near the door scurried away. In a few minutes, Vijaya, a thin middle-class woman in a cheap blue printed nylon sari came in and stood nervously before them. Professor Radhika explained what was required of her in measured tones. Vijaya said meekly that she had two small children, and having to go all the way to the SERVICE offices would add two more hours of travel daily, and she wouldn't be able to manage. No, her husband could not take turns, since he was a clerk in a machine tools factory and left home at six in the morning.

Professor Radhika smiled across the table at Sharma*ji*. 'You see, how the system traps a woman into nothing short of serfdom, with husband, family, children, and then the man nowadays expects her to bring in a second salary! What can one do? It's so disheartening. Right now I am working on a paper I expect to read at the Tokyo Conference next month, which I am calling 'Sisterhood: Hearing the Truth; Responding with Commitment!'' The attender came in carrying a cellphone and said it was from *peddamma*. With a frown Professor Radhika picked up the phone and appreciably raised her voice: '*Amma*! I cannot do anything right now! I'm in the middle of an important meeting! No, I can't leave and come home! You have had these pains before, that's because you eat too much. You must begin to remember that you are in your eighties, and you must stop eating pickles! Well, what do you want, pain or pickles? All right, when I come home this evening—it will be late—I will bring home some fresh curds, yes, I was in a hurry and I upset what we had. Or…get up, slowly, and set some for yourself!'

Professor Radhika gave her gold earrings another shake through her curls. 'I cannot stand it! That's my mother-in-law! It's really a power game she plays with me, but I give it back to her, tit for tat. The old goat can very well look after herself, but she never tires of trying to make me into a docile *bahu*. Me?! You know why she is doing all this drama? She overheard me, I am sure, saying I was planning to go and see this new Aamir Khan film. Well, I will see the film, and she can wait, she and her pains!'

Jyotilakshmi Devi turned to the waiting Vijaya. 'Remember the first discussion we had when we employed you? You are required to be of general assistance at the Centre in developing platforms for Sisterhood. Working in Mr Sharma's office develops such a platform, in a new area. You accepted the job, and you have got to do what we tell you. It is your responsibility to solve your household problems. Understand?' Vijaya nodded uncertainly.

Mrs Janaki Prasad Rao got up and embraced Vijaya tenderly. 'My dear, remember this is Sisterhood, and we think only of your own good. Mr Sharma, Vijaya will bring her children along with her to work, that's all right? I knew it would be. Make available a cell-phone for Vijaya, Mr Sharma, so if she misses the bus she can call and you can send round your car. Remember, Mr Sharma, though Vijaya is junior staff, she is from the Global Sisterhood Centre, and she should receive all the respect you would show to one of us!' Vijaya hung her head. Sharma*ji* assented with a bland smile.

'These simple middle-class girls, they are such gems,' said Mrs Janaki Prasad Rao, after Vijaya had left the room. 'Girls like Vijaya personify the eternal values of our culture. Modernism has had a disastrous effect on what we as a people have stood for for the last five thousand years! If Urmila was not my son's wife, I would throw her out of the house in a minute. I told her, "dear, feminism is not infantile disorder." Feminism respects the deep values we as Indian women have inherited—I am sorry, but I am an essentialist woman. I glory in our essentialism! Urmila wants the dear boy to cook her breakfast himself and serve her in bed! Where does he have the time? And all the money he makes for her, does she think it grows on trees? It's infantile sex play, nothing else!'

Dr Sujatha was frowning, and said somewhat churlishly she wished she had thought of having her husband cook her breakfast, but he could make nothing but boiled eggs. Mrs Janaki Prasad Rao flew to embrace Dr Sujatha and said they both could teach dear John how to cook real Indian food.

Professor Radhika said, please, Janaki, teach my mother-in-law some good recipes, so she could have something interesting to eat when the cook went on leave. Jyotilakshmi Devi cutting in acidly said that it would be far more useful to teach the parliamentary cooks something decent. Sharma*ji* gingerly took leave of them all, and made his escape from the Global Sisterhood Centre.

13. Human Materials Engineering

'For a long time now, materials sciences has been a forgotten, under-funded discipline in India. To tell the truth, one could say the same about Old Europe—manufacturing industries have slipped into low profit margins. Business focus has shifted to Capital Markets Management,' said Vijay Kumar, launched into his PowerPoint presentation at the Ninth Global IT for Development Conference in the many-chandeliered hall of the Sheraton. 'But when President Bush brought the spotlight back on Space Probes, the spot in turn has moved back on *nuu* materials technologies. I'm into hardware, and I tell you guys, come join me! It's the most exciting ride you can get, anywhere in the world!' Applause broke out all over the hall, and young Indian aspirants to an American way of life stood up and clapped, more in celebration of Vijay mixing his American with his broader Coastal Andhra accent. 'We are all into social engineering, right?' continued Vijay. 'This country is changing so *faast*, like you wouldn't believe. And the guys over at the Bank—the World Bank, y'know—at the other, duller end of my country, *wal*, those guys keep talkin' about developing *hooman* capital, but that's yesterday's thought, we should be talkin' about *hooman* materials engineering!' He shrugged his shoulders in an expressive American way, and splayed out his hand, to renewed applause. 'You guys have seen the space shuttle make I don't know how many re-entries into the atmosphere. Temperatures in the nose of the craft go up—oh, I dunno—maybe a couple of thousand degrees Celsius, and you need *nuu* materials to withstand that kinda' heat. It's just like the old way of making alloys, only now it's no longer junior league. The same analogy can apply to Society. We need to harden Society to take the heat of progress, create *nuu* elements through social engineering, and meld them together to hold for take-off!'

The Minister of State for Rural Development was a large, slow, hardened politician who had risen by looking out for the main chance. Though the young speaker annoyed him with his airs, he was impressed by the appreciation the talk received from the circle of American millionaires in the audience, and guessed that sizable investment might flow into his constituency if their support was properly harnessed. The Director of the State Institute for Human Resources Management, a distant cousin of his, then stood up and said he would establish a Chair for Human Materials Engineering if American friends in the audience would help fund it. The millionaires, who had been thoroughly briefed by their staff about the local network of familial relationships and decision-making, stood up as one man and clapped in assent. Everyone of them was busy figuring out channels of profitable investment in fast food franchises, fashion stores, up-market leather goods, Indian textiles re-exported back, and so on.

Quickly, a department grew under the newly established Chair, and several needy lecturers with political connections secured tenures. Though the plum post of the Chair itself was kept vacant till a suitable incumbent could be rewarded by the party in power. Professor Gundu Rao, who had retired as head of the department of mechanical engineering, was billed for the post since he had spent most of his academic career wheeling and dealing with real estate agents for land purchases, as a proxy for politicians in power. However, when his name came up in high party circles, it was blocked by a dynamic young politician, who also happened to be the chief minister's son-in-law. A few years ago, when he was still unmarried and a student, his paper had been ridiculed in a conference by Professor Gundu Rao, who had risen to humorous heights while tearing it to pieces. Blocking his appointment to the plum post was payback time for the political son-in-law, who said disinterestedly that really the post should go to a leader from civil society, who had actually, in the field, so to speak, 'melded human materials to harden society.' This interjection confused the clutch of low-level politicians in the committee, and one of them, thrashing about to understand the new turn of events, came up with Sharma*ji*'s name. Precisely, said the son-in-law, as further humiliation of Professor Gundu Rao who would be passed over in favour of a nobody like Sharma*ji* took place as he was established as a nobody. Since the son-in-law had spoken, all the others assented, and hence, to everyone's surprise, including his own, Sharma*ji* was offered the Chair of Human Materials Engineering.

As he himself told his friends later, Sharma*ji* had expected something grander than the poky little office he was shown, with its broken-down air-conditioner and sticky tape holding together broken pieces of glass in the windows. There was also a faint smell of mouse droppings in the room, which the superintendent assured him would be cleaned with Lysol before he took charge. Sharma*ji* was disappointed to hear from the director that for the present the appointment was an honorary one, since the initial endowment had already been spent in recruiting academic staff, an accountant, and three attenders. However, the Americans had promised an enhancement of their donation next year related to performance, which everyone in the Institute was sure would be exemplary since Sharma*ji* had very kindly agreed to accept the Chair. Sharma*ji* felt dubious about future prospects, but cheered up on hearing that some travel allowance was still available, and that his duties were no more onerous than giving one oration a year during the convocation ceremonies. An attender was appointed exclusively for his use, in the office and at home, stressed the director.

Sharma*ji* had new visiting cards made, giving him the title of 'Professor,' and he made a point of attending several seminars around the country. He spoke with his usual eloquence about the misery of the poor, accompanied by anecdotes about the unacceptably high lifestyles of the rich, how transnational culture made him wonder many times whether he was in Hyderabad or New York, and finally how the need of the hour was to strengthen democracy by strengthening the hands of civil society leaders. He became quite a proponent of human materials engineering, and when young civil engineers, pardonably confused, asked for his advice in some construction project, he did agree to visit the site wearing a hard hat, and nodded sagely at their explanations.

He saw the role of materials everywhere. He commented adversely over dinner to his wife on the material of the dough in his *roti*. He wrote articles in the papers about the poor quality of materials used on the city roads, or for drains, or in city parks. He convinced the director of the institute to spend freely to improve his office, since as Chair of Human Materials Engineering, it reflected poorly on the institute and its prospects for receiving donations if his office were in a shabby state.

But, of course, human materials engineering was his forte. What was 'the tensile strength' of their micro-finance operations, he would ask Dasgupta, when discussing the money-lending activities of his Society. Work plans had to 'gel' better; work teams should be 'compacted' for improved results. Could his colleagues work out a human MOH scale for evaluation? The fad turned into an obsession; he began to believe in human materials engineering. He drew charts, fanciful scales of measurement, and indicators of human materials engineering. He convinced himself that he would put together a new universal model for measuring progress that would knock into a tall hat all older ideas about GNP, GDP, purchasing power parities, and social indicators of the UNDP. It would be the Sharma Index that people would refer to in future.

Venkat had an unemployed nephew, Rajni, who was waiting to go America with his IT skills. He sat in front of Sharma*ji*'s computer with the flair of a pianist to give instant shape and life to any of Sharma*ji*'s fantasies. Rajni took digital pictures of rural women at work and converted them into moving, multi-coloured charts displaying varying human materials. He could convert a block of statistical tables into moving shapes of people, cubistically presented to indicate degrees of hardness. Sharma*ji*'s PowerPoint presentations became the centrepiece of attraction of many an academic conference.

Sharma*ji* was gratified to get a call from the Prime Minister's office one morning, requesting him to address a special meeting of the Planning Commission on the new Science of Human Materials Engineering. He was not at all surprised, taking it as his due, no, as recognition of the science he had been the first to develop in the world. At the meeting, he was introduced generously by the personal secretary to the Prime Minister as a professor, a holder of two doctorates from London, one in social sciences and one in engineering, the recognized leader of civil society in southern India, and the inventor of the new science of human materials engineering. Sharma*ji*, unfazed by the presence of prominent ministers especially requested to attend the meeting, launched into a practised presentation, with Rajni's graphics and his own funny anecdotes, interspersed with moving personal accounts of poverty. Spontaneous clapping resounded round the room when he finished. The Minister for Human Resources Development said loudly and emphatically that at least the central universities should immediately institute departments in the new science. Secretary, Communications and Broadcasting, requested Sharma*ji* to stay an extra day to attend electronic and print-media press conferences. The spokesman from External Affairs said thoughtfully that this could have the laugh on the Americans. The Minister of State for Finance hoped this scientific leap forward would go down well at the next G8 meeting. The Minister for Human Resources Development was impatient with all this talk and snatched back the initiative, since after all this was part of his turf. Pointing an accusing finger at Sharma*ji*, he said he would ask him point-blank if he would be prepared to chair a high-level committee of scientists and work out the broad research parameters of this science, so that proper staffing could take place from conjoint disciplines. Sharma*ji*'s answer was first to be lost in thought and then to come to a decision. His first responsibility was to the poor, he said with equal firmness, whose first servant he was. Everyone in the room said they respected that. However, he said, the development of this new science was also a national responsibility which weighed on his conscience. Quite so, said the spokesman from External Affairs. Sharma*ji* would accept the task in the National Interest. He could maybe spare time for three, or at the most four visits to Delhi a month, not more. He travelled badly, so, to save working time, preferred business class air travel. An office next to the Secretary's in Sastri Bhavan, plus a full complement of staff and staff car and a suite in the India International Centre was all he required to expedite matters. He would accept no emoluments, since this was in the National Interest, but he hoped concerned government departments would be instructed to work closely with his Society in future, in the 'larger interest.' Perhaps, through his Society they would get, not a bigger bang for their buck, but more satisfaction for having done a job well. When he had left the room, many in the room said with feeling that if there were more people like him, India would achieve the high spiritual goals that had been set by Swami Vivekananda and Mahatma Gandhi for the Nation.

14. Sharma*ji* Gets Angry

Normally, Sharma*ji* was calm, considerate, in fact the embodiment of compassion. But now he was very angry, and who would not be, if an aged relative, who should really be protecting his nephews, was trying to cheat them in the most blatant manner? He fumed in the train as they rattled towards Tenali, and even his younger brother, Raghu, a smaller, darker, pock-marked version of himself, who had been dragged along, could not change his mood, or get him off the painful subject.

'Our uncle should have been protecting our interests, instead of quietly trying to make away with our property. It is a shame! What glorious ancestors we come from, and now this!' There was nothing more to be said, especially by Raghu, who sank into his seat. Others crowded round in the unreserved general compartment— 'this is all we can afford, now that Uncle has swindled us' had been Sharma*ji*'s firm assertion at the ticket counter. Everyone in the crowded compartment heard every sordid detail repeated in changing versions by Sharma*ji*. Many shook their heads dolefully at Man's True Nature, others assured the brothers that there surely was a God, and none could escape *karma*; one decrepit lawyer promised to take the case up with the Supreme Court for almost no fees. The dry, desiccated landscape of Telangana gave way to the gentler acres of Andhra, lush fields circled with tall trees threw a greening light into the carriage as they flashed by, and the air smelt cooler and sweet. None of these sights that Raghu immersed himself in could lift Sharma*ji*'s gloom.

One of the few remaining *jetkas* at the station, with an ancient horse whose bones stuck out at every conceivable angle, took them jolting over the narrow curving dust road to their uncle's house. The journey itself was a marvel, for the vehicle, which shook and lurched at every turn, threatened to disintegrate before their very eyes. Sharmaji fought hard against paying the meagre fees demanded by the ancient and gaunt driver, older than even his horse, a man they had known since childhood. The bargaining was brought to an end only when Raghu quietly slipped Salim a ten-rupee note without his brother noticing.

As they walked up to the house, Sharma*ji* pointed out that the *tamarind* tree, their favourite childhood *tamarind* tree, had been felled and sold by their greedy uncle, who had not even notified them, not even one thieving word. Finally, after brusque salutations, they were seated in old but comfortable chairs in the small, tiled veranda, festooned with cobwebs. Buvamma, the cook they remembered from childhood, but now grown fat and toothless, had waddled up with a tray of coffee cups. Just to show how displeased he was, Sharma*ji* had said there wasn't enough sugar in his coffee, and Buvamma had to go and get some.

Their uncle, Satyanarayana, sat huddled in a chair in front, looking as faded as his old *khadi kurta* flapping round his tall frame, all skin and bones now, his sunken eyes peeping out mildly at Sharma*ji*'s solid form sipping an angry cup of coffee.

'It is a shame that our family matters should be dragged into court for all to witness our degeneration,' said Sharma*ji*, with genuine regret. 'I am a very busy man, all the time involved in social work of national importance, without a care for myself. The whole world knows that. What do I care about money? But it is a father's duty—and also an uncle's,' he added pointedly, 'to take care of the succeeding generation, so I had to bring a stay order, much to my distaste, when I heard you were quietly selling our ancestral property without telling us.' A loud snort, and a blow into a large, dirty handkerchief followed.

'I would not cheat you, Veda, or Raghu,' said their Uncle Satyanarayana slowly, drawing shallow breaths. 'This house I built out of the savings from my grain business, when things were going well. When younger brother passed away and left both of you as little orphans in my charge, Sita and I, poor woman, she left me early just like Raghava did, we very strictly saw to it that your father's money was safely invested and used only for your education, when we didn't have our own money to spend. All your normal expenses I took care of, Veda, I told you all this, gave you strict accounts, don't you remember?'

'Well, one can tell anything to a young gullible boy,' said Sharma*ji* sardonically. 'I can't go back and recover the money owing to me now. Let all that go. But to sell the house! The house we all grew up in! In a shady deal, by night, without informing your nephews, your rightful partners! How could you think of that? And how did you think we would keep quiet?'

'Veda, Veda, it is not as you think! I will show you all the papers. I have kept them carefully. The loans I took, the contractors' receipts, everything. I am selling because, like your father, poor Raghava, I have cancer, and the doctors tell me I need the money for treatment. I have to come to the city and stay with your aunt, Lalita Devi—she has said I could stay in a room for a small rent. Otherwise, why would I sell?'

'Uncle, anyone can make up papers. I know too much about the world to be taken in like that. If it comes to that, there are several lawyers—one Supreme Court lawyer even travelled with me today—who can expose such tricks. Tell me one thing. Raghu and I grew up in this house; how did that happen if we were not also owners? Just tell me that, the whole village knows that, by God!' Sharma*ji* was shouting.

'Calm yourself, Veda, think. Remember you, Raghu and my son Shankar were all the family I had left after my wife and your father left me. Now I am all alone; Shankar is also gone, in that terrible bus accident.' Satyanarayana closed his eyes.

'None can escape *karma*,' said Sharma*ji* unctuously to no one in particular. 'We will all get what we deserve. God sees to that.'

Satyanarayana opened his eyes. 'You know, after I am gone, everything, whatever is left will come to you, to you both. Where is the doubt?'

'Whatever is left, whatever is left,' mimicked Sharma*ji*. 'What will be left after you have spent everything foolishly on whatever greedy city doctors suggest? Why can't you try *ayurveda* or traditional herbal medicine? These modern doctors take your money, live in big houses, and never cure cancer; they just kill off their patients after sucking them dry. Even the West now recognizes the efficacy of our native herbs. Thousands of white people are coming to India for cures. Turmeric is the best remedy for cancer, Uncle, believe me, PhDs are being written about its powers. Just tell this Buvamma to put more *haldi* in every dish.'

'The doctors say that the cancer is in the early stage and with therapy and maybe an operation—they can only decide in the city hospital—there is a chance it can be cured. That is why, when everyone advised me, I decided to go in for hospital treatment. If all this had been known in those days, I might even have saved Raghava,' added Satyanarayana with regret.

'I have sacrificed my career, my prospects, everything I had,' said Sharma*ji*, turning to Raghu who kept looking at his feet. 'And look at the grip *maya* has on our elderly uncle with one foot in the grave in any case. He is desperate to enjoy life, God means nothing to him; he will even steal from his family for his pleasures.'

Buvamma had been sitting on the threshold listening to all of them. Now she broke in. 'Don't say such bad things, Vedanna, you always had a hasty temper, from childhood. I have served this house for forty years, I know. What your uncle says is true. He built the house with his money. He spent whatever he could on both of you. Have you forgotten he sent you abroad selling the lands? Have you forgotten that police case he hushed up? You would never have gone to college, only to jail, but for him!'

'So this is your witness!' shouted Sharma*ji* in great anger. 'They will laugh at you in court, I will see to that. That land was my father's. Of course, corrupt people can have all records changed by greasing the right palms, don't I know that? And what police case? It was all cooked up. I tell you, now I know by whom, just to keep me under his thumb! Which boy in this fornicating neighbourhood has not done worse things? Am I to listen to a lecture on morality from this low-caste woman, who has had God knows what relations with my uncle for forty years as she boasts!'

'God will burn out your eyes if you speak like that,' muttered Buvamma getting up slowly and hobbling back inside, towards the kitchen.

Sharma*ji* was beside himself with fury. 'What did that whore say?' he demanded, struggling up. 'I am going to thrash her for daring to address me, me, Vedavyas Sharma, chairman of SERVICE, me, who could have had a career in London, which I gave up to come and help such low-born, thieving, whoring, turds...'

'Veda, I will give you and Raghu half share,' said Satyanarayana suddenly, starting up. 'Will that satisfy you? And the rest you will have after I am gone. Calm yourself, the money will go nowhere.

I shall go and live with my cousin sister, Lalita Devi, in the room she will let out to me. We will see what treatment I can get for the money. You are right—and I thank you for reminding me—there is no reason for trying to prolong life.'

On the train back, Sharma*ji* was pleased. He ordered two plates of *vadas*, and paid for both, telling Raghu to keep his money; it was his duty to look after his younger brother. 'You see, Raghu,' he said contentedly munching his *vada*, dipping it now and then in chutney to add to the relish, 'you must know how to tackle difficult situations. For some people, a straightforward request will do, but for others, you must use a tactic they understand. After all, as they say, you can't get *ghee* out of a jar without using a crooked finger.'

Every now and then, Sharma*ji* pointed out the view, or some building of interest, out of the tinted plate-glass window of their air-conditioned compartment. Suddenly, a thought occurred to him. 'Raghu, out of our part of the money, I will give you one-fourth, that is fair. You are a bachelor, and too much money may lead you astray,' he laughed and winked. 'I have three children, you see; yes, my daughter is married, and Ashok is in Silicon Valley earning ten thousand dollars a month, but Prithivi is a worry. All right? Good! I love you, my brother.' He leaned forward and squeezed Raghu's arm, 'I can't tell you how happy I am to see you.'

As the train entered the dusty Telangana plains, Raghu gave voice to what had been worrying him a long time. 'I think we may have misunderstood Uncle Satyanarayana. Everyone has always told me how well he and Aunty Sita took care of us, when others may have sent us away to a hostel, or even to an orphanage. I remember them being very kind. And he did send you abroad, selling those lands, and he did protect you...'

Sharma*ji* smiled a superior smile. 'Brother, you are naïve. You do not understand the ways of the world. That is why I am always worried about you.' Then a dark frown clouded his face. 'Even if he did do all that he and those people say he did for us, even if he did protect us, even if he sold his lands to send us abroad, I will never forgive him for what he has done!' Sharma*ji* had never heard of Freud, let alone of a Freudian slip.

15. The Storyteller

Maggie Pyne sat on a large cushion, in the middle of a circle of village women, in the mud-built community centre. It was a beautiful day outside, and Sharma*ji* could see two golden orioles on the dark green branches of an acacia tree. He sat uncomfortably beside Maggie, propping up his back against the uneven wall, but with a view of the wet countryside and ploughmen knee-deep in the fields behind their bullocks.

'I am a Village Storyteller,' said Maggie comfortably and very slowly in English. 'They call me Magpie,' which Sharma*ji* easily translated as 'Myna,' to the women. 'First, everyone must touch the hands of the person next to her. Touching each other is very important, we don't do that often enough,' added Maggie. The village women quickly did as they were bid, several of them worried about all the work left undone at home, and also in the fields, now that the rains had started in earnest. 'Why do we tell stories? They bond us in a sisterhood.' Maggie's large white arms made a gathering movement, which needed no translation. All the women grinned and clapped. Maggie was pleased. 'We women are so oppressed by daily life—all our mundane chores—that stories told to each other let our minds and souls soar out into the blue beyond, till we can rise, rise, rise…' Everyone got the picture, and Kamalamma, suiting action to the thought, slipped out from the back to make tea for the gathering and also attend to the cleaning of the village centre.

'These days, people have stopped telling stories to each other. We rush off to work, and our children grow up without hearing stories, as our grandparents used to. This is the saddest part of modernity. We must get back to practising our active imagination, as Carl Jung advised, for it is through our fantasies, our shared whimsy, that we can recreate external reality in balance with our internal reality.' At this point, Sharma*ji* needed her to stop so that he might translate with some difficulty, but all the women nodded intelligently, with worried frowns, which Maggie took as positive engagement.

'Storytelling is simple,' she continued, opening out her hands like a large white lotus in a dark pond. 'We can all start with something natural, nearby. I start with my storytelling name—Magpie—it sounds like my name and yet is not my given name, but it becomes instantly a real name.' A broad smile lit up her face and all the women broke out into relieved laughter. 'See, Sharma*ji*, we women from two corners of the world can understand each other—we don't need men to interpret—we don't need you.' Affectionately, she reached out and gave a playful push to his shoulder, and again the women laughed, and nodded at each other for they too seemed to get the meaning.

Maggie was happily into her stride. 'What does a magpie do? She flits from flower to flower, from tree to tree, telling stories to all the other birds as they gather their morning worms. They gather food, and she helps them gather happiness. So, let us start. This magpie has flown in from far away, from the land of a very bad man, who is a Big Cat, hiding in a Bush, and pretending he is a Bush!' She moved her eyes and hands expressively, and meowed most effectively, asking them to chase the Bad Cat away. Egged on by her, some of the women got up and with brooms shooed away an imaginary cat right out of the door, and slipped away themselves. When order was restored, Maggie resumed her story.

Maggie created a new story right in their midst about the cat that hid in a bush and a poor frightened Muslim mouse called— she asked them to name the mouse, and after several names had been suggested, she accepted the name Hussein. The mouse, she said, had put in its little burrow a choice collection of seeds and nuts for the winter, but the Bad Cat called Bush wanted to eat them himself, because he liked the oil in the Nuts. What oil did they use for cooking? A discussion followed, and the differing qualities of gingelly, groundnut, mustard and sunflower oil were debated. Sharma*ji* pronounced in favour of sunflower oil, and charts were produced to show the health benefits of sunflower. Some women said that gingelly oil was cheap, and they were used to its taste. Maggie wanted to see the seeds from which gingelly oil was expressed, and when she saw the small seeds, she retold her story explaining how a small little seed like that could make a big, big difference in the world of men, cats, and birds.

Maggie was very, very happy over the morning's session, and at lunch told Sharma*ji* that she was willing to fund a training programme for creating women storytellers in his villages. Practical teaching programmes needed to be complemented with working on the Spirit. Sharma*ji* quickly gave a ballpark figure for the proposed programme, and when Maggie agreed quite readily to support it for three years, he felt a little sorry that he had not presented a more generous budget. Everyone had the capacity to be a storyteller, said Maggie earnestly, and the active imagination of everyone needed to be developed for lessening, she could not say removing, the more pressing neuroses of modern life. Could Sharma*ji* arrange more village sessions for her, where the women, in the comfort of being together, could let their imaginations soar, tell stories, laugh, touch each other? Touching was so important.

That afternoon, as Maggie took a siesta in the guesthouse, Sharma*ji* called an emergency meeting of his trusted aides,

Dasgupta, Abraham, Venkat and Rukmini, to work out a storytelling schedule for Maggie Pyne. Groups had to be put together, at least for a couple of hours at a time, during the height of the agricultural work. It was agreed that daily wages would be given to the women to listen to Maggie's stories. Sharma*ji* could not, regretfully, accompany her everywhere, he was quite firm about it. This duty would have to be shared among them, and they should ensure the success of each storytelling session. It was important that Maggie, a new donor, should go away happy that she had ignited the spark of storytelling among village women.

Dasgupta chewed reflectively on some *paan*. 'There is no trouble about that,' he said comfortably, his mouth full of red betel-nut juice. 'They all tell stories all the time—too many stories, that is the trouble. But this programme will be a clear success. I know the mischievous ones in every village—don't they make life hell for me? I shall tell each of them to rehearse one of their stories ahead of time—the sort of humbug they try to fool me with—me? When Miss Maggie is halfway through, they will spontaneously stand up and start on their own stories. This will make her happy!' Everyone agreed this was a very good idea, and that the selected women should be summoned to the centre that very evening—send a jeep to collect them all, there was no time left, said Sharma*ji*—and Dasgupta would give his instructions.

Rukmini was in a reflective mood. Why not show in the beginning that all the women shied away from each other, kept their distance, and then, inspired by Maggie, slowly started to touch each other, till they all happily danced in a circle with arms round each other's shoulders? They anyway danced like that often, that would not be the problem. Getting them to keep a distance between each other in the beginning would be. Abraham had a solution. Why not start by having only a few women in a hall, sitting at a distance from each other, who would then tell

Maggie there was no room for the other women to sit. She would then ask the women to squeeze up, Abraham would translate, all the women would have to do was refuse to move, and then the others could be brought in, one by one, and made to touch each other. Sharma*ji* was reflective. If it was to succeed, it had to be done well, it had to be rehearsed in advance. The women must be told what was needed of them, why it was important, and that a sari would be presented to each of them if everything went off well. Venkat, cynical as ever, assured Sharma*ji* that everything would go off like clockwork; the village women were very smart, they knew the score, they knew that the Society through its foreign donations kept them at a standard of living far higher than that in non-beneficiary villages. Sharma*ji* did not quite like it being put in this frank manner, but he had to agree that Venkat's words reflected the truth of the matter.

'My God! It was such tiring work!' said Maggie Pyne five days later. 'But inspiring, Sharma*ji*! How much the women resisted touching each other! Once I had to get up and actually press a woman's hand down on the shoulder of another. There was such resistance—I could feel her energy, wanting to pull her hand away. It always took us a long time in Des Moines to learn to touch each other. We were all from small farming families, my father had to sell out his eight hundred acres in the end to pay his debts. But the women in Iowa learned to cope. Now, whenever we meet that is the first thing we do—we go round in a circle, not afraid to touch each other. But here! It's been marvellous! How the women have responded! After being unsure of each other in the beginning, which was only natural. And the stories! You should have heard them! How imaginative the women are, once active imagination is allowed to act within each one. It was a marvellous experience, I shall never forget how a little story from me broke open dammed up spirits, how stories flowed out like great rivers!' She cried beautifully, without restraint, like a child.

Sharma*ji* held her hands comfortingly in his own. 'Dear Maggie, our dear Magpie, you have been marvellous,' he murmured. 'We did not pay heed to the spiritual side of our village friends, and focused only on the economics. But you taught us—no, don't deny it—that the heart is more important than the head. That active imagination creates true wealth, that of happiness.'

Maggie Pyne promised to come again next year, but do come in December, counselled Sharma*ji*, when it was not so hot and humid, to be with the marvellous women once again, and help more storytellers come out of their cocoons, like beautiful butterflies. That, Sharma*ji* said, was such an appropriately descriptive metaphor, he would title the project 'Awakening the Butterflies.'

16. The Servant Girl

'**Lakshmi should not be** in the house this evening,' said Sharma*ji* to no one in particular.

'Why not?' challenged his wife. 'Where will she go? In the evenings I don't want to send her here and there. The place is no longer safe. You don't know how wicked men have become. No, she stays home.'

'Why don't you understand?' asked Sharma*ji* irritably. 'But when have you ever understood anything about my work? Some foreigners are coming this evening. Ramulu will bring them home straight from the airport. After an hour's discussion, I will ask them what sort of hotel they want to go to, and send them off. That's all.'

'Oh, foreigners are safe,' said his wife, relieved. 'They won't even notice Lakshmi. They want only high-class women, like you see in pictures. Lakshmi must definitely stay. Who will serve them *pakodas* and tea? Not me, I am not their servant, or your servant.'

'You have a one-track mind,' declared Sharma*ji*. 'Try and understand something—they have just led a campaign against child labour in the North, where they are very cruel to children, not like our people. We are cheated by employing these lazy kids, we spend money on them, and they are always playing outside. Anyway, it will be a big, big misunderstanding if Lakshmi is here when those foreigners come. I am expecting a large grant, and I don't want anything to be spoilt just because of you. Send Lakshmi to Shanta.'

After some discussion, it was settled that Lakshmi would be given bus fare, clear instructions on how to find Shanta's house and packed off early enough in the day. But she should return by the first bus the next day—there would be too much cleaning to do. Lakshmi seemed cheerfully agreeable when Sharma*ji* left for work in the morning. It was raining hard in the evening when he returned. His wife met him at the door with a worried frown.

'I tried to call Shanta all day,' she said, 'but her line is down. In America it snows and there are hurricanes every other day, but the telephone always works, clearer than calling across the street. So why should rain break everything down here?'

Sharma*ji* had no answer, but was relieved to learn that Lakshmi had set off quite confidently, the persistent rain not making any difference to her. These village people are quite hardy, Sharma*ji* told his wife, they survive, and before you know it Lakshmi will come home with three little kids dragging at her skirt. He tried to phone the airport to find out if the plane was on time, but the line was persistently busy. So he sent Ramulu off in any case to wait for the foreign guests at the airport, and bring them straight home whenever they arrived.

An hour later, his wife had made a pile of nice spicy *pakodas*, some of which he gratefully munched with a cup of tea, leaving the rest for the guests. But one by one, the *pakodas* disappeared as the guests failed to arrive, till they were all gone. After shouting at him for being greedy, and predicting he would suffer from gas all night, his wife went back to the kitchen to make another pile of *pakodas*. A heavy thunderstorm broke overhead, and all the lights went out all over the colony. With much shouting, so as to be heard over the lashing of the storm, they closed the rattling windows, dug out some candles, and sat round the table grumbling about the weather, the inconsiderate guests, the inefficiency of the airlines, and corruption in politics, which was at the root of all their troubles.

Suddenly the lights came on in a blaze, and they could hear the buzzing of the phone, which had come off the hook. Sharma*ji*'s wife tried Shanta's number, and declared gleefully that it was ringing. After several renewed attempts, she came to her husband with an anxious look.

'I think Shanta is not in town,' she said in a frightened whisper. 'She did tell me she might go to Shirdi one of these weekends, and that's where she must have gone after locking up the house. I never thought she would do so without telling me. She must have tried, but her line has been down. What are we to do? That stupid girl must be sitting outside the door all this while in the dark. I am scared. You must go immediately and get her back. What will I say to her parents if anything happens to her?'

Sharma*ji* looked at his watch. It was nearing ten. 'It is so late, and I don't have a car, and where do you think I can find autos on a wet night like this? She will be all right huddled up. A little cold, that is all.'

'You don't know that neighbourhood,' wailed his wife. 'You don't see anything, even right under your nose! That colony has bars, men get drunk in the evening, and you know what drunk men are like. They are bad even when they are sober, and they never think honourably about helpless girls. And our girl is a wayward, I know her type, the way she looks at the milkman, I know. What will we say to her parents? What will we say to my grand-uncle, who sent her from the village? If you won't go, I will go!'

When she started looking frantically for her umbrella and *chappals*, Sharma*ji* knew there was no option, and he had to go find the wretched girl so far away on that windy, cold, dark night. His worst fears were realized. He couldn't find an auto for well over half an hour, and when he did find one in a dark street, the drunk auto*wallah*—he could smell his breath even on that windy night—demanded two hundred rupees to take him back and forth. Sharma*ji* was tired, and his pants were soaked with splashes of muddy water. So he got in and said he would add a *baksheesh* of ten rupees if the fellow drove politely and carefully.

'Guru, I am always polite to my customers,' said the fellow, revving up his engine. 'Come, I can take you to better places. You will have the most colourful night of all nights!'

'*Arre*, I am going to get a sick person, not for any pleasure, so drive carefully and quickly. We don't want someone's life on our hands,' said Sharma*ji*.

Sobered that he was on a mission of mercy, the auto*wallah* bumped his way in the dark, splashing Sharma*ji* with more muddy water, and lurching perilously over potholes, cursing the government and corruption among politicians. Shanta's colony had descended into pitch darkness when Sharma*ji* got there at last. He went up to her door, but found no Lakshmi. Where could the girl have gone? He stumbled down the stairs, and along with the auto*wallah* hunted out a *chowkidar* asleep under a flight of stairs.

The *chowkidar* was annoyed and suspicious till he was told he was speaking to Shantamma's father. 'Shantamma left two days ago. There has been nobody here since then. No girl, who will come in this rain? She must have stayed home.' With that he curled himself inside his blanket, calling on *Indra* and *Arjuna* to save him on that rainy night. Sharma*ji* was really worried now. Where could the girl have gone? He remembered a case from several years ago when the whole village had turned up to beat up the employer of a boy who had died of natural causes. God knows! He could be ruined over this stupid girl, even if he escaped a thrashing. The auto*wallah* and he stumbled around the dark housing complex, while he called out her name. They only set off dogs barking, one truculent animal, baring his teeth and snapping at them.

'You said it was some sick person,' said the auto*wallah*, not liking to get sober in the cold wind. 'Now you are after some girl. I can get you all the girls you want. College-educated for a man like you. Starlets!'

'She is my missing servant. Don't you understand?' screamed Sharma*ji*. 'Anything could have happened to her on a night like this! And you are making indecent proposals!'

'*Arre Sahib*, there is nothing indecent about sex,' said the auto*wallah* in a professorial manner. 'How do you think you were born? By your parents doing *puja*? No, no, I mean no disrespect. That girl has run away, they all do that, and earn some money. Don't worry, she will turn up for work tomorrow morning, when you can beat her for worrying you, all right?'

This advice did not satisfy Sharma*ji* and he tried to scour a few more streets. When the auto*wallah* said he would then charge three hundred rupees, Sharma*ji* very reluctantly decided to return home. He was very tired, sick of accosting policemen on the beat, and in any case the search was useless. But what would he tell his wife, and what of the consequences on the morrow?

It was somewhat of a relief to enter his apartment, warm and blazing with light, after stumbling around in the cold dark streets for hours. A pile of backpacks and suitcases met him at the door, and then he saw his three foreign guests sitting around the table being served tea and *pakodas* by Lakshmi, while his wife sat smiling at the head, telling them jokes.

Henk, a burly man in khaki shorts, half rose from his chair, waving his cup. 'Sharma*ji*! We were told that you have been hunting for Lakshmi in the dark, but here she is safe and sound.' Gerd, also in khaki, nodded from Olympian heights, and patted the girl's shoulders. His wife cracked more jokes, setting off happy laughter. The plane had been hours late, it was now past midnight and too late to find hotels. So that night they would all stretch out in the spare room, Mrs Sharma had been so kind as to make all arrangements. Even Lakshmi seemed quite at ease, only hunching her shoulders forward to hide her budding breasts under the unblinking bespectacled gaze of Peter's. At last, all the tall foreigners stretched their arms and said they were ready for bed. Henk threw a hundred rupee note at Lakshmi and told her to get him some cigarettes from any corner shop that was open as he was fresh out. And so they went to bed, Sharma*ji* thanking the Gods that all had turned out well on that blustery night.

17. Sharma*ji* Stands Trial

Instinctively, Sharma*ji* knew from the very start that he should not get involved, that it was folly to do so, and yet get involved he did—he put it down, a period of wrenching, honest reflection later, to overweening pride, to vaulting ambition. It all started that early February morning in his town flat, as he sat in his balcony, clad only in his *banian* and *dhoti*, drinking his morning cup of coffee and reading his morning newspaper. He was reading another report of a police encounter with Marxist-Leninist naxalites, with photographs of six young bodies stretched out in grotesque death among the bushes, when the doorbell rang. Thinking the maid-servant had come unusually early, he went grumbling to the door, tucking in his loose *dhoti*, to find a somber delegation of human rights activists waiting at the door.

'Sir! I am the least qualified to do what you are asking,' he said in a despairing voice, at the third repetition of their request. 'You don't know how much trouble I have with the police myself, whenever it comes to the question of receiving foreign funds. They are very suspicious, and my getting into the picture will not only not help your cause, but most probably I shall have to wind up my NGO!'

Veera Reddy, the 'People's Poet,' as he was popularly known, was a slim man, with greying hair and simple shabby clothes, who would pass unnoticed even in a small gathering, but when he spoke in meetings he commanded the instant respect of several thousands. He looked at Sharma*ji* with a level gaze. 'Sir, you have an established reputation in our country and in the world as a leader of civil society. These so-called encounters are nothing but the murder of young tribal and dalit boys and girls, who have taken to arms as a last resort. I do not agree with what they are doing; I never have; I want to bring about peace in all these jungle villages, where the government is waging a war. We are asking you only to be a member of a fact-finding committee, to help negotiate between the *naxalites* and the government. We have some hope now, because even the ruling party's high command has said it wants peace.'

Though Sharma*ji* continued to protest for another hour, a vision was already forming in the back of his mind, of the glory he would be covered with if a peaceful resolution could be achieved of this intractable political problem. Even a Nobel Prize for Peace might come his way. His resistance to the idea weakened rapidly as his vision grew in depth and detail. He plunged into the peace efforts with his usual enthusiasm, and very much enjoyed being driven about in government cars to meetings in the secretariat, followed by tête-à-têtes with the chief minister, the director-general of police, and once even with the prime minister.

For a couple of months the talks teetered on the apparent brink of success, with much media coverage, only to break down catastrophically, followed by a spate of police encounters that wiped out several groups of young *naxalites*. He was once again *persona non grata* with the police; an inspector from the intelligence bureau visited his office, and all his efforts seemed totally forgotten by the media, which dropped him out of all sight. Grumbling and regretting his fruitless involvement in politics, he went back to his rural centre to get back into the familiar development groove. He found that the paperwork he had neglected remained undone, and, what caused him the most worry, deadlines for submitting accounts, project proposals and budgets had slipped by without securing new funds.

One late afternoon, a week or so later, he was taking a walk along the dusty village road, composing an impressive explanation to his donors for the delay in communicating with them. Of course highlighting the stress he had been under to resolve a national emergency, when an old, mud-encrusted white Ambassador drew up alongside and two young men jumped out. They requested him to accompany them immediately to a secret high-level meeting of the peace committee. They could give him no further details, and he got into the car thinking he might still retrieve some benefit for all the work he had done. The vehicle drove ahead at top speed, bumping appallingly over rutted village roads, even when darkness and dust swirled all around them. Sharma*ji* remonstrated, and the young men said it would just be a few minutes more, but it was a full hour before the vehicle drew up with a jerk in the middle of nowhere. Sharma*ji* got out on very stiff legs, only to be surrounded in an instant by half a dozen young men in olive drab fatigues. He realized with a shock that he was a prisoner of the *naxalites.*

Unceremoniously, with no words exchanged, they hustled him into a decrepit jeep, blindfolded him, and thrust him to the floor. The rear metal gate banged shut, and they were off again on an even bumpier ride, his face bruised by the legs of his captors as the jeep careened down forest slopes. It bounced over ridges, and once settled to twist and turn in the soft sand of a *nullah*. He was thankful when they stopped at last, but his relief was short-lived, as he was forced to walk fast through the dark forest at a pace he had never adopted, even in his youth. Rest came in the depth of the jungle as dawn was breaking, a vile sweet tea was cooked over three stones, and then, after ten minutes, they were off again. When he sat down in protest, the leader unconcernedly pointed his automatic at Sharma*ji* and said he would be happy to kill him then and there if he wanted it that way. Almost blind with fatigue, his chest heaving uncontrollably, Sharma*ji* somehow rose to his feet and staggered on as fast as he could.

Hours later, during a late afternoon rest deep inside a banyan grove, a girl *naxalite* offered him some smelly, badly burnt pork to eat, and kneeling down, told him, not unkindly, that he had nothing to fear, and that no harm would be done to him illegally. With that somewhat comforting thought he fell into a dead sleep, till he was kicked awake and forced to start another rapid journey through the thick forest in the depth of the night. Next morning, when he was gulping down his tea out of a rusted tin mug, the girl who had been kind to him pointed to a little stream below where they sat, and told him to shit, for later he wouldn't have the chance. Normally his bowels moved only after several cups of hot coffee, but he made an attempt, walking down to the stream with his thighs trembling with fatigue. As he unbuttoned his pants, he saw that the girl was perched on a stone, looking at him, her weapon at the ready. She laughed and told him to go ahead, she knew how men shat. He cleaned himself with water scooped up in the mug he had just used for coffee, and the girl laughed again at his grimace.

By afternoon they had reached a remote tribal village deep in the forested hills. It seemed at first glance to be populated only by the *naxalite* groups, most of the tribal inhabitants having discreetly vanished into the jungle, except for a few older people left behind to cook food and serve. Most of the young people lounged around, laughing, joking, or cleaning their guns. He was dumped in a clearing in the middle of the village. He sat nursing his bare torn feet—a sandal strap had snapped a long time ago. He had tried hopping on one leg, then abandoned the other sandal also and had shuffled along on bare feet. His captors all had stout boots, but no one offered him a pair, in fact they had no spare pair to offer. He was filthy from head to foot, and he stank. A grizzled three-day growth made his face feel stiff. In any case, the exhaustion he was in made the village, the trees, the *naxalites*, and the screeching birds, swim round in circles as in an unreal dream.

'Mr Sharma, good afternoon!' said a voice in English, half humorously, and he looked up with a start to see a dark-faced young man with a short clipped moustache, dressed in olive drabs like the rest, with a Sam Browne belt, holster and pistol, seated on a straight-backed chair behind a small table. He was some sort of commander, and he glanced intently at a notebook while sipping a glass of water.

'We can address you in English, Telugu or Hindi, whichever you are comfortable with,' continued the man. 'I chair this People's Court, and with my two colleagues form the Panel that will go into all the charges laid against you.' Two other young men hastily sat down on either side of their leader on upturned plastic buckets. Sharma*ji* stammered that Telugu was his mother tongue, so the proceedings were conducted mostly in Telugu with a free sprinkling of English and Hindi words and sentences, whichever came to their tongues without effort.

'You will address me only as Chairman,' said the leader or commander clearly. 'Remember this is a Court, a People's Court. You can defend yourself. We do not believe in all that bourgeois farce of lawyers and an anti-people legal system. But at this Court we will be fair, take your words at face value, and assess them against known facts. First, you will tell me all facts about yourself, your work, your activities, and why you decided to work against us, against the people as an agent of the police.'

Sharma*ji* was cross-questioned carefully, the commander or chairman going back over his earlier statements, asking the same questions again, checking his answers, asking for clarifications about any perceived discrepancies. Sharma*ji* realized he was fighting for his life, but in his exhausted state, try as he would, he could not be his usual clever self, and the words tumbled out of his mouth as of their own volition.

'I am not an agent of the police, or anyone else!' he cried for the umpteenth time. 'I was asked by Veera Reddy to help, to help save lives, your lives, and lives of people who are being killed in encounters by the police. I tried my level best, and I failed. That is not my fault—and I am not an informer nor agent!'

'That is not the information placed before us,' said the chairman gravely. 'We have strong circumstantial evidence that you are a police agent, and that you deliberately passed on information to help the police kill many soldiers of the people. I would advise you to be frank.'

Sharma*ji* broke down and wept uncontrollably, and a girl comrade was ordered to give him some water. In the interrogation that followed, the chairman showed that he had detailed and accurate information about whatever went on at the SERVICE centre; he seemed to have knowledge about the petty fudging of accounts, the general misuse of programmes and even about Sharma*ji*'s secret relationship with Rukmini.

Sharma*ji* looked around wildly. How did they know so much? Surely this could be only a horrible dream? And then he saw Ramulu, his dismissed driver, looking at him in triumph from under a forage cap. So, the thieving, insolent rascal had become a *naxal*, and was determined to have him killed, but why? Just for throwing him out of a low-paid job?

'The facts as we know are not as you state. You are of bad character, and you run a bogus organization. Everything points to you being a mole of the police. Cunningly involving yourself with our innocent bourgeois friends, you got a perfect chance to betray us to the police.'

When he heard this cold damning statement from the chairman, Sharma*ji* realized his end was at hand. There was nothing further to be done. He was too tired, exhausted, fed-up with this stupid life in which he had struggled so hard to make a living, gain a name, support a few people. Death was at hand, and he preferred death to living with everyone around him then, and everyone else he knew, with their stupidity, their arrogance...

'Before we pass judgment, Mr. Sharma, we want you to realize that it is a just judgment. We are not murderers like the police, like your callous bourgeois society. We are Marxist-Leninists, following the shining path of Mao Zedong!'

'You are nothing of the sort,' said Sharma*ji* light-headedly, well past caring. 'You are just a bunch of ignorant kids, playing with guns, and after killing fools like me. You will get killed as well, without even knowing why you are dying!'

The chairman or commander looked at him with interest. 'As a bourgeois you can see the world only through a lens of false consciousness,' he said earnestly. 'We are not here to kill and be killed. We want to complete the New Democratic Revolution in India, cunningly thwarted by the ruling class and their political parties. These compradors, after decades of pretence that they are nationalists, have now become open lackeys of America in its re-colonization of the world. Our hammer blows are aimed at that principal contradiction between the poor of the third world and the new imperial power.'

'You don't even know what is the principal contradiction,' laughed Sharma*ji* weakly, almost enjoying yourself. 'You speak like a bourgeois professor, full of empty theory. Marxism is all about material reality. Lenin and Mao created Revolution by knowing what the real facts were. Forget America and the bourgeois world. As far as you and your comrades are concerned, the principal contradiction is between you and the police!'

The commander signalled to him to go on. 'And you know what is the principal aspect of this contradiction?' continued Sharma*ji* in delirium. 'It lies in their superiority—not in arms, or courage, but in numbers, inexorable numbers. If you think you are like a fish in water, you are drinking up all the water, and you are flapping like fish on the beach, ready for slaughter.'

'You are just meaninglessly abusive, like any bourgeois, braving out the moment of your death,' said the commander judiciously. 'You have not said anything meaningful, or of material reality.'

'Oh, no? What is your understanding of the unity of opposites?' Sharma*ji* challenged. 'You confuse it with one divides into two don't you? You think that only means you winkle out who your hidden enemies are, don't you? Wrong!'

'Well, instruct us,' said the commander in a level voice, as Sharma*ji* lay back on the ground, tired to death, with eyes closed.

'Listen! Don't think you fellows are the only ones ever to wish for Revolution,' said Sharma*ji*, levering himself up on his elbows. 'We all wanted Revolution when I was a student. And I had an excellent history teacher, but you have only these badly translated pieces of paper. The Unity of Opposites is a deep philosophical concept, a powerful Maoist *mantra*. It means whatever good you do, it will have a bad side, a dark side, and your strategy must minimize its effect always. You are trying to protect these tribals, but you are also driving them away in fear. They are the water for you fish, but all your water is receding fast in fear!'

The commander leaned forward to say something, hesitated, and then started to speak again. But at that moment a series of low whistles broke out at the periphery of the clearing, and a new group sauntered in led by an older woman.

'Greetings! Comrade Nehru,' said the woman, addressing the commander apparently by his *nom de guerre*. 'What is going on? A People's Court? I know this fellow,' she added, looking indifferently at Sharma*ji*.

'Vasantakka, Mr Sharma is charged with being a police agent,' said Nehru standing up deferentially in front of the legendary woman, and he rapidly told her of the charges laid in detail by Comrade Ramulu.

Vasantakka seemed mildly amused, though she was mostly disinterested in the business. 'Sharma was in jail during the Emergency and tortured. He used to be a firebrand in those days, till he decided he would rather be a bourgeois slob. That's the fate of people who live in cities. Do what you like with him, but also make sure there are no hidden reasons for the charge laid against him. I am tired. I will rest for some time.' And with that pronouncement, with scarcely a glance at Sharma*ji*, she disappeared into a hut.

Commander Nehru went up close to Ramulu, and looked him up and down. 'You were trying to settle some personal scores by laying the complaint, were you not?' he asked softly. 'And do you know the punishment for making a misrepresentation for selfish reasons in front of a People's Court?'

Ramulu trembled, and sank to the ground, clutching his commander's knees. Nehru turned away abruptly, his mind made up. 'Blindfold them both,' he commanded.

Sharma*ji* heard gun bolts being drawn back, and knew he was on the brink of eternity. He heard the shot even as he felt a terrific blow to his head, and he was falling away, far away into blackness, into nothingness.

***

A splash of water woke him spluttering, he tried to lift his head, but then sank back, his head throbbing with pain. A tall, thin man with a black beard was leering at him from on high.

'Ah, ha! You have been visiting *annalu*,' said the man. 'Yes, it's elder brothers' signature all right. They always pistol-whip their unwanted guests and then leave them by the roadside for us truck-*wallahs* to transport back. Get up! Get up! I haven't all day. You can come to the city with me, or sleep here, if you like.'

The truck-driver, and his much shorter cleaner, a lad in dirty black half-pants, Sharma*ji* noticed without curiosity, pulled him groaning to his feet, and into the high front-seat of the truck. The cleaner handed him a cup of tea as they started, a silvery cut-out figure of the God Ganesh swaying in front of his tortured eyes. The truck-driver was a jovial fellow, asking him questions, and then without waiting for answers, launching into anecdotes of others he had rescued on the roadside.

'They could have killed you easily. You are lucky,' he said sagely, as Sharma*ji* at last closed his eyes and fell into a fitful sleep. They were already in the city when he was nudged awake. No, he thanked them, he didn't want them to take him anywhere. He would get down and catch an auto. The truck-driver left him with shouted advice about rubbing gingelly oil into his sore head, and then fomenting it with hot water. An auto-*wallah* looked at him with contempt, but a customer was a customer, so with scant respect, he seated him, after slowly lighting a *bidi*, and they were off homewards. Sharma*ji* could picture his wife's consternation when he got home, and her questions, and the questions of his staff who would stream in, and of curious neighbours, followed by the inevitable visit from the police. His mind distantly turned around thoughts of various stories he could concoct, of being too clever by half for the simple-minded extremists; or of defiance; or of daring escape. Then, for the first time in his life, he decided to say nothing, nothing at all.

18. A Day to Remember

The President of the United States of America broke through the swarms of people around him. 'Hey! Sam—may I call you Sam? I liked what you said. You are a good man.' He pointed a forefinger like a gun at Sharma*ji*'s nose. 'Next time you are in Washington D.C., give me a call and we will have a drink together.' And then he was gone, with the swirling crowd of businessmen, Indian politicians, security guards and media men following him to his car. But he had spoken loudly for all to hear, and already a respectful circle of the subaltern business elite was beginning to form around Sharma*ji*.

A brief visit to the one-day 'Consultation: Business Aids the Poor' had been scheduled for the President at the last minute, and even though the President's security had been for hours at the seven-star hotel venue of the conference. None of the Indian business organisers had actually expected the President to show up. Just the announcement that he might drop in for a few minutes had made their day. Hastily, the Secretary, General Administration Department, was asked for names of key people who should be invited. In the list sent up, Sharma*ji*'s name had been slipped in unnoticed, the government's stock rep of civil society for all meetings. When he had arrived at the super posh hotel, he had been largely ignored and given a seat at a table at the back, where he had sat comfortably, stuffing himself with canapés, admiring the chandeliers, and already making up stories for the future on how he had single-handedly defied—that was the only word—the corporate might in defence of the people.

In the midst of the three-minute welcoming speeches for the President, the American Ambassador had stood up and asked to hear voices from civil society. A brief uncomfortable silence had followed, which saw Sharma*ji* rise slowly to his feet. He had not been cowed by the irritated tone of the chairman of the federation of industries when asked to identify himself, but had loudly and firmly informed the audience that he was surprised that a conference on assistance to the poor had included only himself and not several of his more famous colleagues.

'We from Civil Society do not ask for hand-outs—the Poor do not need them. We only ask that you treat us with Respect. We do not ask for your Aid. We ask only for Business Opportunities!' When the President of the United States himself stood up and applauded, the whole large congregation of the elite business world leapt to its feet and cheered loudly and long. Sharma*ji* had sat down, preening himself for choosing the right message for the occasion.

When the session resumed after the President's departure, Sharma*ji* was cordially invited to the dais, a large name card hastily printed out that almost hides half his face, was placed in front of his nose. Before the presentations started, Miss Kirti Desai of Media Buzz described all the trials and tribulations her team had undergone for the production of the coffee-table book, *Challenge! The Face of Poverty*, with five hundred beautiful pictures of the poor and hungry, photographed from all over India. Complimentary copies were handed to every delegate in the room by her staff.

During the presentations that followed, Sharma*ji*'s opinions were referred to with cordial regularity. Businessmen, famous in

India, and several of them well-known in the United States as well, came up in disciplined procession to the podium to make ten-minute PowerPoint presentations, projected onto a giant screen at the back. Their trained voices carried around the vast room through a specially installed Bose system. The chandeliers dimmed expertly at every presentation, always followed by just thirty seconds of applause from fellow businessmen.

A seafood exporter showed how a fleet of ultra-modern trawlers could increase fish catches by an order of ten; a seed specialist pictured vast fields of GM grain, burnished in the golden sun of several other countries; a ready-made pre-fab house was seen to be assembled ready for occupation within one hour; several pharmaceutical giants presented drug technologies in the pipeline that would eradicate disease; varieties of beverages to please every taste flashed from slide to slide; an auto manufacturer projected yet another people's car; a combined display of IT greats showed that education for all was only a mouse-click away; and there was even a presentation on women's empowerment by an institute for fashion technology. Two corporate houses, which had adopted a village each, showed pictures of smiling village people, one to the accompaniment of a Carnatic *kirtana*, for the village was in Tamil Nadu, and the other to the sound of a Hindustani *alap*, for that village was on the banks of the Ganga. When the presentations ended, the screen dissolved into a picture of Aishwarya Rai smiling over her left shoulder.

Industry rose for a sumptuous lunch, fusing over the culinary traditions of several Asian countries, with renewed confidence that they could do the job of eradicating poverty and making the start of the new millennium an Indian century. Sharma*ji* received another standing ovation when he summed up with Winston Churchill's immortal words: 'Give us the tools and we will finish the job.'

He, of course, sat at the high table with his side pockets bulging with the business cards thrust upon him. He daintily determined to taste every one of the forty-odd exotic dishes laid out for the gathering. He was secure in the knowledge that his new friends would surely give jobs to several of his nephews, nieces, and other hangers-on.

As he was dithering over which set of desserts to go for, a thin young man in a loud check shirt came up to him. 'I am Sitaram,' he said simply. Most people knew the legendary billion dollars he had made in Silicon Valley over a year and a half, and then given up IT to head a group of venture capitalists who funded socially relevant cutting-edge technologies. Despite his obvious charm and suavity, he was also known for ruthlessly cutting off a hopeful presentation in the first two minutes if he thought it was a non-starter.

'I want to convert my home village in Krishna district to look exactly like the President's hometown,' said Sitaram shyly. 'Give the same street names, and rebuild an exact replica of his town square in the centre of my village. What do you think?'

'I think it is a great idea,' said Sharma*ji*, helping himself to all the three different kinds of gateau, being unable to decide between them. The conference chairman then hustled him away to a secluded corner for a serious talk.

'Indian business will be making a major presentation in Detroit this fall,' said the chairman, his accents switching between a major of broad coastal Andhra to a minor of mid-western American. 'We will all be there. We would like you to make a keynote presentation on private sector-civil society partnership. We will of course cover all expenses, and there will be an honorarium of ten thousand rupees a day. We mean to make it a dynamic occasion. I am sure you will enjoy it.'

Sharma*ji* thought for a bit. 'Ten thousand rupees—that's about two hundred dollars a day, right?' he asked in mild enquiry.

The chairman busily rustled his papers, and said with an amused laugh at himself: 'Sorry! What am I thinking! Of course it's an international conference, and the honorarium would be at international standards—around a thousand dollars—no, two thousand dollars a day.'

There was a pause. 'These days, what with my health not being robust, I always travel with my wife,' said Sharma*ji* pleasantly.

The chairman tapped Sharma*ji*'s knee confidently. 'Leave it to us. We will fly you both out first class, of course, and the President's suite at the Sheraton—unless of course he turns up to hear you!'

They both laughed together at the joke.

'I will have to ask my wife, of course,' said Sharma*ji*, and then to leave no matter in further suspense, added: 'But I am sure I can convince her. It's for India, and we are all Indians!'

While the chairman was busily noting down cell-phone numbers, times to call, and the office address, Sharma*ji*, who had briefly adopted the well-known pose of Rodin's Le Penseur, lifted his head and said with a worried frown: 'We should make better use of this opportunity, you know? I mean, take the initiative forward to have lasting effect.'

Securing the chairman's undivided attention, he sketched out a training programme to be conducted some time in the future by his own organisation, aptly named SERVICE, and why should it not be of service to business?

'Fantastic idea, Mr Sharma!' said the chairman decisively. 'I can see you are a man of vision. I think we can settle this right away!' Rising, he snapped his fingers familiarly at the dean of management studies, who was ambling around vaguely with a cup of coffee, and took him into a huddle with a few other colleagues from Silicon Valley. He came back to Sharma*ji* a few minutes later with a satisfied smile, with the dean in tow.

'It is too early to say, but there is a feeling going round that we should institute a chair in the management school. We would like you to be the first person to hold that chair—of course, we know you are very busy, so don't say no! A lecture a term is all that is asked for, and a keynote on Convocation Day! Come on, Mr Sharma! Help us out!'

After some persuasion, Sharma*ji* was made to agree.

'This is a landmark day for private sector-civil society partnership!' said the chairman enthusiastically. 'I see only progress and profits for people ahead of us!' They all shook hands on that.

19. Sharma*ji* Meets his Match

Lesley Tuck had reached the end of his undistinguished professional career as the Regional Director of the British Council in the city. A good-natured but ineffective fellow, he had got by in a third world town with his self-deprecating clowning, his attempts to push the envelope on behalf of several local indigent groups, and the low profile he had studiously adopted within his departmental hierarchy. He had been put out to grass at this, his last posting. But hidden within that colourless exterior burned a desire to achieve, to create an event that would be long remembered as the Tuck Initiative.

He got a startlingly imaginative idea during the tea he organized to facilitate the free distribution of old books on British Sport, for which there was no more room on the crowded library shelves. With a flash of brilliance, he thought of a cricket tournament among local NGOs, the winning team being awarded two tickets for a weekend visit to London during Jubilee Year, and tickets at the Lord's to see the final of the ODI series. He was surprised when his superiors took up the idea with alacrity, instead of the usual dismissive wave of a hand. Within weeks he was authorized to organize the local tournament; a small but adequate budget had been allotted, and he even received a short letter of praise for his initiative from the minister for international development. Lesley Tuck positively glowed with importance. His career would end with a bang, a golden hued bang, which would bring back memories of his one brief year as slow left-arm bowler for the Minor Counties.

With unwonted energy he got around to organizing the tournament, which after some consultation he agreed had to be a short knockout series, rather than the more elaborate league idea he had started out with. Most of the NGOs in receipt of donations from Britain signed on, many secretly recruiting fresh staff with some knowledge of cricket. While taking part in the matches might be tiresome, they thought it was worth their while to get the recognition of the British government, which had suddenly loosened its usually tight purse strings and was shaking out guineas in all directions. An ancient jewel had been prised out of its crown by the tragedy that followed its triumph in the Second World War; old colonial connections were allowed to wither away as Her Majesty's Government dithered between Europe and nostalgia, but the ceremonies attendant on the Jubilee Year brought back a rush of enthusiasm to win back the minds and hearts of a people who had once without much complaint built up their lost Empire.

Very quickly, the one-day games that were played on a variety of badly maintained club grounds winkled out most of the competing teams, who were happy to retire from the scene with a handshake from Lesley Tuck and a Certificate of Participation in the Jubilee Year Cricket Tournament of Civil Society Organizations. The winner could possibly be SERVICE, with its long tradition of Saturday afternoon cricket, Sharma*ji* carrying on an earlier belief he had inherited from his physics teacher in school that exhausting cricket was better than allowing his staff to scheme during their idle hours. Or, the winner would be the Foundation for Advanced Urban Geriatric Health [FAUGH], a rich NGO, which had recruited jobless sportsmen as male nurses.

SERVICE and FAUGH faced each other at the finals one afternoon over the Gymkhana pitch, a well-rolled affair, surrounded by a tidy oval-shaped ground. Not only Lesley Tuck but the British Council Directors from Delhi had turned up for the match, and were seated in the pavilion along with the town's sporting elite. Both SERVICE and FAUGH had quickly and in unanimity rejected the idea of permitting 'unknown' neutral umpires to preside over the fate of the day. Lesley Tuck reluctantly agreed that Sharma*ji*, on behalf of his team, and Vemmalapudi Sastri *garu*, the thin, stooped, authoritarian head of FAUGH, should be the two umpires. When Sastri *garu* shook hands with Sharma*ji*, there was already a condescending assumption in his voice when, looking down on his opponent's bald head, he wished the best team all success. Sharma*ji* grimly determined not to let that 'corrupt fellow' have the last laugh, come what may. To his discomfiture, the FAUGH captain won the toss and naturally decided to bat first and fresh in the morning.

The runs rolled out easily for the enemy team, and if the batsmen got out at regular intervals, it was more because the male nurses settled scores by running each other out. An astonishing six wickets were lost with batsmen stranded in the middle of the crease while Sharma*ji*'s gleeful finger remained pointing rigidly towards heaven. The grin on the face of the remaining batsman would soon be wiped out as he was paid in full by the colleague who followed. FAUGH were all out for 127 runs. Sastri *garu* refusing to speak with Sharma*ji* or anyone else at the leisurely lunch that followed, breaking his silence only to Lesley Tuck with a remark about the glorious uncertainties of the game. Tuck nodded dreamily, totally oblivious to the suppressed tensions around the table. Sharma*ji*, on the other hand, was loud and jolly, and related well-known anecdotes about Dr W.G. Grace, winning the condescension of the British Council directors. The head of FAUGH tried to make amends over dessert by stressing that he had tried all his life to inculcate cricketing values among his colleagues, but unfortunately to little avail. His team returned his glowering look with blank smiles.

The male nurses, being good trenchermen, did full justice to the lunch, and hence were sluggish when they took to the field; however, they were confident that their opponents could never make up enough runs to win. Sastri *garu*'s pace attack became understandably breathless in a few overs, and the runs came easily, though to Sharma*ji*'s mounting concern wickets also fell at regular intervals, Abraham at thirty-five closing his eyes to sweep to leg, missing completely, and getting bowled. With his in-form batsman gone, Sharma*ji* called a drinks interval, loudly seconded by the fielders despite Sastri *garu*'s disapproval, and under cover of the happy chatter of the players, Sharma*ji* counseled caution to his batsmen; telling them to focus on the ball right up to the bat, and take their time. He even desperately promised vague rewards to follow victory.

The only one to take his advice seemed to be Dasgupta, who despite his dragging left leg seemed miraculously to be stuck to his crease, snicking boundaries over the outstretched fingertips of the fielders. Gamely, he stood at one end, his nimble runner stealing singles whenever the ball bounced out of reach. Thankfully, Sharma*ji* was at the bowler's end to consider an appeal when a straight ball rapped Dasgupta on the pads. After a very short struggle with his conscience, Sharma*ji* ruled in favour of his batsman. After all, he reasoned, you cannot give a man out for being unable to move his polio-stricken leg well out of the way of a ball intentionally hurled at a physically challenged batsman. But Sastri *garu* fumed at this totally moral decision. He said loudly, to the sniggering of his fielders, that he was sorry that poor sportsmanship was marring the good name of cricket these days. His chance came twelve runs later when from square-leg he loudly called 'run out,' though no appeal was made, and Dasgupta's runner seemed to have dashed well past the stumps.

As his star batsman dragged his way back to the pavilion, Sharma*ji* grimly declared war without considering the niceties of the Geneva Convention. A skied ball to mid-off was declared no ball by him before it landed in the fielder's hands. Fifteen more runs were needed for victory, which he felt honour bound to secure for his team. Were they to be cheated by this paltry quack, who everyone knew terrorized his aged patients? He and his wife would go to London with the winning tickets, and she could shop at Marks and Spencer's to her heart's content, and they would lunch at Wimpy's.

As they crossed over, Sastri *garu* came up to him officiously and sneered: 'Sharma, can I lend you a copy of the Rule Book?'

'Read it yourself, Sastri,' shot back Sharma*ji* hotly. 'I hear many of your patients are launching public interest litigation against FAUGH for cheating and cruelty. Better hurry away and bribe some officials, and leave cricket to players.' Sastri *garu* was beside himself with fury at this disrespectful address to him, who was far senior to this fellow Sharma, but he realized that the English were watching and would not demean himself on the field with further words. He determined to act.

When only nine runs were needed for victory with three wickets still in hand for the SERVICE team, Sastri *garu* coolly held two batsmen leg before wicket off two successive balls. He smiled with avuncular triumph at Sharma*ji* at the end of the over. Grimly defiant, Sharma*ji* decided to do away with all convention. He declared every ball a no ball, even as it left the bowler's hand, and Venkat at the crease picking up the cue smashed two boundaries. But in his eager carelessness to score the winning run, he slipped and fell heavily, straining his bad back. To Sharma*ji*'s chagrin there he lay in the middle, like a beached whale, while Sastri *garu* quite loudly and unnecessarily shouted run out.

The match had ended in a worthless tie. Without a word said between them, Sharma*ji* and Sastri *garu* walked back to the pavilion to gathering applause, while the players helped poor Venkat to his feet and half carried him back.

Lesley Tuck gushed: 'I must say, what a magnificent end to a super tournament! We have two winners! SERVICE and FAUGH! But we have only two tickets,' he continued in less enthusiastic tones, 'so I am afraid, you'll both have to share them. One each I mean.'

Sharma*ji* and Sastri *garu* looked at each other with dawning comprehension. They would not be able to take their wives. They would not have to hang around shops, spending money they did not have. They would not have to have their London holiday spoiled with wifely strictures. They could spend time in a pub. They could go to places they could not visit with their wives.

Sharma*ji* turned and smiled graciously at the happy crowd in the middle of their sumptuous tea in the pavilion. 'We could not have had a better result for the Jubilee Year Tournament,' he said with a broad smile. 'At Lord's, I would have missed the companionship of my good friend, Sastri *garu*. We have always been together, at work and at play, in serving people and in playing cricket. God produced the tie, though, of course without that freak accident, we would have won.' He went up and pumped Sastri *garu*'s hand, who though not fully placated, and not having forgotten or forgiven any remark, was wily enough to express pleasure at the outcome. He peered down at Sharma*ji*'s round smiling countenance. 'Let us plan our London trip together, so that we may bring back new ideas to serve the people,' he said audibly enough for the happily smiling Lesley Tuck.

As he expected, so it happened. Their memorable London visit ended one evening in the warmth of an English pub. London had been home to so many Indian myths and legends over the last hundred-and-fifty years, and they relived several in repeated well-known anecdotes. Then, mellow and happy, they ordered familiar cold Kingfisher beer from India for their last drink. Sastri *garu* looked fondly at Sharma*ji*, who smiled back, already in the haze of nostalgia to be recollected back at home within a few days.

'Well, we laid it on with a trowel, about their sportsmanship,' said Sastri *garu*, 'till they were bursting with self-congratulation, though as you know, Sharma*ji*, the English are the worst cry-babies in sport.'

20. Sharma*ji* Meets the Learned

Sharma*ji* never had any doubts about his own worth to society, so he treated as a matter of course the invitation he received to chair the key session of the annual conference organized by the Nuclear Scientists of India. He was told the focus of the conference would be on 'The Energy Needs of the Poor,' and who better than himself to chair such an important session? As further and unnecessary inducement, he was told the Prime Minister himself would be on the dais. Sharma*ji* made detailed notes of all the issues he would raise during tea-time with the leader of the country.

The local chapter of the Indian Association of IT Industries offered to host the two-day meeting in their own Grand Hall, which was linked by a covered walkway with the banquet hall of the latest seven-star hotel. All the distinguished scientists of the country, most of whom had been retired from directorships according to strict government service rules, would also attend, all hoping like Sharma*ji* to get the undivided attention for a few minutes of the most powerful person in the land. The first inaugural day was when it would all happen, and the second being reserved for 'technical sessions,' only of interest to the younger scientists who would share news of the latest research. A session which everyone knew would be dull, boring, and quite pointless.

The Prime Minister arrived punctiliously on time—well, no more than twenty minutes late, which everyone considered uniquely praiseworthy, since previous incumbents had kept scientists hanging about for hours on end, involved in the more vital tasks of settling power-sharing disputes among local politicians. After all the garlanding, the lighting of inaugural lamps, and the singing out of tune of invocative hymns from the Rig Veda were over, the learned audience settled down for the morning session. Seizing the occasion, Sharma*ji* said he would open the meeting with the 'Chair's Remarks,' since he was in no position to express an opinion on the learned talks that would follow. He would do his duty by pointing out to the august assembly the actual living conditions of the poor, with which, he was confident, only he was familiar. He gave them many anecdotes about the struggles of rural women to fetch water from miles away, the stygian darkness that prevented young girls from reading, how living forests had to be felled for cooking some thin gruel over charcoal fires, and the lack of connectivity that left innumerable unwarned villages at the mercy of tsunamis. His remarks met with thunderous applause, and Dr Bhattacharjee, President of the Association of Nuclear Scientists, seized the moment to say he could not listen to Mr Sharma dry-eyed, and hoped that they, the gathered scientific elite of the country, would rise to the call of the hour, to lay the ghost of poverty, and put their combined shoulders to the scientific wheel, and move the bullock cart of the state into the jet age of the future!

They then settled down to hear the keynote address on 'The Energy Needs of the Poor,' given by Dr Srinagesh, the former Director-General of Nuclear Fuels. He was a distinguished scientist with thirty-five years spent vehemently arguing the case for a total energy focus on the nuclear option, since there was no other imaginable source of power that could supply all of the country's immediate and growing developmental needs.

Once, he had painted an alarming picture of a pandemic of cancer if one more coal-fired thermal station were added to the grid. Pleas for examining renewable energy sources he had laughed away to scorn, becoming quite witty in the process. The great man had reluctantly given up the chair of office, informing the government dispassionately 'as a scientist, that the country would face a grave crisis were he to step down at this critical political-energy juncture.' With its usual somnolent conduct of the affairs of state, the government had not heeded his dire warnings and after retiring him, had appointed a younger man in his place. But in his 'devoted commitment to the people—not to any transient government,' Dr Srinagesh had said on having to quit his post, he would 'happily get back to solving some of the key problems scientists faced in basic research,' which he had had to discontinue, though on the threshold of epoch-making discoveries, to shoulder over the last thirty years the weighty administrative duties thrust upon him by a thankless state.

Most of the audience who had previously heard his impassioned presentations on behalf of nuclear energy thought they would see some of his familiar PowerPoint presentations, but they were in for a surprise.

'Mr Prime Minister, Dr Sharma, Distinguished Colleagues!' boomed Dr Srinagesh, 'I should first of all like to thank my colleagues and friends, who, without informing me, got together with Jeannie Larmont to set up the Srinagesh Foundation on the eve of my joyous return to science from the ranks of the bureaucracy,' he paused to beam at his successor, 'my return to the work-bench of science, if you will, to devote myself to the Goddess of Knowledge. Something I was not able to do while Director-General, though, of course, I represented our country at all of the crucial scientific gatherings in the world and established the scientific reputation of our country. Jeannie, please stand up so that we can all give you a big hand!'

A thin, faded American millionairess stood up shyly to applause, many of the assembled scientists openly envious of Dr Srinagesh for landing such a rich girlfriend.

'Jeannie has been able to persuade me to take a re-look at the scientific facts that stare us in the face. There can be no doubt at all, Mr Prime Minister, that with over thirteen hundred joules of sunlight streaming down on every square metre of our great country over three hundred and thirty days of the year on an average, we have no option available but the solar energy option! We must exploit this God-given perennial source to provide energy for our billion people. My Foundation is ready to do its part. I have already calculated that for a small initial investment by government of no more than a hundred *crores*—which is around twenty million dollars—I would be able to energize a hundred villages with eternal light! I shall now proceed to give a brief oversight of the potentialities, and the installation processes I shall adopt.'

The enthusiastic discussion that followed his presentation highlighted other renewable energy options. Retired nuclear scientists seemed to have experienced a spectacular change of heart, and spoke of the exciting path-breaking work they were doing with their own foundations with wind energy, biogas, energy woodlots, and many hybrid systems that could solve the country's energy problem, provided a few *crores* of public investment could be made right away into foundations under informed scientific leadership. Dr Ghotge, a well-known elder figure of the nuclear establishment, then rose, dressed in *khadi kurta* and *dhoti*, and sporting a flowing, saintly white beard. After several lengthy mumbled quotations in the original Sanskrit, he said it was vain to think of harnessing

Nature while Man himself chose not to toil. He had developed several simple mechanical devices which would enormously—that was the only word—increase the effect of human muscle energy. When you think of a billion people working together as a community—as Gandhiji had wished—one could readily imagine the energy transformation of society. His society, aptly named Man for Energy or ME—to emphasize personal commitment— would show the way. He asked for no government support, but as a Gandhian he would not prevent them from partnering with him.

Dr Subbaraman, former director of the Cement Institute of India, agreed with all the views expressed, but said everyone was missing the point by 'externalizing the poor people's need and use of energy.' It had to be integrated in their housing. He would say without fear of opposition that the indiscriminate use of cement was the bane of the countryside—a view which he would have shouted down two years earlier when in power. What the poor wanted was the use of mud for buildings, friendly mud, with which they grew up, and in which their last remains were interred. He showed slides of different styles of traditional mud housing still in practice around the country, and said simply that he was even now willing to serve the country at half the compensation he would receive as a United Nations consultant.

The question of 'food energy for the people' was also brought up by a group of life scientists who as a cooperative group had bought out five hundred acres from poor farmers in the Nagarjunasagar left-bank *ayacut* region. Despite better profits that would accrue from the market, they were willing that the government should procure all their produce at a price to be mutually determined to ensure food security among the poor.

In consequence of so many excellent presentations, lunch had to be put off by half an hour. The Prime Minister and

Sharma*ji*, along with a few top-flight in-service scientists, were taken to a small special room by Dr Bhattacharjee, the President of the Association of Nuclear Scientists, for a cosy chat over lunch. When they were all seated in deep sofas, with plates piled high with food balanced on their knees, Dr Bhattacharjee turned to the PM with a smile. 'Sir, my retired colleagues, despite their advancing age and other infirmities, have shown you, shown us all, the vigour in science exploration. I am sure they will produce some good results, even if it is only to educate our school children to look at all sides of a question. But as you rightly said in parliament, Sir, we are staring down the barrel of an energy meltdown. Our hydro dams are silting up fast, and do not produce power as expected. And this despite causing immense suffering to displaced farmers—electoral losses in three state assemblies I put down to this single fact! Our cities—I don't need to tell you, Sir, living as you do in the capital— are made unlivable by thermal power stations. There is no option but to go in massively for fast-breeder reactors! I am as peaceful a man as Dr Ghogte, but I am also a patriot.' He dropped his voice to a chummy conspiratorial whisper. 'Let's face it, we are surrounded by neighbours who do not necessarily wish us well. We must be prepared. We all know the dual uses fast-breeders can be put to, and it gives us a necessary margin of nuclear weapons safety.'

The Prime Minister, perhaps unwilling to discuss security concerns among relative strangers, then rose and said he had to go. The scientists jostled each other at the door in their eagerness to press their separate cases while seeing him to his car. Sharma*ji* was alone in the small dining room. He went up to the side table and helped himself to a few desserts. After he had eaten all he could, he wandered back to the conference hall to find that most people had disappeared somewhere. Those who were there were riffling through their papers and gave him a blank look. He looked around to say thank you and goodbye to any functionary, but he could find none. So, he made his own way out, and went home for his habitual siesta.

21. The Great Canadian Curd Churn

Barney Hall, the youngest untenured professor in the department of veterinary sciences at the University in Calgary, had been told off, in no uncertain terms. He had either to produce papers in refereed publications or get research grants if he wished to extend his stay at that establishment. His previous attempts at reading papers at conferences had been uniformly unsatisfactory, and even dangerous. A small review paper of his on the usefulness of growth hormones at a one-day workshop organized by the cattle industry had roused loud protests from green fiends and health freaks; another oral presentation in his own university on improving the quality of veal by close-penning calves led to an animal rights activist rushing to the dais to stab him with her ball-point pen. He was now genuinely scared that if he attempted to publish a paper he might get a letter-bomb by return post. The only option was to go for a government grant, but the bureaucrats in Ottawa were now cagey after public outcries against them for spreading mad cow disease.

During this unhappy period, he was invited to dinner by an Indian colleague from the department of electrical engineering who had gained fame by inventing a rugged non-breakable light-emitting diode, which was encased in a patented Canadian plastic holder, could be stuck onto the seat of one's pants at night as a safety measure, to warn motorists that there was a pedestrian ahead.

Though his sensibilities revolted against the smell of curries, he went along, hoping to pick up a tip or two on how to swing grants his way. His Indian friend was too full of himself to listen to his veiled requests, but enlightenment came when he was served curds and rice. They helped to mitigate the sharpness of the curries, and if he remembered right his undergraduate course on nutrition, live curds also contained useful microbes that helped break down food faster, and promoted the absorption of the 'B' family of vitamins. Curds were produced from milk, and milk came from cows, which were part of his turf!

With great excitement he focused his research on curds, how they could be made to the highest Canadian health standards, and how their quality could be improved in terms of quantity and nutritive value. By the time the first few shoots of green grass broke out of the eternal snows blanketing the campus, he had completed an exciting proposal about how Canada could teach the poor of the third world to benefit by eating curds. The head of his department was equally thrilled, to whom all this was very new stuff, never having ventured even to try a fruit yogurt, since the very name had a threatening French sound to it. In any case, the university was hungry for money, and it would do him no harm if a junior of his caught the fancy of the bigwigs in Ottawa.

The two professors need not have worried so much about what reception they would get in the capital; the vice-president of the Canadian International Development Agency [CIDA] immediately saw the advantage to himself, his department, and his country, if this project were to be supported, and throwing his arms round Al and Barney he led them to the cafeteria for a cheap lunch. At the upcoming review meeting for reallocating budgets, he sponsored the project, added more expenses, and asked for ten million Canadian dollars to be given to the university to set up a separate foundation to further the ongoing research, and extend its benefits to all non-terrorist countries. He was able to convince the Canadian government that the grant spent on this project would bring back home five times as much money in earnings through exported curd churns of the latest Canadian design, and by consultancies of Canadian curd experts—to be insisted upon by Canadian donor agencies—and sale of curd technology and curd starters to third world non-terrorist countries.

Since India was a major player in the Aid Recipients Market, it was decided by CIDA that the Canadian Curd Mission would see its birth in that country. Barney's success at garnering a large and stable grant had suddenly made him very popular with the higher echelons of academia; he was even invited for a barbecue fest in the vice-chancellor's back garden during a quickly warming June Sunday. Grant money gave Barney new poise, and girls, instead of trying to stab him with ball-point pens, were willing to be asked out to dinner. During a brainstorming session in the basement of his department, several of his new girl admirers spontaneously came up with the name for his foundation: It was to be The Great Canadian Curd Churn! Over a million dollars Canadian were spent on designing the foundation's chic booklets and leaflets, with inevitable pictures of starving African children on the cover and a smiling Indian girl at the back, skipping along eating curds out of a plastic cup with a visible logo of The Great Canadian Curd Churn. The National Film Board of Canada sent teams to thirty-odd countries to film trees, colours, lakes, and silent sands, with quick glimpses of local people making, eating, relishing curds. The film won several awards round the world and continued to be considered a high point in Canadian filmmaking history. A lot more money was spent on organizing talk shows and other media events, and Barney had the time of his life flying to Sofia, Nairobi, Stockholm, and Madras, to introduce his life's work.

Sharma*ji* was well aware of all these developments, since he always kept his nose close to the well-known points of grant generation. He was one of the first to congratulate Barney on his fundamental scientific discovery, and suggest that a partnership between the foundation and his own society would help immediately in saving lives.

Barney listened wide-eyed to the tone of feverish urgency in Sharma*ji*'s voice, and held himself in readiness to save the lives of the poor children he had seen so often on the cover of his brochure. The CIDA official in New Delhi invited the Press Corps to witness the gift of one hundred curd churns of the latest Canadian design to Sharma*ji*. The broadly smiling Canadian High Commissioner was flanked by a team of Canadian Curd Technologists, who had been taking anti-malarial pills for a month, and had brought their own portable Canadian water-purifying kit for use during the arduous training programme in Sharam*ji*'s villages. In New Delhi itself, Sharma*ji* held an orientation meeting for his guests, showing blown-up pictures of cobras, kraits, and Russell's Vipers for easy recognition in case they found them in their bathrooms or in their shoes. The non-poisonous varieties were to be gently shooed away, while the poisonous ones could only be gently removed by his own trained staff. A young Canadian curd technologist wondered if Sharma*ji* could teach her how to gently remove poisonous snakes herself, since she couldn't bear to kill any living thing other than spiders, which she dreaded.

A small tent township was erected by Sharma*ji* near his rural centre for the international electronic media teams of CNN, BBC, German radio, France One, and of course CBC, who camped there for a fortnight to create live programmes on how Canadians were saving the lives of poor women and children by teaching them how to make and eat curds.

However, Canadian nutritionists warned on several talk shows that Indians being 'non-Caucasians' would be lactose-intolerant and hence unable to immediately assimilate milk or a milk product, such as curds, and great care must be taken in introducing curds into India. Emeritus Professor Mike 'Hogwash' Adamson, who had justified the sobriquet he received in his youth by winning the Canadian Jakob Creuzfeld Award for high-protein engineering of cattle feed, declared himself cautiously hopeful. Filmed on his cattle ranch in Alberta, he took the viewer carefully over the intricate science involved in making a 'Non-Caucasian' drink milk, and came up with a 'unique all-Canadian theory,' in Rosaline Blabberwell's words! The TV crews, intent on fair reporting, also showed a five-second clip of Indian malcontents holding up placards in Indian dialects with slogans about Indians having eaten curds everyday over the last five thousand years.

'I have watched Masai tribesmen drink milk,' said Professor Adamson, shaking his head in wonder and pursing his lips. 'Now the Masai are also non-Caucasian, and yet they can drink milk. Scientifically, this has never been explained! I kind of guess it could come from drinking raw blood from an opened vein in the neck of a cow, calf, or bull, you take your pick. Look, I will show you.' As the camera followed him, he trotted into his barn, slit open the neck vein of a small calf and bent down to drink the blood.

'How does it taste, Hogwash?' asked Rosaline excitedly.

'Oh, I dunno, it kinda tastes like, I guess, raw blood,' said the professor, straightening up and wiping his mouth with his handkerchief. 'There, I ruined that handkerchief, dunno what Elsie is going to say when I get back in. But science is demanding.'

'Canadian science is making small but important breakthroughs like this every day to help people living under difficult conditions all over the world. One day soon, Mike 'Hogwash' Adamson's novel idea may help save an Indian child's life, but unfortunately the Hindoo religion might prevent millions upon millions from making use of this simple measure. This is Rosaline Blabbermouth taking you back to the CBC studio in Calgary, where a group of young Baptists are even now with Swami Biryaninanda, who runs the Yoga clinic downtown. Let us see if religious taboos can be lifted to permit millions of starving children to drink raw cow's blood!' When Sharma*ji* was interviewed by the CBC in his rural 'unit,' he said that with the help of the Canadian Curd Training Programme he had been able to induce the first learners to eat a little bit of curds. When the camera went into the canteen, it showed rows of frightened women refusing to eat curds, 'till Sharma went over and spoke to them in their own, I guess, Hindoo dialect, and then after a few hesitant mouthfuls, the enthusiastic response of the poor women to this Canadian food was really, really overwhelming!'

When the Canadian High Commissioner was interviewed in New Delhi, he said proudly that his own kitchen staff had been asked to include curds in every menu, and he and his diplomatic guests from now on would eat at least a symbolic spoonful of curds to show that Canadians empathized with the people of India.

22. The NGO Living Book

The Norwegian was a young, slim, pleasant-faced diplomat in a simple white shirt and khaki trousers. He could easily have been mistaken for a student. He smiled apologetically at Sharma*ji*, looked out of the large French windows onto the trim embassy lawns, and then pushed the excellent cup of coffee closer to his guest.

'I suppose I should have come down to Hyderabad to make my request,' said Ashbjorn Trigvisson gently, 'instead of sending you the air ticket, but I have to be on call all the time here now that the ambassador is on leave, and I hope you forgive me. We want your advice, and to enlist your help.'

Sharma*ji* nodded his agreement.

'You know how people learn, grown-up people, I mean,' continued Trigvisson. 'They don't know something, they go to a library, take out books, and find there isn't enough information in them, and take out more books. Finally, they take a course, because a person can teach better than a whole lot of books. This is where we want to help in a unique way, using our small aid funds to best advantage. We want to fund the setting up of a Living Library, really a team of experts, who will advice NGOs or local governments, or any development agency, on request, who can be taken out like a book to help people who want advice. And we want to start with a really Big Book, like the Bible of Development. We want you to be that Bible!'

Sharma*ji* was dazed, to say the least, at the intended honour, and at the same time scared of how he would be used by several NGO leaders he knew. An image of torn pages and scribbled margins came vividly to mind. He recoiled in horror, and said quickly that cognizant though he was of the honour done, the pressure of work at home, etcetera, etcetera. Trigvisson looked quite crestfallen.

'I know it's too much to ask,' he said. 'But you are such a fund of vital knowledge, like a Bible, as I said, and India needs you to share it. I cannot think of two other persons to replace you, but I respect, and regretfully accept your declining the offer. In fact, there is no money in it, and it is such a bother, I know.'

Sharma*ji* congratulated himself on not falling into a trap. Somehow he had sensed there was no money in the offer, just a painful social obligation. Every scoundrel who wanted to make a fast buck by starting an NGO would have been after him to share not knowledge, but leads to his best donors. No way, old boy, thought Sharma*ji*. Trigvisson continued anxiously to ask his advice about who else he could call. There was no money, which was a big handicap in getting the right person. The fund could afford no more than a thousand dollars per day of advice offered, and of course all expenses paid, business air travel, three-star hotel accommodation, that sort of thing.

This news completely changed the picture for Sharma*ji*. There were several of his friends out there who could keep him busy for at least a hundred days a year, and that would mean a hundred thousand dollars a year, plus all expenses for star hotels.

'Ashbjorn, I am willing to help, only temporarily, mind, till you have the whole thing properly set up. By then, I would have helped you select the next 'Bible' as you say, and I will be back in my villages. No more after that, okay?' Ashbjorn accepted gratefully.

The next day, his new-found friend, Ashbjorn, took him round to Sastri Bhavan, the government's control centre for all educational institutions, to meet the Secretary for Human Resources Development, who did the controlling. After the statutory half-hour wait in the crowded waiting room, with walls reddened with eons of betel nut spit, they were ushered into the presence. The Secretary, a squat balding man, listened to the idea, enthusiastically welcomed Sharma*ji*'s induction as the first Living Bible, and said that he would personally watch over the progress the proposal made through the various departments and ministries of government before the funds could be accepted and the Living Library set up.

Sharma*ji* flew home on the wings of his jet and his soaring hopes. He was sure his calculation, give or take ten thousand, was accurate, he would get all the money he wanted in one swift package. Ashbjorn was a good trustworthy guy since Scandinavians were all trustworthy, especially the Norwegians. Apart from the money he would make, he was happy to be helpful to the nation. It was an honour and a duty, which only he could perform. As soon as he got home, he would celebrate by buying a new red Maruti. He had always wanted a fast red car, and he, at last, felt justified in spending lavishly on himself.

Sharma*ji* enjoyed his new car; he loved to drive it and to be seen driving it. He called on friends and offered lifts. He started going out to expensive restaurants in five-star hotels; after all, he should get accustomed to entertaining his clients in such places. His monthly expenditures went into the red, but his conscience was untroubled. Ashbjorn continued to be enthusiastic and supportive. Everything was going well, Sharma*ji* knew better than most how slow the government machinery worked, and his case was safe in the Norwegian's hands. Of course, section officers asked too many questions and fresh notes had to be prepared. Of course, the department of economic affairs raised some queries, and the file had to be re-written all over again. Of course, for the umpteenth time, Sharma*ji* had to send a fresh version of his curriculum vitae. But the patience and youthful exuberance exhibited by Ashbjorn was exemplary.

Joji George walked in one day into Sharma*ji*'s office. He was a tall, powerfully built man with a black square-cut beard that framed one of the widest, friendliest smiles on the face of a NGO leader. The Kozikode Women's Crafts Foundation had received a very large order for coir mattresses and coir doormats from New Zealand buyers, and Joji had come in search of extra coir raw material supplies, though the Andhra variety of coir was decidedly inferior, but then it had to be cheaper also, right? Sharma*ji* placed a car at Joji's disposal, and all the attention of his staff for the next two weeks was diverted to helping Joji in securing his supply chain.

'Thank you, brother, you have been the Nizam of Hyderabad to me,' said Joji, laughing deeply and embracing Sharma*ji* before leaving. 'You are a great guy. Why don't you come to Kerala, God's Own Country, sometime?'

'I might, Joji, I might, but good friends like you must invite me,' said Sharma*ji*, placing his hands on the tall man's shoulders. 'You should ask me to come and advise, or something. I have the funds for it you know, and now I can spend a week or so with you.' Joji George laughed happily again. 'If you have the funds, brother, come for a month at Onam time. Or come and see the snake boat races, or visit the Periyar national park. I will fit you out with a boatman I know, he will take you out through all the backwaters, show you the Kerala few visitors see—special only for special guests,' he added with an elaborate wink. After he had left, Sharma*ji* searched for the address of another old friend who worked on organic tea in Kurseong. A fortnight spent in the high

Himalayan hill stations, while he earned a thousand dollars a day, would be very bracing.

When six months had passed and no word had come down to him, he made another long-distance call to the Norwegian and learnt that the Indian government wanted to consider the proposal in the coming financial year. During the next summer, Ashbjorn came down unexpectedly to Hyderabad to give the good news in person to Sharma*ji* that the project had finally been approved by the Indian government, and not only that but the Indian government itself was enthusiastic to contribute funds, real *funds*, to establish the Living Library! They both had dinner at an expensive continental place, and Ashbjorn and he polished off several bottles of the best wine available. Peeking over the Norwegian's shoulder, Sharma*ji* was stunned at the bill, but steeled himself with the thought that he had now moved into a higher bracket in life.

A few more months passed, and over the phone Ashbjorn sounded hassled, but still positive. Then he was away on long home leave, and no one else in the embassy seemed to know about the fate of the project. After several inconclusive telephone conversations and irritated answers from haughty Indian women receptionists at the embassy, Sharma*ji* desisted from making further calls and decided to wait it out till Ashbjorn returned to Delhi. After the rains had ceased, he was surprised to get a letter from one Mr Janhunen, who said he had taken over from Trigvisson, and was renewing acquaintance with all his predecessor's contacts. Mr Sharma would be hearing shortly about the progress of his project. Three months later, Sharma*ji* got a short note from Mr Janhunen that he was glad the project of the Living Library was at last in operation, and that Mr. Sharma had been empanelled as one of the Living Books. He would soon be hearing in detail from the Indian Human Resources Development Ministry, under which the Living Library had been established.

Three weeks later, Sharma*ji* received a long coarse envelope, with his name and address printed in cheap smudged ink. The several cyclostyled sheets listed the rules and regulations governing the establishment of the Living Library and the required duties of all the 'Living Books.' A key section detailed how the Living Books would be selected from the empanelled group by the chairperson of the empowered committee, who incidentally happened to be the Secretary he had met two years ago. All the other Living Books were retired Secretaries to Government. Sharma*ji*'s name was appended at the end as 'conjoint category' to be used in conjunction with the above named. Unemotionally, Sharma*ji* looked out of the window down at his red car. Even if he sold it now, he would lose at least two lakhs rupees. He looked at the sheaf of papers he held in his hand and knew he would never be called, even as a 'conjoint,' and tossed it into the wastepaper basket. The point was to survive, and he was a survivor.

23. Sharma*ji* of the SAS

The Secular Association of Socialists [SAS], had first been formed during the dark days of Indira Gandhi's Emergency by a group of brave academics as a way of showing up the falsehood in Mrs. Gandhi's political protestations. And for establishing the true meaning of both secularism and socialism in the public interest. Feverish closed-door midnight meetings had been held in several campuses during that dark period, and notes passed from hand to hand in complete secrecy. Even a code had been elaborately constructed, which turned out to be too complex for any intellectual, and which led to too much drinking of coffee and whisky in several cafes and bars. And though many professors had willingly agreed to join the SAS and sacrifice careers, and even their own lives, for the sake of Truth, somehow none of them could find the time to address public meetings. Sharma*ji* had been a student in those heady days, showing off noisy commitment and rash courage—accounts of which he embroidered and exaggerated to his own advantage in later years. It was almost inevitable that he would be conned into becoming the founding president of the SAS. He eloquently addressed several open meetings, though only on campus, and mostly in the student hostels, and consequently he was picked up for questioning by the police.

The next ten days had been the worst he ever had to experience. He remembered for the rest of his life that while upholding democratic principles was the duty of every citizen, such an act or for that matter any act that might draw the attention of the police, was best carried out symbolically, like a religious ritual, for instance. He then understood the practical wisdom displayed by his elders in the movement. In fact, though, the police had merely amused themselves by making him go through all the early phases of interrogation, while demonstrating to their raw recruits how a prisoner can be made to change from defiance to sullenness, and then to pleading, and finally to abject surrender. None would ever know, except for a few senior officers, what effect a mere visit to the electrical room had had on him, and after they perfunctorily took down what information he had, all of which and more was already known to them. He left their premises, the college, and the city, thoroughly shaken, and retired to his uncle's house in his ancestral village.

A few months later Mrs. Gandhi lost the elections, and overnight he became a national hero as the martyred founder-president of the SAS, and began his rapid advancement as a spokesperson and budding leader of civil society. The SAS was de facto discontinued, since there seemed, at that time, no further need for such an organisation.

One can imagine Sharma*ji*'s surprise then, when several decades later, a delegation of lawyers, retired judges, and active academics came to his flat one morning to suggest a revival of the SAS, now that globalisation threatened the very values for which he had sacrificed his liberty long ago. In the past he had spoken with his usual eloquence about that earlier threat to Indian democracy, and how he had with Gandhian courage taken on all that a neo-colonial system could fling at an Indian, and he spoke of it again. He assured the delegation that despite his failing health, and the pressure of enormous duties on his time, he would undertake the re-formation of the SAS.

A few phone calls assured him that Christians Everywhere would be proud to fund such an organisation, and that he should not be his usual parsimonious self when working out the budget for the first conference. With Dasgupta's help, a generous proposal was dispatched, and he was able to acquire in short order a couple of air-conditioners, a washing machine, a microwave, and a large flat TV, which made his wife very happy, as well as some communication equipment for the office. He was also able to take on a long lease, and on very favourable terms, the Conference Centre of the Federation of Textile Industries, which could no longer afford such excellent facilities.

Global Event Managers, run by his cousin, were hired to promote the International Conference of the SAS. The BBC, Associated Press, CNN, German radio, France One, all the local and national TV stations and the Press were to cover the event. Lady Scilly decided to come with a small staff, but only as an observer, since she said she came only to learn and hear. Every evening would be graced with an ethnic cultural performance and dinner hosted by a leading business house of the city. The municipality arranged for fireworks on the opening night.

Sharma*ji* beamed at the great circle of distinguished academics, jurists, doctors and activists around the conference table, with supporting students and staff seated behind their leaders. After media had taken all the pictures they wanted, they retired behind the glassed-off cubicles arranged for them, and the conference got under way with a stirring inaugural speech by Sharma*ji*. As they broke for coffee, he was able to see in the TV sets placed in the corridor grabs of his speech being relayed by several networks.

'You have arrived,' said Pauline Lefevre, smiling down at him, and he smiled back and moved away uncomfortably, for memories of that unsuccessful evening he had spent in her flat in Paris still haunted him. Robert's praise was unequivocal, without any tinge of sarcasm. 'You laid into them, old man, great show!' said the lanky Brit, dipping his biscuit into his tea, village fashion. 'They will have to take notice of SERVICE and Christians Everywhere now. Grand job. I wish I was an orator like you!' and he moved off, thumping Sharma*ji* on the back. All his other guests wanted to meet him then, and a few anxious students asked complicated questions, which he could neither hear nor understand.

The main plenary discussion turned on what was meant by secularism, particularly in the post 9/11 age. Anti-spiritualism was rejected out of hand by all, but none could agree on what 'spiritualism' signified. Even accepting that the term meant something, which they all understood, or better still felt, in a non-intersubjectival way, they asked what signification should be given within the political context of secularism. Swami Vithalananda referred to several texts that a saffron-clad acolyte sitting behind kept handing to him. After fifteen minutes, the gist emerged that nothing existed but the Spirit, and that 'spiritualism' was the recognition by the Mind—which itself was an ephemeral creation of the Spirit—of this sole Truth, and secularism could be an approach by which all could share this Truth. The academics respectfully would have none of this simplification. The discussion returned to the Problematic.

After tea-break, David Kriegmann of the New York Dialogue Committee showed a ten-minute clip of the fall of the World Trade Center. He said that this film should be shown in all *madrasas* along with another, which he had with him, showing Moslems, Jewish people and Christians all praying near each other in Jerusalem, but his ramble was cut short agitatedly by Angela Hanley of the New Age for Peace, who broke into tears, and stammered: 'It is not so much the death of three thousand people that shatters me, horrifying—horrifying—though the very thought is, I mean I could mourn, mourn, for a friend, but my God, three thousand?

But then Death is the billowing debris in David's film, don't you see? Darling, this is not a criticism of your film, but the thought that humanity is billowing towards destruction, global warming melting huge glaciers, tigers gone within the decade, all those magnificent creatures—has anybody seen house sparrows lately?—and every morning I get up with a single image etched in my mind, the face of that lovely African child, with his large eyes, dying, dying in his mother's arms...' and then she ran out of the room, followed by Kriegmann and a dozen girl students.

Retired Professor Godbole, his shiny bald head sticking out over wispy white hair, tried to bring the group round to what worried him. 'I have a great difficulty in accepting, without challenge, the Nehruvian concept of Secularism,' he said in a whisper. 'All societies are basically religious—I will qualify my statement—they follow certain cultural practices, which have grown organically out of their own religious beliefs. To negate this is to negate a vital element of their cherished identities. If we are to bring peace between communities—and that is the purpose of the secularism project—we must remember what Gandhiji said: "There is no path to peace. Peace is the path," and so...'

Vyjayanti Iyengar, Professor of English, broke in sharply, as she always did when Gandhi was mentioned: 'I thought Dr B.R. Ambedkar said that?' she challenged.

Dr Susie George, Director of the Institute of Immunology, lifted her patrician head with its beautifully coiffured halo of white hair and said softly but decisively: 'Sir Syed Ahmed first mentioned it at the inaugural of the Anglo-Mohammedan Oriental College at Aligarh—in 1886, was it...?' and she looked round for corroboration.

At this point, Sharma*ji* decided to up the ante, and take charge: 'That quotation has been used by several great people, but you first find it in Kabir's fourteenth-century poems,' and since there was no one in the group of intellectuals who had read Kabir, he launched into an oration about the need of the hour for everyone to come together under one banner, irrespective of caste, creed, or colour. Out of the corner of one eye, he saw Lady Scilly silently applauding. 'I work with the simple people in the villages,' he continued. 'In our villages they are all one, Hindu, Muslim, Christian, or Gond. We should not confuse the religion—the religiosity of the urban middle classes'—he gave a short laugh—'with the true religion of the simple people. For them it is a way of life, it is not an opium of the masses.'

A delicate cough reminded everyone that Dr Feroz had sat silently throughout, incessantly smoking one cigarette after another, each lit from the stub of the preceding one. A deep frown between his hooded eyes with their faraway look. Everyone knew he had staunchly maintained his communist principles, despite a trying twenty-five years with the Ford Motor Company in Detroit. The delicate cough also brought to mind the whispered rumour that Dr Feroz had not long to live, though he had always stoically refused to speak about his health, much to the admiration of his friends.

'Marx said religion was an opiate,' he said with aristocratic precision, and continued in the same nuanced style. 'Religious suffering is, at one and the same time, the expression of real suffering and a protest against real suffering. Religion is the sigh of the oppressed creature, the heart of a heartless world, and the soul of soulless conditions.'

Pin-drop silence followed, as everyone took in not only the words but also the manner of their delivery.

The delicate cough was repeated. 'This is, perhaps, the one unsolved—the one unsolvable—question that has revolved in my mind,' said Dr Feroz, fixing his eyes steadily on the flowerpot in front of him. 'How do we ease that sigh? How can we bring the soul back? Back to soulless conditions?' And then he looked at them all as if waking from a dream, and laughed softly till a cough blew out a cloud of smoke. 'It is a torment of mine,' and then, as if no one else existed, he got up and went out into the veranda to smoke a fresh cigarette. A large girl with a large bosom rushed out to be of assistance.

The discussion was picked up again. A thin-faced, spectacled activist with a thin, straggly beard asked Sharma*ji* loudly: 'Are you saying then that you, you, support all kinds of religious ideas, actions? Do you support fundamentalism?'

'Certainly not!' said Sharma*ji* stoutly. 'The very meaning of my remarks makes it clear that I oppose fundamentalism of all kinds, religious, economic—the Americans are economic fundamentalists, cultural…'

Farook Ali Khan Sahib, the curator of the Hyderabad Medieval Records Library, could not let this pass: 'Sharma Sahib, there is a distinction we must make here between correct religious belief and erroneous religious belief. A person with correct religious belief could also be termed a fundamentalist scholar, and he could lead a completely peaceful life.'

Sharma*ji* squirmed a little. 'Well, words have different meanings in different contexts,' he said. 'I am referring to fanatical behaviour, which I condemn.'

'What do you call fanatical behaviour?' challenged the activist with the thin, straggly beard. Loud voices cut in from all directions at this stage, with a consensus being reached after ten minutes that they would accept violent behaviour as fanatical behaviour.

A girl in some kind of religious robe, who had been looking fixedly at a long-stemmed rose she held in her hand, now got up, allowing her unbound hair to fan around her down to her knees, and asked Sharma*ji*: 'Do you now regret that you ever were a revolutionary, and do you reject and condemn all revolutionary acts?' Many young men glared at her and him in turns.

Sharma*ji* tried to use all his skill and tact in trying to work around the question, when Dr Shankar Rao, the chair of The Voice of the Dalit Nation and head of the Department of Political Science, jumped up and shouted: 'God damn it! I am sick of this *Brahmin-Bania* farce. I came here only because I thought some few of you may have the guts to demand social change. I will have nothing further to do with such trickery!' He kicked back his chair and made for the door, but Professor Godbole held him back by main force. A number of young men shouted: 'Inquilab Zindabad! Long Live Marxist-Leninist Mao Ze Dong Thought!' The girl with the rose shrilled: 'China Out of Tibet!'

Sharma*ji* looked round helplessly for Dr Feroz, but he along with the large-bosomed girl had disappeared.

Lakshmi Srivatsav, the doyeness of the feminist movement, was standing and tinkling her pen against her glass. Silence fell over the room. She was a large woman, 'nobly planned,' as Wordsworth would have said, and she commanded the attention of the gathering with little effort.

'Whenever we discuss political matters, or matters of faith, as we do today,' she said with impeccably regurgitated received pronunciation, as if she was chewing on something tasty, 'we tend to forget that there are others in the world apart from the men'— she paused to let that sink in—'apart from the men who take all the decisions. I have been sitting here all day listening to you debate this point and that, and not one of you have voiced, or realized, what hardships women have to bear because of your decisions. You talk of peace as if it concerns only you—almost as if everything is a game—I am sorry, but it is not! It is women who are killed and tortured, and not you comfortable gentlemen.'

Lady Scilly went up spontaneously and kissed Lakshmi Srivatsav, and their eyes were glistening when they unclinched.

It was time for SAS to come out with a concrete action plan, suggested Professor Godbole. Mr Krishna Prasad, Head of United Publishing, adjusted his elegant tie and said that they should bring out a book, or even a series, well researched, and using modern terminology, which would highlight the similarities of thought in all religions. He could help with publication, if some financial help were guaranteed, he said. All the students seemed to think it was a great idea, while the religious leaders sank glumly into silence. Sharma*ji* quickly saw the dangerous shoals to which such an enterprise could lead, and cut short the debate by saying roundly that they did not have the expertise to make summaries of religious books without giving offence, or even the skill to modernize the texts, which itself would require years of work by qualified religious leaders. Farook Sahib nodded assent, and the matter was dropped.

It was close to dinner time, so they adjourned and asked Sharma*ji* to draft out a release for the Press. After a sumptuous dinner, he drafted out a carefully worded innocuous statement out of the mishmash of notes presented to him by the rapporteurs.

He got up late the next morning and sat in his favourite chair, overlooking the busy street, waiting for coffee to be served to him by his wife. He picked up the first newspaper out of the neatly laid out pile on the side table. There was a flattering colour picture of him speaking. '*Sharma of SERVICE condemns fundamentalism,*' read the caption. The short account of the conference, written hastily by the reporter, focused largely on him, he noticed smugly—no doubt as a return favour for the lavish bar he had kept open all day—but as he read on he was appalled to find himself made out into some sort of heroic crusader against fundamentalist religious fanatics of all religions. The reporter made him out to be a fearless opponent of all bigots, one who wanted to cleanse society of all religious superstitions. Not a word of his press release had been used. With a nerveless hand he picked up other papers, but all the rags carried a similar theme, written by worthless, drunken idiots. They put in words he had never used, or remembered using. It was all taken out of context.

The telephone jangled his thoughts. 'Sir, there is some crowd gathering here outside the office,' said Dasgupta's voice. 'I don't know what the problem is, but I am closing the office and I have called the police.'

He was deep in thought as his wife brought him his coffee. He took her hand. 'I am very tired. I need a holiday, and I want to give you a holiday. Let's both go to Darjeeling for two weeks—no, three weeks. Let's leave today—this morning!'

She looked at him in amazement. What had come over him? They didn't have the money, and in any case they would need time to make all the arrangements but he brushed aside all her objections like an eager young lover. They would go to Darjeeling that very day, that very morning. He would ring up Indian Airlines and they would collect the tickets at the airport.

'But it is November!' she said, half in doubt, half happily. 'The best month to go to Darjeeling,' said Sharma*ji*. 'All the tourists would have gone. And you have never seen snow, have you? We will roll in it!'

And happily, hand in hand, they went off to pack their bags.

24. Death and the Maiden

Sharma*ji* found it hard to digest his meals. When he attended long seminars, he found that gas obstructed his ability to speak, especially after lunch. Then, regretfully, he needed to fart often. He really would not have cared had it not been for all the foreign girl volunteers. If he suppressed the pressure building up inside him, he felt like a balloon trying to lift off, and in any case such control could not be maintained for long without letting go of a disastrous burst. The worst of it was that the girls did not titter, it was almost as if they expected it of him. He visited his doctor.

He was shown charts relating age to height and weight. There was no getting round the fact that he was thirty kilograms overweight. The doctor also informed him in plain terms that every kilo of excess weight shortened life. If he did not start a regime to reduce his weight, he could end up with a heart attack, or worse, a disabling stroke that would leave him incapacitated in a wheelchair. A nutritionist was brought in and a chart was prepared for a typical week. There seemed to be very little on it of anything, and nothing of what he liked to eat. Further, diet control had to be supplemented with daily walks in the park. His circulation was in bad shape, and he had a tendency to fall prey to arthritis. But he should not overdo anything in his enthusiasm. He had wrecked his body over the years, and if there was to be recovery, it also had to be a slow process. It would not be good to tire himself out with very long walks—at his age he might be prone to atrial fibrillation. More charts were brought in upon his enquiry to explain the matter. The consultation left him extremely depressed. The doctor seemed to suggest in a polite way that he might have very little time left.

The best time to walk of course was in the early morning, but that was always a difficult proposition for Sharma*ji*, who got up late, and wanted several cups of coffee made by his wife before he could even look at the newspaper. At the same time the doctor had put the wind up him properly, so he thought he would make up for those mornings when he slept late by walking through the park at dusk, when it was a little cooler.

Tired after a day at the office, panting because he had been unable to restrict himself at lunch to frugal helpings. He would lumber through the park in the gloaming hope that the exercise was doing him some good. But fears about his failing health began to prey upon his mind, and he started to read the obituary column in the newspapers first thing in the morning to note with horror that several men of his age had began to pass on. Many seemed to be overweight men, at least by the photos that were printed, and all seemed to have been suppressing a burst of gas when the picture was taken.

He started to note omens: the call of an owl, a black cat across the street, and inauspicious remarks made by his wife to him when he was contemplating his health. He learned how to consult I Ching and Tarot cards but they gave him little comfort. There used to be a saying that dogs could see 'Death,' and he looked at the dogs in the compound of his apartment building to see if they were looking at him in any strange way. There were stories in the *Puranas* that some people had come face to face with Death and rescued themselves by clever argument. If anyone could argue his way out cleverly, surely it was himself.

One day, while wandering through the park, he felt that some dark shadow was following him. He hid behind a tall hedge and waited, but no form appeared. Shaking off this feeling he took to his walk, only to spy a dark figure vanish rapidly round a bend. What could it be? He slept fitfully that night, and dreamt that *Yama*, the God of Death, stood on a huge black buffalo in the park and laughed at him in a sinister way.

The next evening, just as he was turning homeward in the park, a quick lonely figure clad in a jet-black *burqa* passed him by, but seemed to give him a meaningful look. He was rattled. If it had been a Muslim woman, she would have slid by respectfully, self-effacingly; she would never have walked so swiftly and looked straight at him in that meaningful way through the slit, with her dark mesmeric eyes. That was no Muslim woman, but who else would wear a *burqa*? Maybe it was a dark creature in the semblance of a woman in a *burqa*. For the first time in a long time, he prayed before he slept, again very fitfully, with strange dreams that he could not recollect later but which left him with one impression— they boded him no good.

A few days passed without incident, and he was regaining his courage, when once again in the dark the swift, seemingly *burqa*-clad figure passed him, almost without putting foot to ground in his imagination. Again he thought the figure shot a keen meaningful look at him. What could it all mean? He dreaded going for his walks in the park, but a fatal attraction drew him there in the evenings, more to see if that embodied bad omen pursued him than for any reasons of health. Just when he felt that at last he had shaken it off, he would spy the dreaded figure where he least expected it, as ever swift, vanishing round some corner in the park in an unearthly manner! There could be no getting round the reality of that vision. He began to be deliberately kinder to his wife, praising the food she cooked, asking after her health, sighing heavily, and seeing the world for what it was, a mere painted veil, a tale told by an idiot.

Then one evening, he spied the figure lurking round a corner before him and turned back to avoid whatever spirit *Yama* had sent to prepare him for the inevitable. There was a sound of flying feet, an unearthly scream, and, turning in fear to face his last hour, he saw Ramulamma, the midwife of his own centre, the *burqa* shrugged off, holding two struggling boys by their ears.

'I am glad Sharma*ji* is here to witness your shame!' she screamed. 'You think none of us will know? You think you can lurk in this park and squeeze girls' breasts and no one would tell? I hid in this *burqa* to catch you rascals! So you want to see my breasts, you serpents? See my breasts, go on, I brought you into this world to do this!'

The boys were down on the gravel path, weeping, saying they would never do it again, they were ashamed, deeply ashamed.

'Go home, you rascals!' commanded Ramulamma. 'If I really had been a Muslim girl, you idiots could have started a riot! Do you realize that, you good-for-nothing loafers? Go!'

The boys ran away as fast as they could.

Ramulamma turned to Sharma*ji*. 'I was hoping you would be near when I caught those stupid boys. I hope they will not forget this lesson.'

25. Sharma*ji* Battles Dark Powers in the Air

Sharma*ji* liked nothing better than re-telling tales of yore, of his derring-do, to a young and doting audience. And the Rathskeller in the little Swiss town, on a cold autumn evening, offered the best setting. He was seated on a bench at the middle of a long oaken table, surrounded by the youth group of the human rights seminar, which had just concluded. They wanted to hear more from him, and two beautiful girls were snuggled up on either side to keep him warm. He was drinking his third large glass of red wine, and washing it down with a variety of whole-grain breads and swiss cheeses spread on the table. If he turned his head past the perfumed curls of one of his companions, he could see the placid stream, which ran under the window at the back.

'Everyone holds up the Indian example as the greatest democracy in the world,' he mused, staring at the melting wax of the candle in front, 'but you must remember that people have to fight for their democratic rights, all the time, all the time, and never more so than now, when America threatens us with re-colonization!'

This was a familiar and popular theme. 'You said something during the conference about your personal fight with the Indian police,' suggested Joost, the Dutch boy at the table. The others leaned forward expectantly, and Sharma*ji* could feel the breast of the girl on his left pressed against his arm. His moment had arrived.

'You must all have heard of the dark days of the Indian Emergency, when Mrs. Indira Gandhi suspended civil liberties in India and prorogued Parliament indefinitely?' asked Sharma*ji*, but it was clear from the blank looks round him that they had not heard of that momentous occasion, and he could see, in fact, that several had not even been born in those times. He gave them a rough picture of what had occurred, the incarceration of all democratic leaders, including himself, he was careful to add—but he would say not a word about the tortures he himself underwent, for that was not the 'Gandhian way,' and in any case several other leaders had almost faced the same hardships. It was plain to all from his words and his look that he was dissembling modestly.

'No! But I will tell you,' said Sharma*ji* with emphasis, 'about an incident during that time that illustrates how quickly a democratic country with a democratic heritage of five thousand years can be brought down to fascism!'

Joost rose, brought back a fresh bottle of Beaujolais Nouveau and replenished Sharma*ji*'s glass.

'I had just come out of custody—in fact I escaped—but that is another story,' said Sharma*ji* smacking his lips, 'and I would have been re-arrested at the public meeting I addressed—what did I care in those days! I was young, and they had done all they could to me without breaking my spirit. As I was saying, the police were there to re-arrest me, but they received orders not to do so in front of that huge crowd—you know, there is only so much people will take? Well, a few days later, I received a phone call from the Chairman of the Indian Council of Historical Research and was told he was sending me an air ticket to go to Delhi to meet him. I was still a student, but my scholarship was beginning to be known. That is what I advise all young people, let us be activists, but let us also stand first in the class!'

Some sheepish glances were exchanged around him.

'I had never been on a plane before; how could I, coming from a very poor family even I could never afford such an expense. You know I had to read my textbooks under the street lights, since we couldn't afford even an electrical connection. Well! I was seated in this plane, afraid, but willing to try anything!'

Indulgent but at the same time respectfully appreciative laughter broke out round the table.

'This man in the front seat—I couldn't see his face, only the 'Gandhi cap' on his head—started abusing the stewardess. He was demanding to know why the take-off had been delayed by half-an-hour—just half-an-hour, mind you—that she should call the pilot to him. He wanted a full explanation, and so on and so forth. The poor girl tried to pacify him, but he seized her roughly by the shoulder and shoved her staggering towards the cockpit door. My blood was boiling, I tell you, after all I was a young man then, but I think I still would do what I did that day. I was going to rise and give him a slap, but then I knew that airline rules forbid a fight in mid-air. Even as I was debating with myself, an elderly gentleman also sitting in front said politely, "Doesn't matter, Sir, we are on our way, so why don't you relax?"

"Relax! And who the devil are you?" shouted the fellow, standing up, his fat face red with fury. I could see he was some kind of politician. "Do you know who I am?" he shouted for the whole planeload of passengers to hear. "I am Govindas Munshi, a Member of Madam's Advisory Committee!"

'A chilled silence fell all round me, for in those days Indira Gandhi's name was associated with terror, though history has now given us a more balanced view of her as a great patriot, having been misled by fellows like this Munshi. By then the co-pilot had come into the cabin. Munshi turned on him and bellowed: "Inform Delhi Airport and Tihar Jail that I have caught an Anti-National," pointing to the hapless old man. "He is to be transported straight to jail for interrogation!"

'That gentleman was now fully terrified. "I beg you, Sir, I did not know who you were! I meant no harm!"

"You don't have to tell me anything," said Munshi with a devilish look. 'You can tell them in Tihar Jail when you are caned!" 'I could take this no longer. "Fascist! Fascist pig!" I shouted. Govindas Munshi's eyes went red with hatred. "How dare you, you scoundrel!" he yelled, waddling towards me. Before anyone could interfere, I had sprung forward like a leopard, and with a light touch sent him screaming to the floor of the aisle.

"I don't care if your fascist police assassinate me!" I said, for as you can imagine, my blood was also boiling hot. "I may die later, but you will die now, you pig. Apologize to this lady and this gentleman!" I was young then, and I have asked forgiveness from God many times for my behaviour.'

The group round the table willingly forgave him on the spot, and a few pairs of female eyes cast moist glances in his direction.

'He was after all a bully and a coward, and he whimpered that he had only been doing his duty and begged me to spare him. "Take him into custody for causing trouble during a flight!" I told the co-pilot, who was very willing to do so. The other passengers had taken courage, and assured me that they would keep a careful watch over Munshi. Though I was the youngest in the plane, my actions made me a natural leader. When we arrived at Delhi Airport, an Inspector General of Police was in attendance, and totally flabbergasted to see Govindas Munshi take humble leave of me—a student! And you know who that old man was whom I rescued? He was the Managing Director of one of India's biggest corporations in Calcutta—you can guess which one! I did get an offer of a high executive post from him, but a revolutionary does not work for corporations!'

A chorus of congratulatory laughter greeted this story, and the young people crowded round Sharma*ji* for more. He did tell them a few more anecdotes, but the Munshi story had been the best of the evening. Well past midnight, they all decided to go to bed, and the two girls on either side of Sharma*ji* supported him back to the modest hotel where they were staying. Several bottles of red wine had been emptied over the evening, and he was not quite steady on his legs. In any case, he liked their young bodies next to him, recounting on the way back over the cobblestones that Gandhiji himself had been so supported by his nieces in his old age.

They helped him take off his shoes and jacket. While the tall blonde slipped out after kissing him goodnight, the shorter dark beauty, whose breast he had felt pressed against him most of the evening, stayed back to tuck him in. His eyes were glazing in a golden haze of wine and fiction, when she leaned over him, her face indistinct and inches away, and whispered from far away: 'Shall I stay, dear Sharma*ji*?' but he was far away in his own world, and he felt her lips lightly brush his, and then she was gone, switching off the light.

It had been a great evening, full of admiration, food and wine, he could ask for no more. With every rendition the Munshi story had became more real in his mind, taking on ever so many more details, his mind hearing the words spoken so long ago even more clearly, seeing the events in all their sharp and new detail. Somewhere, in some corner of his mind, like an un-believed fast-fading version of some ancient myth, was a bleached-out memory of his old history professor telling him a tale of shame in a breaking voice, of such an incident when the whole plane had sat in cowed silence while the corporate executive was marched off to jail. But his version was more true, if not in fact, then in his own mind, for he willed it to be true. By retelling the story his way he had gloriously removed the stigma of shame from his professor and all other passengers on that plane, and ruined Munshi's reputation one more time by historical rumour, in revenge for the evil he had wrought that day.

26. An International Wedding

The news broke upon him with all the suddenness of a monsoon thunderstorm. He was alternately bewildered, angry, confused, and also glad.

'I don't believe it!' said Sharma*ji*. 'You mean Rukmini—Rukmini—and Robert—Robert Todd—are going to get married? How do you know, and why was I not told before? Why am I always the last person to be told anything? Am I just nobody? I can't believe it, and I won't until they tell me personally!'

A few minutes later Robert entered his unit, accompanied by Rukmini, to join Abraham the bearer of ill-good news. Her silky, dusky cheeks were blushing darkly, and her eyes sparkled as she looked at Robert.

'Sharma*ji*! You can throw me out on my ear if you like, but I have come to ask your permission—your permission, Sharma*ji*—to marry Rukmini,' said Robert in his shy, open way.

Sharma*ji* had pulled himself together. He ran out from behind the table, embraced and kissed Robert on the cheek, and saluted Rukmini with equal fondness. This was the happiest day of his life, he announced loudly, everything was to be left to him. It would be a grand wedding, and people would remember it for the rest of their lives. Rukmini was a blessed girl, he knew it the moment he had set eyes on her, and Robert was the luckiest man as he could see their children being the light of the world. Abraham, there was so much work to be done, and what were their plans, and so on, in a bustling manner that would have done credit to Jane Austen's Mrs Bennett.

As he said himself, there were a million things to be done. A SERVICE staff meeting was called, a critical path chalked out, and duties apportioned. While the couple had said they would prefer a Hindu wedding, Sharma*ji* insisted it should be followed by a Christian wedding, as was only fit and proper, in the Wesley Church. He would arrange everything with his friend, the pastor. The church choir must be rehearsed, and Abraham, as the Christian on the committee, must see to it. Gandhiji, said Sharma*ji* with his customary respectful pause at the name, had liked 'Lead Kindly Light,' and this must be sung. The marriage *pandal* on the *mutt* premises was the obvious choice for the 'Hindu' wedding. After much debate, it was unanimously decided that since the elite of the city and government were to be invited for the 'wedding of the season,' the rural centre was ruled out as a venue for the reception. All the events must take place in the city, but the key question was, where?

The choice of venues stretched from Sharma*ji*'s own neighbourhood, as that would be 'homely,' the bride being almost a 'daughter of the house'—a statement that raised many discreet eyebrows, and brought out not so discreet smiles hidden behind sari *paloos*—to the Raj Bhavan itself, since Sharma*ji* was a known friend of the Governor's, who patronized NGOs in general and SERVICE in particular. Ultimately, the Botanical Gardens were accorded the great honour of hosting the Reception, since the Horticultural Society in any case was a partner in providing planting material for the 'Green' SERVICE programme. Venkat would be in-charge of the Reception, and he would keep Sharma*ji* informed of every move first thing every morning. Three busloads would bring women from all the villages to the reception, and Dasgupta was to oversee all transport arrangements, including decking the 'bride's car,' their society's SUV with roses, and hiring special taxis for the city's notables.

After much discussion with the pastor of the church and the priests of the temple, Sharma*ji* reluctantly agreed to the church wedding being performed first, though by rights the girl's religion should have had primacy. What clinched the issue for Sharma*ji* was the appetizing prospect that straight after the 'Hindu' ceremony, they could all partake of a chaste lunch, cooked on the temple premises in the traditional manner. Many times in the past several months he had been tempted to offer a special *puja*, to be followed by a lunch at the temple, but had desisted for fear that the Gods might take umbrage at his insincerity. But a marriage was a fitting occasion, especially so since Robert, a foreign 'outcaste,' would be given Gods' grace for once in his life.

Organizing the menu for the reception was an altogether tougher proposition, since the elite would be coming, Muslims, government officials and Press people, whose friendship he could cement during the evening. It went without saying that a bar must be kept open during the function. But someone had to keep a watchful eye on it and on the servants, otherwise he would be beggared. Of course, all expenses would be met out of the society's funds, but even then, he could always find good uses for money saved. After worrying at length, he decided that no one in the staff could be trusted, and that he had no option but to ask his brother-in-law to take charge of the bar. Of course that fellow would take advantage of his helplessness by offering free drinks to all his cronies, but that was a better option than to let any one of his staff loose on the drinks.

Sharma*ji* decided he would take personal charge of ordering the food. He prided himself on his epicurean tastes. He would meld Andhra dishes with Hyderabadi cuisine—each dish should be a delight on its own, and yet no more than one organic highlight among many of a gastronomic evening that would be remembered by all. He was pleased with this fancy, with himself, and even with Rukmini, for enabling him to be the 'giver of food' to all, and what food it would be! He threw himself into organizing the food with an enthusiasm he had not felt for anything else in a long time. Clearly no single cook could be entrusted with the whole menu, but different experts must be called in for preparing the dishes that had brought them special renown.

His wife had sniffed at his enthusiasm, remarking pointedly that his own daughter's wedding had been a shabby affair, while he was now making a fool of himself over this other woman. He had snapped back that they were not spending a rupee of their own money, and that this was a business occasion when he could please so many important people. Her eyes had widened at this new perspective, and she had said no more, but she continued to show her displeasure in the way she banged down his coffee cup every time. As he needed her help, he decided to overlook her ill temper.

'Look, all the government secretaries will be there, from the Chief Secretary downwards,' he told her one evening. 'They are almost all North Indians who have never had a chance to eat proper food, our food. You must conduct them to the Andhra table and show them how to eat, how to appreciate every dish. No one can do it better than you. We must buy you a silk sari for the evening. We will do it this week. Now we must get the best cooks— you know them better than anyone else, since you yourself are the best cook.'

She was not impervious to this praise. She smiled, sat down, and they amicably discussed dishes, cooks, special vessels to be borrowed, and who had them. 'What you need to do is engage Kamalamma,' she said after due deliberation. 'My mother learnt cooking from her, but she fusses all the time, and she hates to come to the city. But I know she needs money. Her son is an IT engineer and a good job has been offered to him in California. He has to pay for his own ticket, so she will cook. But you must send a car to fetch her.'

Kamalamma, when she arrived, turned out to be a rather large woman, very unsteady on her legs, but with a commanding voice all the same. Refusing to sit on a chair, she lowered herself groaning onto the floor of their flat and ordered Sharma*ji*'s wife to get her some hot coffee and a few soft *idlis*, if she had any. Sharma*ji* was amazed to see his wife being obsequious, which she had never been before, even on their wedding day, even to his own aunt. After half an hour, during which the women exchanged many stories about distant relatives and cures for constant aches and other disorders, Kamalamma turned to Sharma*ji*, who had sat by patiently, and told him that she and her three assistants, no more than boys really, would stay at the temple—she could not stand dirty city apartments—but next morning he was to come with them to buy provisions.

The shopping expedition stretched over four days, with Kamalamma negotiating the crowded narrow lanes with surprising agility, though she never ceased to complain of the city, its filth, and her own ailments, which had brought her to death's door. She rested her large, panting self on narrow ledges or stools set by the door of shops, and held long animated conversations with the shopkeepers. They all seemed to agree readily with her that the vegetables or oil or grain on display were not of the fastidious quality to which she was accustomed. Some blamed it on the government and its policies, some on the present generation, and a few on the Iraq war. Sharma*ji* tagged along, disgorging money whenever she declared herself reconciled to the choice available, vainly wishing he could be sitting in his cloistered office, under his fan, and waiting for his tiffin. But he was determined that the feast at the reception would be such as would be remembered in fable and in song, and so he soldiered on.

Kamalamma was pleased that he had danced attendance for four days without complaining. There were not very many husbands like that, she reminded his wife, who should count herself lucky. Sharma*ji* was amazed to see his wife blushing demurely, and glancing at him coyly, as if to hint of other services he performed to her satisfaction. Upon being told he would no longer be needed to accompany them to the shops, he organized a taxi for them, gave his wife all the money she demanded, and hurried off to consult his good friend, Wajid Hussain, about the Hyderabadi section of the menu.

He entered his friend's gate, tucked away unobtrusively in the corner of a mean little street, and, crossing a wide courtyard overrun with children, puddles, and chicken, climbed a few shallow stone steps to the deep veranda, where Wajid sat in an armchair, fanning himself. His friend would hear of nothing till he had had a cup of tea and tasted the sweets made just that morning. Wajid and he had been at school together and smoked their first cigarette together at the Palace Theatre's matinee show. So he started straightaway telling Wajid to get off his armchair and find him the best Hyderabadi cook there was, why he needed one, and how important the party would be. Wajid heard him out languidly, and then seemed to sink into sleep. Sharma*ji* waited patiently, knowing the great mind was working.

'You need Afzal *mian*, if he is at all free that evening,' said Wajid with deliberation. 'We will go and see him, but after lunch. You never come home these days, so I must insist. Then, we will start up my old Austin Eight, I haven't taken her out for a spin in a long time, and this could be a perfect afternoon.' Sharma*ji* knew nothing could induce Wajid to change his plans once his mind was made up. So after a leisurely lunch, which he enjoyed, and after tinkering for half an hour with the carburetor of the old car, which he hated, they set off to the other end of town, proudly honking their brass horn. They were received with ceremony at Afzal *mian*'s place, a long low structure which combined a large cookhouse, a small neat frontal office, and residential quarters at the back.

Afzal *mian* did much consulting of his diary, shouted at sundry young assistants to fetch him his 'order book,' used two of his cellphones to apologize to various customers that despite his earlier promises he would not be able to cater for their parties; what could he do, his hands were tied by honour, and life would be meaningless without loyalty. After thirty minutes spent assuring them that he would help make alternative arrangements, Afzal *mian* turned to Wajid and said, '*Bhai sahib*, see what trouble he was creating for his old friend?'

Wajid took all this with equanimity. '*Arre bhai*, what are friends for if not to give trouble?' he asked. 'If you have a dish of your excellent *qubanni* I would like it very much now.' Afzal *mian* hurriedly shouted orders, and a dish of sweet *qubanni* with thick cream and apricot nuts was served up to both of them in old porcelain dishes. Contentment reigned for a while, and then Wajid and Afzal *mian* put their heads together to design the menu. It was immediately agreed that chicken in *biryani* was a modern abomination, and not to be thought of, but Afzal *mian* said dejectedly that the market did not have the quality of rice he used for his *biryanis*. When Sharma*ji* intervened to suggest that he could have some *basmati* sent down from Punjab, they looked at him in silent disdain, Wajid explaining that that sort had no real fragrance, the secret of good *biryani*. After more phone calls, Afzal felt somewhat comforted that loyal friends might send some special rice from Karimnagar in time for the feast. While Wajid knew of a man who could be depended upon to sell them good quality dried fruits, there was no hope of genuine saffron being available anywhere, so certain dishes were ruthlessly eliminated.

Before they left Afzal *mian*'s place, Wajid asked him to give them his best price. Afzal *mian* objected. He could not charge anything; this was between friends, it would be like a function in his own house. After much haggling, it was agreed that Afzal *mian* would charge something—not fees—that was impossible, but something to cover the minor expenses of his assistants. Since he had several assistants, Sharma*ji* was sure it would be a large bill, but thankfully not exorbitant.

As the preparations progressed, Sharma*ji* found that he was working with an energy that surprised him. He went to bed planning, leapt out of it before anyone else was about, and organized the day meticulously as he had never done before. His exhilaration grew with the successful operation of every step; this was one 'project' that would really happen, for which he would not have to write a long report about why things went wrong. He was exhausted but triumphant. On the eve of the wedding, he was tense and relaxed in turns, like Napoleon who had scrupulously planned a victory and waited only for his forces to carry out his vision. On the day itself, there was nothing further for him to do but savour the accolades that were showered upon him, for in truth he was too tired and dazed even to do justice to the meals he had planned with such anticipation.

After all the guests had left late that evening, and Robert had pumped his hand one last time and Rukmini had kissed him on the cheek, he was all alone with himself. For once in his life he had done something from which he derived no benefit at all, but all the same he was happy.

27. The White She-Buffalo

Sharma*ji*'s wife whispered to him hoarsely in the semi-privacy of their bedroom that she didn't like 'the white she-buffalo'; in fact, never had even when she first heard of her, and now she was sure she didn't trust her. Never mind how much she smiled, or said in a fake Punjabi way, 'Mummyji, how beautiful your sari is,' or 'Mummyji, you must teach me how to cook such delicious Indian food for Ashok.' She was not 'her Mummy.' She was poor Ashok's mother, and this tragic marriage would surely kill her soon. Why couldn't he have married her brother's daughter, Deepti? A beautiful, respectful girl, who was herself a computer expert. It wasn't as if she had asked him to marry a village girl! Deepti would have made him happy, there would already be a grandson, and she would never have tyrannized over her son like this huge 'white she-buffalo.'

Sharma*ji* didn't care for Margaret either, but for different reasons. She was three inches taller than him, for one, muscular like a man, and he was sure, much stronger than Ashok. She was out every morning by six, with the hedges still wet with dew, her bare white thighs flashing in the rising dawn and her hard buttocks encased in tight black shorts pumping behind her as she ran, her blonde ponytail swinging from side to side. His neighbours must already be sniggering at him, him, Vedavyas Sharma. Not that she was attractive, how could anyone so big-boned be attractive? Apart from her repulsive muscles though, her face was always rose-petal soft. It never took on that sexy golden oily sheen, which lit up a woman's face like her diamond nose-ring, and sent his pulse racing, even at his age. But it was poor misguided Ashok who would have to live out this tragedy, that is, if it lasted. At first he had not thought anything of it when Ashok kept writing about this American girl from Buffalo, who was his research partner—in fact his wife had laughingly started calling her the 'white she-buffalo.' Later, when he read between the lines, he had chuckled stupidly, thinking Ashok was only sowing his wild oats, but he never ever thought his son would be stupid enough to marry an American woman. And now here they were, spending their first Christmas together with him in India.

Margaret was back from her run, and sat in a low cane chair in front of him, her sweaty thighs crossed, drinking a mug of hot coffee. 'Dad! I have been here now, what, eight days? And I have not seen one person out running. And with all the oily food you eat here, it is a one-way street to a heart attack. Even Ashok doesn't want to run. OK, he is in good health, but boy, will he lose it fast if he doesn't shape up every morning. Ashok! Ashok! For crying out loud, it's seven already! Get up! Now, Ashook!'

Well, that's what came of marrying American women; they bully you in front of their father-in-law. Ashok came out of their room in his *dhoti*, grinning sheepishly, wiping his face with a towel, the black stubble of his beard still unshaven. 'Meg, remember this is my holiday?' said Ashok on his way to the kitchen to beg a cup of coffee from his mother. 'I am regressing, Meg, and let me, after seven bloody hard years working for Simon Legree. And four more days and it's over!'

'I thought you both worked in Cal-Tech; what has happened? Has Ashok lost his job?' asked Sharma*ji* in alarm.

'Dad! You are such a dude,' said Margaret, laughing, and rose to kiss his cheek. 'I think I will go help Mom in the kitchen. I do want to learn how to make those crisp *dosas*, and I will, even if it kills me!' Sharma*ji*, suppressing an uncharitable wish, got up with a sigh and made his way to his own bathroom for a thoughtful shit and a bath. As he sat long on the toilet, he reviewed the scene and came once again to the regretful conclusion that there was nothing he could do. The real problem would come if there were children before the break-up. It would kill Ashok; when too late he would bitterly regret his fascination for white skin. At least he could have married someone small and docile, as they showed in films these days, but then he himself had been unlucky in his own marriage— that had been the fault of that scheming uncle of his. Ashok had fallen into this trap of his own free will; there was no uncle to make his life miserable.

As Ashok drove them both to the Gymkhana courts, he kept looking sideways at his son. Yes, Ashok had changed, in many ways. He seemed to be bigger, and maybe thanks to Margaret, he had developed hard biceps that popped out of his tee-shirt sleeves. He was very confident nowadays, not at all like the shy lad he had seen off in tears so long ago at the airport. He spoke easily to anybody, in that nasal American way, which, to start with, Sharma*ji* found intimidating.

'Well, Dad! I know neither you nor Mom cares for Meg,' said Ashok with a wide grin, negotiating round a herd of buffalos in conference. 'We laugh about it at night when we are alone. Meg thinks you are both cute. And our first son will be named Bison, just to tease Mom!' Ashok was laughing happily to Sharma*ji*'s consternation. So his wife had not been so secretive after all in her whisperings. He tried to bluster his way out.

'Dad, we don't mind, honestly. Meg is one in a million. She's seen some hard times, and back home, you know, the whole world is there, living next door, falling in love, marrying, divorcing, you see it all. And don't worry, Dad! We're never ever going to divorce, and if we do, we will do it like friends, okay?'

There was nothing Sharma*ji* could say to this son of his, who was no longer like the boy he had brought up, who was, let's face it, no longer an Indian. He had not wanted to face this truth that had been presented to him in a myriad ways in the past, but which he had shied away from seeing. His son was no longer an Indian. He ate his mother's cooking, but Sharma*ji* knew instinctively that Ashok no longer relished it; in fact Margaret liked it much more. Ashok was just regressing, as he himself had said, just for two weeks, to recollect a part of his life now definitely a historic past, glimpsed like a myth. He moved about his hometown warily, like a man in a strange jungle. He smiled at, got up to help, and fetched things for all the elders he had grown up among, but Sharma*ji* knew it was just a time-bound ritual. They were all strangers to Ashok now, though, incredibly, Margaret was busily making friends with all of them, taking down addresses in earnest, figuring out if she knew any of their descendents back in the States, offering to carry pickles, parcels, and letters back to them. Margaret cared about Indians; Ashok no longer did.

They were in the club where Ashok had first learned to play tennis. Ramesh Gangadhar, the former star tennis player of the club and one of the richest men in the city, had taken an interest in the boy and had coached him personally, every day, every morning from six to eight. Sharma*ji* had been very proud that he could give his son the chances in life he himself never had, and had always swelled with satisfaction at seeing his son play tennis and mix in such high circles. For his son's sake, he had accepted with dignity the slighting way the high and mighty Ramesh Gangadhar treated him. And now, he had come with Ashok to watch the Club Tennis finals between the still 'evergreen' Ramesh and his own son, who had returned in time for the tournament. Mr Gangadhar had been very complimentary at the way Ashok had developed his game in the States, improving his serve and his two-handed backhand shots. Now that Sharma*ji* had come to be respected as an NGO leader, he even unbent enough to address him politely, and offer a seat beside him to watch the matches.

All the club *'koihais'* were there, reminiscing about the good old days, retelling known anecdotes for the umpteenth time, berating the government for its corruption, laughing at how they had fiddled their income-tax returns all legally, and fussing over their tea. Ashok was a great lad, earning, y'know, a hundred thousand bucks, bucks not rupees, and Ramesh was one of their own. It would be a hard-fought contest between the Older and the Younger Titan. But it wasn't to be. Ashok's shots were flawless, his service powerful, and his placing had that egotistical Gangadhar running all over the court, panting like a grampus. A few claps fell away into silence when Ashok won the first set 6–0. A few well-meaning, and hurt-assuaging pieces of advice were shouted across from the pavilion. 'Ramesh, old chap, change that racket, it's half-an-ounce too heavy for this weather,' or 'sand your palms, old chap,' or 'Bearer! Take that bottle of lemonade for Ramesh Sahib, *jaldi.*' Of course, to show fairness all round, the members did murmur, 'Well played, Ashok, damn good form!' Sharma*ji* was inwardly very happy; Ashok, his son, was humiliating that ass Gangadhar. This was payback time for all the snide insults he had heaped on Sharma*ji*.

The second set started ten minutes late, after the club marker had massaged oil into Gangadhar's knees. The first game Ashok won as easily as he had the others. In the second game, after a couple of deuces, he broke his opponent's serve, Ramesh already panting with the strain, and wiping his eyes with his sweatbands. Ashok started the third game two up in the second set, and served an ace. Then as he was stretching up to serve for the second point, he let out a loud cry and fell to the ground, obviously in great pain. Ramesh Gangadhar was over the net like a shot and beside Ashok before anyone else. He, the marker, and a couple of others helped Ashok back to the pavilion. Even after fifteen minutes of hot-water fomentation and liberal use of the club's standard pain-relieving embrocation, Ashok was hardly able to stand on one leg. He regretfully conceded the match to Ramesh, who refused to accept it at first, saying that he had been beaten fair and square. But the best of three sets had not been completed, and the umpire, one of the club's oldest members, held that they could not use their own discretion in the matter, the match was Ramesh's. Sharma*ji* then set off in his car in a flurry of worry, with his son, the runners-up plaque, and shouted good wishes trailing behind him, to find a doctor.

After a couple of hours spent on X-raying the leg and pain-relieving treatment, Sharma*ji* and Ashok, now in a wheel-chair, were escorted by two nurses into the orthopedist's room.

'There's nothing to be alarmed about,' said the doctor slowly and unconvincingly. 'There is nothing organically wrong with that leg. No bones broken, no torn ligaments. It must have been a severe cramp. This is a very dry climate, and I always advice athletes to drink a lot of water. One loses water without one's knowledge; and then it catches up with you during a match, as has just happened, when you are already under strain...' The doctor seemed to lose interest in the whole business and concentrated on his fingernails. Satisfied with their condition, he lifted his head and said with some impatience, 'You should be okay for the journey home, in fact you should be okay by the evening. If there's any problem tomorrow, come back and let's look at you again.'

Sharma*ji* was very relieved, but he was still disappointed that his son had not given Ramesh Gangadhar the thrashing he deserved. He helped him carefully into the lift of his apartment building, and with an affectionate arm round his son, helped him to bed, telling his wife testily that it was only a sprain, and she should get some coffee and *upma* ready for their son. Without waiting to be further questioned by Margaret, who had stepped out to buy some things, he went to his office to answer some letters. He was much later getting back than expected, and he was just reaching the lift back home when Ashok came bounding down the stairs with a whistle. Seeing his father, he came to a dead stop with a guilty look, and then without a word, limped out.

Later that evening, when Sharma*ji* was alone with his son, sitting in the veranda of his flat, drinking a pint of cold beer, he asked simply, 'You were not really hurt in the Club, were you?'

Ashok was silent for a bit. 'No, Dad! I wasn't. I didn't realize how much better I had become, or how much Ramesh had aged. If I had beaten him 6–0, 6–0, it would have humiliated him, Dad. He was my guru, Dad, he taught me tennis, and how could I do that to him in front of his friends, in his own Club, where he had been president three times? I couldn't live with myself, Dad, if I did that. I thought of hitting the ball out of court a few times, but that would have been condescending, and he would have known like a shot.'

Sharma*ji* looked at his son silently, speculatively.

'I know he wasn't always nice to you, Dad,' said Ashok looking down, 'but that's because of the way his set of people are brought up—he's quite decent really, deep down.'

'So, there's still some Indian left in you,' said Sharma*ji* slowly. His son smiled affectionately at him, in a sheepish way. 'Oh, I am Indian all right, deep down,' he said.

28. Shanta Threatens Divorce

'**Yes! Appa, I am** getting a divorce. And nothing you can say or any of this hypocritical meaningless nonsense can make me change my mind!' Shanta said firmly, slapping down on the dining table her black leather work-bag, full of exam papers to correct. His wife was rattling pots and pans in the kitchen of their flat, whether in support of her daughter's statement or in agitated response, he could not tell.

It was a hot summer evening, with mosquitoes buzzing round his head, adding to his discomfort. 'But Shantu, what has happened? I know you have had disagreements with Ravi; which married pair does not? I can help sort things out. Ravi—I know Ravi—leave it to me, and he will come round. Don't I know how to do it?' Sharma*ji* was trying to regain control. This was not the time for a scandal. He was held in very high esteem. He was trying to glue together a coalition of civil society organizations, with himself at the head, which would use EU money—he forgot which DG it came under—but essentially for cultural purposes to revitalize traditional values. But people would laugh if his own daughter went in for a divorce at this time.

His daughter's plump figure was heading towards the kitchen with her hair cut short in a 'bob,' swaying defiantly round her shoulders. 'Shantu, Shantu! Don't be disrespectful! This is your father speaking, not one of your modern academic friends, who doesn't care about values. I will not let you ruin your life! What else do I have in life, except my children? Everything else I have sacrificed to the nation!' Sharma*ji* got up ponderously from the dining table, leaving behind his plate, periodically filled with hot *pakodas* by his wife. 'Let us discuss this; listen to your mother!' he cried in desperation, following her into the kitchen.

His wife was calmly giving some hot *pakodas* to Shanta, who was eating them as if nothing had happened. 'Give me a list of what Ravi has done; let us be rational. He is a good fellow, you modern people should appreciate him. He never took a rupee in dowry; even I with my high principles was surprised at that noble gesture. And you have hardly been married two years, and you jump up and say you want a divorce? You, why don't you speak sense to your daughter?' His wife, her ample back turned towards them, continued to make *pakodas*, but the way she handled the ladle, he knew she was angry about something. Maybe the silly woman would help him, just this once.

'Appa, this is none of your business,' said Shanta calmly, munching *pakodas*. 'If you like Ravi so much, marry him yourself. That will give Amma a break.'

Such effrontery was not to be tolerated, but Sharma*ji* was at a loss how to regain control. Shouting at his daughter would make her more obstinate, he knew. If he put up with insolence it was only to bide his time; but he must bring this cocky stupid girl round, manipulate her somehow so that she did not spoil everything.

He laughed a dry laugh. 'You are angry, my little girl! Whom I have treasured more than life, seen through every little trouble, protected her, taught her, spent lavishly on her wedding'—he regretted the allusion he moment he said it, this was no time to talk of marriage—'she is now angry with her poor father. Be angry, but I will continue to love you!'

His daughter seemed unimpressed. She continued to munch *pakodas,* as if they were discussing something totally inconsequential.

'Appa, you have made a pretty good life for yourself. You twist everybody round, everything round to satisfy yourself. You are the greatest manipulator there is! But you cannot manipulate me! I know you too well. I know all about this precious SERVICE society and its scams. And remember, I know that poor grand uncle Satyanarayana passed away without your lifting a finger to save him. So, no talk of values to me, okay? I will live my life. I just thought I would let you know, rather have a neighbour tell you.'

Sharma*ji* was getting livid. His rough tongue had made many others back down; maybe a tongue-lashing would make this girl bend to his will. 'Thank You! Thank You! Thank You!' he said viciously. 'We now have no family! These modern women don't care if they kill off their parents! You have squeezed everything you want from me, and you don't need either of us any more, I see that! What a fine example you set your students! No wonder, with teachers like you, the country is going to the dogs! Dogs, I tell you, male and female!' He had avoided the word 'bitch,' his skills in wordy duelling were finely honed.

His wife spoke suddenly, unexpectedly. 'Shanta wants a divorce, and she must get it. You will never understand.'

Sharma*ji* was stunned. He had never expected that his traditional wife, and moreover, one over whom he ruled, gently but firmly, would support such non-Brahminical attitudes to marriage. 'What is this, what is this I hear?' he demanded, moving threateningly towards his wife, who turned her back on him calmly. 'So, you people have been discussing this for some time, have you? Without telling me? Behind my back, while I was slaving in the *pariah* cherry, rubbing shoulders with Muslims, why, to feed you? Ah ha! What loyalty, what family feeling! I see now, when you said get a large-screen colour TV I knew that the rot had set in. It is these films with their degrading dances that have corrupted you. This is why our Manu Dharma Shastra has said that women must be controlled by men, or else society is lost, dharma is lost! What a fool I was not to have seen all this before! What a fool to be soft towards women! One thing I will tell you, listen to me, woman! I will not permit any divorce in my house! That is final!'

With that he went to the bedroom and lay down without switching on the light. His wife did not come to him immediately. He would take it out on her later. After some time, the dark, the quiet and all the *pakodas* he had eaten had their effect, and he was dropping off into a sullen nap, when his wife came in.

'Come, dinner is ready,' she said simply.

'I will not eat,' he said. 'You have given me a pain in my chest. You have killed me.' His wife went away. He grimly closed his eyes.

'Come, Appa, don't sulk,' said his daughter, indecently cheerful. 'Amma has made brinjals with that special *masala* you like, and the curds are really thick. So come before we eat it all up!' What arrogance! But why should he suffer for their sins? They should be taught a lesson, not himself. He got up, and went into the next room, blinking in the light and trying to look both ill and aggrieved. The food was already on the table, and he sat in his customary place and made quite a good meal of it, taking whatever was offered with ill grace.

After the meal, he sat in his easy chair, fanning himself, and satisfied himself with the *paan* his wife had made for him. 'Eh, you!' he called out to her. 'What has happened to you! Is this the way to make *paan*? My God!' His daughter was talking in the kitchen with his wife, helping to clear away, wash, and dry the dishes. As she left, she wished him a cheery goodbye, but he deigned no reply.

He had hoped that the whole thing would blow over, that his daughter had thought it all up just to harass him, but such was not the case. The divorce petition was to be heard in court. He tried meeting Ravi a few times, but each time his son-in-law was pleasant but evasive. He was surprised that Ravi himself was not going to oppose the divorce. How could a man be so lost to shame?

The meeting of the NGO coalition to protect traditional values took place in the Dange Hall, named after the famous communist leader of olden days, communists being more interested in the matter of traditional values than anyone else. The walls of the hall were covered with printed iconic portraits of Marx, Engels, Lenin, Stalin, Mao and Ho Chi Minh. Over the entrance hung the large oil portrait of Dange himself. Delegates crowded in, many from rural areas, straight from bus stations. On the high dais was a long table, covered with the standard red tablecloth one expects in left-wing functions. Several chairs were ranged behind the table, and in front of each chair, on the table, were a small flower vase with plastic flowers and a sealed drinking water bottle.

The high dignitaries took their places. To the right of the central chair was seated Mr A.K. Nilakentan, former Chief Secretary to government, who, after retirement, had become the leading spokesperson in any left-wing forum. To the left was Dr R.P. Chatopadhyaya, famed and retired atomic scientist, who never failed to espouse the cause of world peace and disarmament. At the very edge of the table, next to the lectren, sat Mr S.D. Damodhar, retired Director General of police, the latest leader in human rights activities. The central chair was of course reserved for Sharma*ji*. Forty-five minutes after the function was supposed to start, when all were seated and the hall had filled up three-quarters, young Gopalan, who managed such affairs, welcomed the audience and said something rambling for ten minutes about the value of values. *Slokas* in Sanskrit followed, recited by the last surviving follower of Mahatma Gandhi, who explained the *slokas* by repeating them again, but more slowly, in Sanskrit. Then came the time for the Presidential address.

Slowly, with head bowed but with determined step, Sharma*ji* made his way to the lectern. Then followed the traditional business of tapping the mike, making a gesture to the technician fiddling with the amplifier, who turned a knob that let out a deafening screech. Finally, after taking a sip of water and clearing his throat, Sharma*ji* began his address.

'Mr Nilakentan, Dr Chatopadhyaya, Mr Damodhar, dignitaries on the dais and in the audience, friends, all citizens who have come here to uphold our traditional values, our Indian way of life, Hindu, Muslim, Christian, Jain, Sikh and Dalit brethren and sisters, Greetings! I have been asked to undertake the heavy burden of the Presidentship of this new coalition, which holds so much promise for our people. I declined several times for I knew there were many others far more worthy to hold this office than myself. Please don't interrupt, believe me, I know I am unworthy, I thank you for reposing confidence in this old man, I thank you for your affection and regard, but I want to share with you today, in open assembly, an innermost struggle I am waging, a struggle between duty and truth! Can there be such a struggle? Yes, my friends, this can happen, and is happening! You all know—why should I hide anything from you, my real family—that my daughter has disobeyed me and filed for a divorce. I said not a word to her! It is the inner conscience that must be stirred. I hope it will, I can only pray it will. But when such an act is being contemplated by my own daughter, I can only see it as my own sin. I cannot remain your President. I therefore request Shri Chakravarthy—the last remaining follower of Gandhiji himself'—pause—'to take the chair!'

This was a masterstroke. The centenarian, after the exertion of waiting two long hours in the hall and reciting the *slokas*, had already been whisked away home. Sharma*ji* could have nominated the civil servant, the atomic scientist, or the policeman, but he shrewdly sensed that any of them would have gracefully accepted the post. There was near pandemonium in the hall. A few men rose, from organizations supported by SERVICE, and with quavering voices insisted that he and only he should be their President. With great reluctance, Sharma*ji* accepted to shoulder the burden, unworthy though he was.

29. The Heart Attack

It was turning out to be a splendid conference. The various coloured grains were spread out on the side table, all neatly labelled in Latin and half a dozen South Indian languages. A bevy of girl students studying art and history were gathered around the table, taking notes and photos, while the Press, for whom the display was intended, had paid it only a cursory glance. Most of them had accepted Sharma*ji*'s handout stoically, and were fidgeting for the Press Conference to end so that they could go the bar SERVICE had thoughtfully opened in the next room, though it was not yet noon. However, a stringer for an agricultural weekly was persistent.

'Our population now exceeds one hundred *crores*,' he announced, referring to a clutch of papers, as if to the latest government statistics, 'and there is persistent malnutrition among thirty to forty percent of rural children'—with another glance at his papers—'can your system feed so many people? Do we not need modern technology for modern times?'

Sharma*ji* beamed. 'That is a very important question,' he said, ignoring the side-talk gathering in volume and urgency from the Press. 'Biodiversity ensures a balanced production of all nutrient foods for all men—human beings—and our livestock also. If we take care of the land, we take care of people also. This was the essence of Gandhiji's approach'—he paused in respect—'our leaders in a mad rush for modernization, for profits, have forgotten his wisdom. What use is modernization when it leads only to malnutrition? Why go in for Vitamin A supplements when the humble drumstick will suffice? Why abandon our *ragi* porridge, rich with calcium, just to swell the coffers of rice millers, feed rats to government *godowns*, and export excess rice to fat Americans, depriving our own people of their right to food?'

From the corner of his eye he could see that the girl students at the table had half turned to listen. 'What shall we do with Americanisms?' he boomed. 'With five-star hotels, fast foods, coca-colas, five-star clubs, even five-star hospitals? What we need are the simple things of the earth, our Indian earth!' A tall girl in tight jeans, whose long lustrous plait caressed each buttock in turn as she moved, gave him a slow sweet smile.

Sharma*ji* was fairly launched into one of his favourite speeches, and no amount of fidgeting among his guests could distract him from holding forth for a good quarter of an hour. He then invited all the assembled to gather round the display, so that he himself could explain in even greater detail the benefits of crops grown to maintain biodiversity, rural health and livelihoods, and recover— he stressed this point—the ageless wisdom of our forebears.

Some of the stragglers at the rear had already wandered off to the bar in the next room, when, with inner satisfaction for having done his duty, even at risk to his own life, Sharma*ji* hurried out, called his driver impatiently, and had himself driven to his doctor. He was not an alarmist, only a cautious man, a well-educated London-returned scholar, who had dedicated his life to the service of his fellowmen, and he deserved better from God than to be struck down in the prime of his life. His heart raced as he thought of his suspicions, as the car threaded its way through the chaotic traffic, and Sharma*ji* was torn between the desire to chastise the driver for blowing his horn so incessantly when his master was in extremis, as it were, and his impatience to order the fellow to drive faster. Had he been like the rest of his fellowmen, mindlessly going about their way like buffalos, he would have been spared this anxiety, drawn from a sober, educated consideration of the facts.

Dr Padmanabhan, his physician, was a consultant at *Vaidya Narayani*, the latest five-star hospital with all the gadgets found in any American hospital, and more, for its hotel wing was already full of NRI and white American medical tourists who had flown in for expert speedy treatment at cut-rates, with exotic elephant rides and temple visits thrown in for free. Entering the large, clean, air-conditioned, marble-floored reception area, with its comforting medical smells, Sharma*ji* began to feel a renewed sense of hope that it might not yet be too late. After agonizing delays at the counter, and then in the waiting room, he was at last face to face with his doctor, on the examining bed, and turned this way and that by firm hands, while his friend and doctor seemed hardly to listen to his urgent self-diagnosis.

'You can put on your shirt,' said Dr Padmanabhan from his desk, as he scribbled rapidly on a notepad. 'I want you to take these tests—my nurse will show you where to go—and then you come back here by four, shall we say?'

A dark, pimply Keralite nurse was ushering him out of the consulting room, when Dr Padmanabhan, giving him a wintry, professional smile, asked him not to worry. But worry he did through all the long dreary tests and the waiting, paying appropriate high fees, at every step as through a cloudy daze. It was early afternoon when they finally let him go, well past his lunchtime, not that he had any appetite left. To kill time till the dreaded verdict from the doctor, he went into the bowels of the hospital—causing him to wince at the thought—to spend a few hundred rupees eating a plate of tasteless *idlis* followed by tepid tea.

'Blood in the stools does not mean cancer,' pronounced Dr Padmanabhan coldly. 'You should know better than to stress yourself out with half-baked knowledge. I could have told you that at the start, but I wanted these tests done to prove it to you, you inveterate hypochondriac!'

Relief poured out of Sharma*ji* in blessed sweat. He really didn't care about the doctor's scolds; after all he was a good fellow, but uncouth like most of these professionals.

'You've got constipation; I've warned you about that before, and that's induced piles,' continued Dr Padmanabhan. 'I am prescribing some medicated cream for your arse-hole, but see that you clip those dirty nails of yours first.'

Sharma*ji* was already feeling very much better, and getting irritated at the doctor's manner. He got up to say goodbye but was waved down by the doctor, who sat down himself with a frown.

'These reports are not all they should be,' said Dr Padmanabhan, cresting his hands like a lotus in front of his face and looking seriously at them. 'Don't get me wrong, there's nothing alarming—as yet. You eat too much for your age—you are fat, your cholesterol levels are too high, and if you go on like this, there could be an event, earlier than we expect. And while you are not a diabetic, you could become one—all South Indian Brahmins are prone, and bad eating habits hasten the process. You must start walking in the morning—go to a gym, start gentle exercises, nothing strenuous—but most importantly, you've got to stop eating rubbish, throwing all sorts of things down into that paunch. Cut down on eating; I know that's difficult, but you must try. Fill your stomach with healthy things. You were on TV this morning; why don't you eat what you prescribe for others?'

Sharma*ji* looked back on that morning's glory, and even further back on SERVICE's biodiversity patches with their straggly crops. There was nothing there for a healthy man, but it would be futile to educate this medico on the issues involved in restoring national biodiversity.

Dr Padmanabhan recommended a health cookbook, which he promised to buy. The one practical piece of advice he got from the doctor was to switch to whole-wheat brown bread for breakfast.

But that advice was not as practical as he first thought, for whole-wheat brown bread was nowhere to be found, despite his loyal staff scouring the city for a health-conscious bakery. It seemed the few bakers who had offered an explanation had said there was no market for brown bread, making Sharma*ji* fume at his fellow citizens' crass eating habits. His assistant, Dasgupta, broke into a diatribe to suggest that when the auditor of Christians Everywhere came in three weeks' time, he should be asked to bring along a bread-making machine. It seemed that one of his friends in Calcutta had such a machine, which was inexpensive and simple to operate, and made all kinds of breads—all one had to do was shove in whole-wheat *atta* and the machine did the rest.

A month later, Sharma*ji* brought home a large cardboard box and carefully unwrapped a glistening new machine on his dining table. When he looked at its sleek streamlined shape, he was sure it was worth the few thousand rupees he had paid for it, but his wife raised a protest.

'What will this do that I don't do?' she asked stridently. '*Chapattis* are as good as bread; they are made with the same flour! You just throw away money on gadgets that will break down in a few weeks, and no one can repair them anyway. You remember that electric ice-cream machine you bought in America, and that coffee-maker in Italy? And I am still filtering your coffee with my mother's copper filter, and I still have to turn our old ice-cream maker by hand in its old wooden bucket. You never buy anything useful, just clutter up our small flat with rubbish!'

Sharma*ji* paid no attention to his wife, accustomed as he was to her views. He told her sternly that she wouldn't have to bother with the bread-making machine, since she didn't know how to handle modern machines. He would make bread himself, for his own health, so that he could continue to work to support his family, as was his duty. His wife retreated to the kitchen, retorting that he was very welcome to step into the kitchen for the first time and learn cooking. After this passage of words, he was too proud to ask her to make bread, nor did she offer to do so. He waited a few days, hoping his daughter would drop by and bake the first batch of breads, but she didn't turn up even over the weekend, and he couldn't bear his wife's snorts every time she passed the machine sitting on top of the sideboard.

So late that next Sunday afternoon, he plugged in the machine and tried reading the instructions, neatly written out in German, French, Spanish and Italian. It was confusing, to say the least, but he was now on his mettle, and having decided what the diagrams meant. He went into the kitchen and loudly asked for measuring cups, flour, butter, salt, oil, sugar and so forth. His wife stood by in amusement while he made a bit of a mess in the kitchen, which she good-naturedly cleaned up later, but he triumphantly packed the machine and it started whirring. He peeked into it at regular intervals, and by dinner time, there was a hot loaf standing beside his plate on the table.

The bread didn't taste as good as he had hoped, but the crowning pleasure of having cooked something himself made him overlook all its faults, and he beamed when his wife, who took a bite, said it wasn't all that bad for a first attempt. He kept eating chunks of the hot loaf along with his regular meal—just as they do in England, he thought—and he finished the whole large loaf in one sitting, eating bread with his *sambhar*, his *rasam*, his curds, and his vegetables. Early next morning, in the bathroom, a sharp pain jabbed him just below his heart, and his breath caught. Was this the event that Padmanabhan had talked about? Cold sweat poured from his brow, which he knew was a bad sign; he made his way back to his bed and called his wife. She came in saying something casually, but was transformed into scared alertness, like he had never seen before. She covered him swiftly with a blanket, rolled him gently to his side, and the next instant she was ringing Padmanabhan and asking for an ambulance. He was in a daze as the ambulance carried him to the hospital, its sirens wailing, his wife by the side of his stretcher, her hand gentle on his brow, smoothing his hair. At the hospital it was like the films, the doctors and nurses ready and hurrying his stretcher into the ICCU. Their presence reassured him, and the sedative calmed his nerves. He lay perfectly still, trying to meditate to protect his poor injured heart, when Padmanabhan's cheerful laugh startled him into opening his bleary eyes, to see his wife's broad kindly face grinning at him as well from behind the doctor's shoulder.

'Your heart, old fellow, is as good as it has ever been,' said the doctor smiling down on him. 'You are full of gas! But you know that already, don't you?'

30. Desert Flower

Chinna or 'small' **Latchmama**, or Latchi as she was called by all, had been left, though not exactly abandoned, at the village centre, by her mother *Pedda* or 'big' Narsamma, who had been 'set aside' for a younger woman by her husband, a drunkard and a wastrel, and yet with some compelling attraction for women. The absence of her husband made no difference economically to Narsamma; in fact, much more of her daily wages now remained in her hands, except when he came around occasionally in the dead of night to snatch away her money for a drink. Though she had complained bitterly when she had been his only wife, now she would gladly have given up all her earnings if only he would be by her side. Tired, depressed, and lonely to the pit of her stomach, she decided to leave the village and look for work in some housing construction site in the city. She could not take her daughter with her to a city slum, full of unknown drunken men, so after a palaver with Sharma*ji*, she left Latchi in the safe compound of the SERVICE rural centre, where in return for some light work, the girl would get food, cast-off clothes, and shelter at night.

Latchi herself seemed quite happy with this arrangement and was always seen taking on any work given to her without complaining, and in fact offering to do something or the other, which seemed odd to the others. She would smile all day if one of the older women gave her a sari they did not want any more, or a helper gave her a pair of discarded tennis shoes, two sizes too large for her bony feet. She always waited till everyone else had finished in the canteen before eating herself, and then at night, when everyone else was going off to bed, would be seen cleaning the canteen all by herself. She slept on the office veranda, covered by an old blanket and using a rolled-up skirt as her pillow.

Sharma*ji* didn't notice her at all after the first few days, when he had tried to judge if she was a thief or of bad repute in any way, and then satisfied that she would be content to behave herself if fed and sheltered, he had lost interest in the child. Early in the morning, while he was still half awake, he would hear her sprinkle water on the dust in front of his 'unit,' before drawing a *muggu* design in front of the steps with rice flour. Idly one day, as he sipped coffee on his veranda, he noticed the perfect symmetry of form in her design, and its perfect curves and straight lines, which formed a rather unique pattern. He wanted to ask her where she had learned that design, but forgot the matter later in the day. Then, the next day, he noticed she had changed the design; the new one was much simpler but equally elegant. In the days that followed he started to notice her *muggu* designs, each very different from the preceding one, each seeming to reflect her feelings for the day, somehow creating a motif which he carried in his mind, which started to influence his thinking for the day.

He questioned her closely one day when he was up early enough to catch her, but she only hung her head shyly and said she didn't know how she drew the *muggus*, or why she changed the designs, or why she drew them. *Pedda* Narsamma appeared one day, looking more cheerful than when Sharma*ji* had seen her last. She had a new sari on, was chewing *paan* and had a string of jasmine in her hair. She ran laughing to her daughter, who stood shyly by, and gave her a box of sweets she had brought from the city. The girl would eat one piece only after all the others round her, including Sharma*ji*, had taken a piece. Sharma*ji* complimented *Pedda* Narsamma on the way she had brought up a good girl, and then asked who had taught the girl to draw such beautiful *muggus*.

'*Saaru*, who would teach a poor girl like her,' laughed *Pedda* Narsamma. 'She just does whatever comes into her head. Hey! You answer *Pedda Saar*. He is being kind to you! Did you learn by watching others?' The girl nodded uncomfortably.

Sharma*ji* forgot about the matter till he attended a gender conference in Delhi sponsored by Christians Everywhere. In the lobby of the Sheraton, where the conference was held, he saw huge panels with photographs of *rangoli*, the *muggus* of North India.

Pramila Choudhury, Chairperson of Women in Craft [India], entered the lobby in a richly brocaded silk sari, and wearing a large intricately carved antique silver and onyx pendant at her throat. She was shepherded by the American Ambassador. Young Kamal Chand, scion of a former princely house and Minister of State for Textiles, drew up a chair for her.

'Thank you, dear boy, I am glad so many people are interested in *rangoli*, the unique art of the humble,' she said, speaking with remote haughtiness in an Oxbridge accent. 'Its discovery, like Jawaharlal's discovery of India, is really self-discovery. We have not found something new in the India all around us, we have found something new in ourselves. Art as conceived by modernity is dead art, it was art yesterday, when shaped by the living hands of the artist, it becomes a dead commodity today in a gallery or a museum. Money and art can never live in the same space-time,' she added with condescension, the light from the chandeliers flashing dazzling shafts of ice-cold blue from the sapphire rings on her fingers. 'The pictures of this uniquely feminine and at the same time empowering art have been taken by three of the foremost young photographers from New York, who agreed to work with me, thanks to a small grant of two million dollars from the Adams Foundation.' Three bearded men in black clothes stood up to applause.

Well, thought Sharma*ji*, the *rangolis* were not all that superior to what little Latchi drew every day, in fact they were definitely not as good. And two million dollars for this, and the American Ambassador dancing attendance to boot! Pugnaciously he determined that he would hold a show of Latchi's work, which he looked forward to seeing every morning when he woke up.

Whatever this heavily made-up lady might say, the *muggus* gained respect and money not when they were seen in the dirt for any dog to walk over, but only when beautifully photographed, enlarged, and presented on panels in a five-star hotel. He would bring Latchi's art to Delhi, and teach these Northerners that people from the South knew more about art than would ever enter the thick heads he saw around him.

The problem was getting the pictures right. He made Venkat, Rukmini and Abraham all take photos of Latchi's *muggus* with the society's field camera, and, in desperation, tried his own hand, but all the photos came out drab, and the designs looked disproportionate. Whatever it cost, he would have to get professional photographers to take the pictures. He was good friends with Syed Hussain, the best-known cinematographer in the region. The first opportunity he got, he asked Syed *bhai* to shoot photos of Latchi's *muggus*. Syed Hussain had just come back after a long shoot in some villages, had had a fight with the cheeseparing producer of the budget film, and was already into his fourth *patiala* peg of Scotch. But he was a good friend, and mellowing, took to the idea fast, by the sixth peg.

'Sharma*ji*, dead photographs are absolutely *passé*. Who wants to see them, when not sponsored by some rich American and followed by Scotch and a lavish dinner? Nobody! Film is the medium everyone understands. It is quite some time since I made a documentary. We will make one on your little girl and show it at Cannes!' As the night progressed, both of them became completely convinced that they would make a documentary out of Latchi's *muggus*.

Money was not to be a stumbling block. Syed *bhai* would organize someone to pay the shot. He and his entourage turned up at the rural centre after a couple of weeks, complete with several movie cameras, a generator van, a small crane for vertical shots at the drawings, and a travelling film-editing kit. There was a lot of good-natured excitement for the next couple of days, with Sharma*ji* and Syed *bhai* happily partying round the campus, and visiting interesting sites in the vicinity, for background colour.

When finally the cameras were all set up, and everyone was up early despite the grumbling of Syed *bhai*'s assistants, and when all was focused round the spot in front of Sharma*ji*'s unit, Latchi was asked to make a *muggu*. A crowd had gathered by then, and Syed *bhai*, dressed in black, with a black cap on his head, shouted tensely for the cameras to 'roll.' Latchi was trembling, tears started in her eyes, and she did a very quick small *muggu*, which really by any standards was only on par with the worst one could see. Abraham shouted at her, Latchi cried, Rukmini went up and put an arm round her and told her to try again. The girl tried several times, but none of the drawings were in the least appealing. Tersely, Syed *bhai* ordered his group to 'pack up,' and they all retired to the canteen for lunch. No one noticed or cared that Latchi did not eat that day.

Next morning, when the cameras were set up again, she did not come running when called. A search was conducted, and she was nowhere to be found. After shouting for her, and scolding loudly that she was a disobedient, ungrateful girl, they packed up again, and Syed *bhai* retired to Sharma*ji*'s unit to steady his nerves in the morning with some more Scotch. Two days later, a driver caught the girl in a village some distance away and brought her back. With everyone clustered round her, Sharma*ji* spoke to her sternly; asked her if she knew how much money had been wasted because of her, money that could have been spent feeding hungry people, and then he softened his tone as he saw her standing there weeping silently, and asked her whether she ever wondered what her mother would say if she had run away for good? When there was nothing more to say, she was dismissed, and the crowd dispersed, with Sharma*ji* mulishly telling Syed *bhai* that they should try again the very next morning.

The next morning, they had very little trouble with the girl; she was already waiting in front of Sharma*ji*'s unit before anyone got up. When all the cameras were set up and the shouting abated a little, she did exactly as she was told. She drew when she was ordered; swept the mess clear when asked to do so, and started again. They all gave her advice. Rukmini brought out a book on Irish Lace and suggested that Latchi could copy some of those designs. The girl tried her best. Abraham then looked at the work and suggested alterations. Latchi made them. The cameras kept rolling. That afternoon, while looking at some rushes with the travelling editing-kit, Syed *bhai* said that they were not to worry, and while the designs they had captured were indeed mediocre, he had some superb shots of her at work. They should have patience, and let her settle down. He had learnt patience through wildlife photography.

But it was not to be. That very evening Syed Hussain got a frantic call from the producer of the budget film—only it was no longer to be a budget film anymore. The producer spoke for half an hour; he said he had raised a great amount of money from interested angels and sold the distribution rights through five territories already; Syed *bhai* should rush back. When the cinematographer's group were loading their vehicles the next morning, Syed *bhai* embraced Sharma*ji*, assured him that everything was working out just fine, he would have more than enough money to do an even better documentary on Latchi. He was committed to it, and Sharma*ji* should wait and see. However, within a few weeks, Syed *bhai* was called away by an American company for location-shooting in the Himalayas, which, as he told Sharma*ji* over the phone, had a unique storyline, he would laugh when he told him everything, but it was also radical, taking a dig at everyone. Syed *bhai* said he would send a big box of Bombay *halwa* for Latchi.

Time passed and what with new worries created by new projects and canards spread by his jealous enemies, Sharma*ji* got involved in many other things. If he did notice Latchi's *muggus*, it was only casually, for he had lost interest in them and her; sometimes he would show deliberate irritation when he saw her early in the morning, for he was still sore at her for thwarting his art project.

One morning, he was woken early by Abraham knocking on his door. Abraham said in low tones that they should send right away for the assistant civil surgeon from the district hospital to look at Latchi. Sharma*ji* was going to burst out angrily, but seeing the look on Abraham's face he instructed that the jeep should be sent to the hospital. He dressed very slowly, and when at last he went over to the office building, he saw a small still group of women with their sari *paloos* drawn across their faces, staring silently at Latchi, who was stretched out on her old blanket. The assistant civil surgeon was just getting up from his examination, and Abraham was shouting orders.

'We cannot determine the cause of death by a cursory examination,' said the doctor unemotionally, 'but maybe we can if you request an autopsy. Do you want one? I would not advise it. The girl is gone. I shall give a death certificate stating death due to illness. They say she was coughing a lot. Maybe TB or pneumonia; in this weather, even a little chill can polish off a person of her class.'

'She has not eaten for weeks,' said the sweeper, looking down on her ruminatingly, which seemed to surprise everyone mildly.

Sharma*ji* looked down at that small still form, her ragged bodice drawn tight over her bony ribs, and for no reason he could name, tears streamed down his face. Many times before, when he showed emotion before his staff or at a meeting, a part of him would stand back to watch the effect he had created, but this time he did not care, he felt humble and he wept. 'I am in charge here,' he said to no one in particular, 'and I shall cremate her.'

'She is a Christian,' said Venkat, who had come up. '*Pedda Narsamma* is a Christian, and so was her father, so she should get a Christian burial.' Sharma*ji* was surprised he had never known this. He ordered for the body to be prepared and then carried to the Christian graveyard next to the Baptist Church. The padre would have to be sent for.

The padre, a large man with blood-shot eyes, arrived around noon at the graveyard. He was displeased at having his routine upset and even the thousand rupees that Sharma*ji* thrust into his hands did not mollify him. With a grunt he shoved the money into the side-pocket of his white habit. It was a brief ceremony, with the padre reading from a Telugu Bible. Sharma*ji* said he would say a few words, since he was in the position of a father to the girl. He praised her sweet nature, her simplicity, her dutiful behaviour, and her skills. 'I am reminded of Grey's *Elegy Written in a Country Churchyard*,' he said in English to the padre. 'Full many a flower is born to blush unseen and waste its sweetness in the desert air.' With the padre making no response, Sharma*ji* looked around at the barren landscape, the brown empty fields, the few sad trees, the shabby huts, and then, taking up a clod of earth, he looked at her face for the last time, and tossed the earth into the grave. Tears came again, but this time it was for himself, for what he had become, a fraud, an essentialist fraud.

31. Sharma*ji*, Padmashree

Over the last few years, Sharma*ji* had started a rather painful early morning routine, having been sufficiently scared by his doctor. His paunch had been growing, and he could no longer thrust himself into his trousers without feeling constricted and slightly out of breath. He had tried to go for gentle walks in the evening accompanied by Revathi, who had replaced Rukmini, discussing new ideas for women's empowerment. Such walks had only given him a healthy appetite, and he would finish the evening with a sumptuous meal. Not only did his girth grow but his nights became disturbed and uncomfortable with flatulence. The suppressed joke of the campus was that his explosions sometimes reached point six on the Richter scale. He had consulted his doctor back in the city, who had wanted a complete, very expensive check-up to be carried out. The news had not been good. His bad cholesterol was too high, and his doctor had said, 'We don't want an event, do we?' A brief early morning workout under supervision in a gym was recommended.

He had begun a routine of walking his way to a nearby gym before six every morning, feeling rather proud of the figure he cut in shorts, tee shirt and white Adidas shoes, which his wife cleaned every afternoon when she was through with the housework. He would cycle for ten minutes, chat with the coach for fifteen while drinking cups of sugary coffee from the gym's dispenser, and then, under prodding from the coach, try standing exercises for another five minutes. By six forty-five he would be back home, feeling virtuous, and would loudly demand a cup of fresh home-filtered coffee from his wife. If he was feeling peckish, he might even ask her for a plate of *upma* right then, served up with potatoes. He did not seem to lose much weight, to his surprise, but he was able to struggle into some of his clothes, though the way he bulged in tiers round the middle added a note of cheer to schoolboys waiting for the bus near his flat.

On the January morning in question, he was late going to the gym, feeling grumpy because of over-indulgence the previous night. His wife was a gifted cook, even he acknowledged that, and the previous night, her brother and his wife had dropped in for a meal. Sharma*ji*, despite the warning looks given by his wife, had not been able to restrain himself. So his grumpiness was understandable to himself, and refusing all conversation, he concentrated on his cycle in the gym. Gas seemed to rise in bubbles up his throat, and every now and then he would stop cycling and belch and fart loudly. He also tried drinking some coffee and cycling again, but he was not comfortable. He slowly began to realize that everyone in the gym was looking at him in a rather peculiar manner. He surreptitiously checked to see if his fly was open, but it was not. Perhaps there was a tear in the seat of his pants, and he tried to feel if it was so, but his arm could not stretch that far round his backside. Peeved, he left the gym with a curt nod at the coach. These fellows, who were they? Nobody.

Waiting for jobs they would never get, envious of big men like himself. They had no culture in any case, so it was not surprising that they gave him such stares. But still he felt uncomfortable.

As he walked past the small shops that lined the street leading to his locality, he noticed, now that he was aware that something was wrong, that shopkeepers paused in the process of getting their shops ready for business and craned round to look at him. What the devil was the matter? It could not be anything to do with his clothes. It must be some rumour everyone had heard. Anxiety gripped his heart. Everyone was always trying to ruin his reputation; no one, not even his wife, despite all the good he had done everybody, was grateful to him. He knew it was human nature. He would follow only the dictates of his conscience, his duty to God, the nation, and society. Let dogs bark, it was their nature to do so. No one could touch those under God's special protection.

But still, it was worrying. What had these rascals heard? It could not be the matter about that accounts slip-up at SERVICE. He had had an anxious two weeks at the Income Tax Department.

To be called up for what happened a few years ago was atrocious, but these fellows tried to trap you and extract money. He had been threatened with legal procedure, leaving him ill and perspiring. He had explained how his staff, inefficient and lazy, and had let him down. How could he afford properly trained accountants, when every penny had to be saved in the interests of the poor? No, there should have been no muddle about the travel expenses. The donors who had invited him—the only delegate from India at the International Conference on Sanitation for Poor Countries, in Paris, it should be noted—the donors themselves seeing his poor health had made all arrangements for a two-week rest cure in the south of France. How could he show any letters from them? It was an ad hoc, last-minute intervention on their part. They had insisted, kidnapped him in fact on his way to the airport, when he was desperately trying to get back to his project in rural India. No, there was no doctor's report either, for the French are very strict about medical confidentiality. Anyway, the matter was settled one way or the other; Dasgupta, that rascal who had got him into this trouble, and greasing some palms no doubt. God knew he and the poor were being swindled at every turn.

On second thoughts, it could not be the income tax matter, for nothing had come out, Dasgupta had seen to that; he would have fired him on the spot if he had not patched up the whole matter, he didn't care how it was done. It was something else, but what? He was very sensitive now, and was aware of locality people, people he never even talked to, coming to their windows to look at him as he walked back. Oh my God! They all knew something. The city must be agog with some filthy rumour! He had returned to his flat only late last night and gone straight to bed, without waking his snoring wife. That woman! How he had been cheated by that uncle of his into marrying a penniless woman without family. And now she was faithless too. Why had she not stayed awake to tell him what everyone was gossiping about? Is this how a loyal wife should behave? Perhaps she had heard about that incident with Revathi. A cold hand gripped his heart. Yes, that was it! All these immoral scoundrels, who sleep with each other's wives all the time. How he had to put up with living in the midst of this steaming filth, but how could he afford to live in a locality befitting his stature, when every penny was to be dedicated to the poor? Yes, these fellows must have heard about what happened with Revathi. It was all innocent, mind you, as she herself had explained to the rest of the staff. She had come to 'his unit' on campus in the evening, as was her duty, to discuss project matters. Despite his headache he had reluctantly agreed to go through the files. His headache becoming intolerable, she had gone into the kitchen to make him a soothing infusion. He had followed her and, blinded with pain, had tripped at the door, and falling had clutched onto her, bringing them both down onto the durrie. Badly winded, he was struggling to get up, when both Venkat and Dasgupta had come in carrying more files. It was only when he saw their astonished look that he noticed for the first time that his hand—which he had held out for support— was on Revathi's breast.

So, that was it. How filthy minds were ready to believe that even the God-fearing were as filthy as themselves! He would never cease to be amazed at people's depravity. So, they were all trying to bring him down. No doubt that Venkat and that Dasgupta wanted to seize control of his NGO. He would see them in hell first. A new suspicion dawned. Maybe that whore Revathi was an accomplice! How he had been mistaken in promoting her! He had been beguiled by her smiles and her pliant manner. He remembered now how she would deliberately sway towards him, not wearing any bra, but lifting her large breasts shamelessly to his face. He was so naïve, so innocent! He should have known she was a practised whore egged on by those snakes in human form, Venkat and Dasgupta, who were out to ruin him. But he would not be ruined. He had nothing to fear. The donors, government officials, all good men, knew him for what he was, a patriot, a tireless worker for people's welfare. Brushing aside the grinning lift-attendant who came forward to insinuate something, he slammed the gate shut and went up to the third floor all by himself. For one awful minute, he feared that a retinue of neighbours would be waiting for him, but mercifully the corridor was empty. He shot into his flat and bolted the door with relief.

He sat in his easy chair grimly, perspiring, without calling out to his wife. He would be stern and dangerous, and cow her into silence. In time this miserable episode would be forgotten. Maybe he would buy her those new gold bangles she was always pestering him about. She was an old woman; how could she complain if he, a virile man, had manly needs?

'Good morning, Padmashree, Sir,' he heard at his elbow, and there was his wife, smiling fondly, bearing a steaming cup of coffee, some freshly made *vadas*, and the local morning newspaper on a tray. He was confused and agitated; he didn't know what was going on, till his eye fell on the folded newspaper. There was his photo on the front page, not taken from the best angle, but undoubtedly it was him. *'Vedavyas Sharma Awarded Padmashree for Social Service,'* proclaimed the headlines. He had been included in the Republic Day Honours List!

The next several minutes were too confused for him to remember later. He had patted his good wife and promised to buy her gold bangles as part of the celebration. Not four, they could not afford so many, but two he could buy. He must buy himself new clothes for the investiture. He could not go to the Rashtrapati Bhavan looking like a beggar. He would get himself a good-quality black suit, no, not a European jacket, but a closed coat, as befitted a nationalist. And yes, Florsheim shoes, nothing less. There would of course be a Press Conference at the SERVICE campus. He had read somewhere that the Sixth Nizam at the Delhi Durbar had been similarly attired in severe black, and had called his ministers his jewels. He would do the same. After all, those splendid fellows, Venkat and Dasgupta, deserved praise. They had their way to make in the world. What did he care for such gewgaws? He cared only to serve humanity. And he would not forget poor Revathi either. He himself would call her to the stage and help her up, being careful not to brush against those breasts of hers. Sharma*ji*, Padmashree! He savoured the title. In a way the President was honouring herself by honouring a simple servant of the people like himself.

About the Author

Vithal Rajan, O.C., B.A. Hons [McGill], Ph.D. [London School of Economics], has worked as an officer at Canadian Industries Ltd [I.C.I.], Canada; as a mediator for the Church in Belfast in the 1970s; as a founding faculty member for the School of Peace Studies, University of Bradford, UK; as Chair of World Studies, International School of Geneva; as Director, World Wide Fund for Nature International, Switzerland; and as Executive Director, Right Livelihood Award, Sweden [also known as the Alternative Nobel Prize]. He has founded several Indian NGOs and he was made an Officer of the Order of Canada for his life-long service to humanity. He is the author of several books of fiction and plays, including *The Legend of Ramulamma*, Writers Workshop, India 2007; *Holmes of the Raj*, Random House India, 2010; *The Year of High Treason*, Rupa Books, 2011; and *Les Mangues de Tara*, Heures Bleues, Montreal, 2011.

Made in the USA
Middletown, DE
14 December 2018